Unbalanced

The Order, a faith built on sacrificing the sisters, has discovered them again.

Courtney Shepard

Unbalanced

Courtney Shepard

Unbalanced

This is a work of fiction. The characters, incidents and dialogues in this book are of the author's imagination and are not to be construed as real. Any resemblance to actual events or persons, living or dead, is completely coincidental.

Published by CS Press
Salt Spring Island, British Columbia, Canada

~~~

Second Edition 2022

eISBN: 978-1-77155-150-2

Cover Art by Courtney Shepard

www.unbalancedseries.com

Version_2
~~~

To all my sisters...

Prologue

Spain, Middle Ages

The Master held his body hunched as he scrutinized the pitiful people. Soldiers purged every home and building, dragging shaking villagers from bed to huddle in the town square like sheep. Parents hushed their children and held them still with fearful grips. Herded by his men, the oldest and slowest souls followed with hesitant steps, pushed into the mass to cower before him and await his instructions.

He'd had enough. He found the same weak, pathetic people in every town and village, and he would not abide their silence a second longer. His men had erected the pyre during the night. Now, displayed before every set of eyes, the mob's reaction rewarded him. Their palpable terror at the wooden structure charged him with renewed vigor, and his blood lust reared, battering against his control.

It was time to set an example.

Sunlight cut through the gray, wet morning as the sun rose behind the shabby stone inn. He was close, so close. The crowd's fear was like sweet wine in his parched mouth, and it drew him forward. Facing them, his gaze stopped on one face and then the next, searching for his prey.

"Where are they?" he shouted, breaking the silent spell. "Tell me the truth, and no more harm will come to you."

Silence.

He raised his face to the rising sun and let his mask fade away. His gray hair darkened to shining black, his wrinkled skin smoothed, and he straightened his hunched posture. Relaxing his face and rolling his lips, he dropped the old priest's harmless and inquisitive expression, revealing his natural, more menacing visage. Gasps and whimpers rose from the crowd.

"Where are they?" he roared again. In the single pulse of heavy silence, he savored the people's pale faces. No one met his eyes.

"We are here."

The words, sharp and clear as glass echoed across the square. Before the last note faded, a chilling breeze cut through the air and blew his robes, snapping them back.

The Master closed his eyes and shivered with the wind. He stared past the crowd to the slight, cloaked form standing beyond his guards' perimeter, and swallowed past his fluttering heart.

She slid her hood back and her long, white hair lifted and floated in the breeze. Her light-gray, chilling eyes were big and round in her small face.

A child?

"And here," another voice called.

He scanned to the left, spotting a second cloaked form. Her gleaming blue eyes flashed and narrowed from behind her curtain of black hair.

He'd found them, but they were too young. These children could not be the ones he sought, the source of their obsession. He hunted women, not children. It couldn't be. He had been searching longer than they had lived. The sheep stirred, turning and looking with him for the other two.

Because there were always four.

He leaned forward, and his heartbeat kicked and stuttered. The ground shimmered and rippled like rings in a pond flowing between the sisters. Two more girls rose from beneath the earth holding hands. One was hooded with her shoulders hunched and her face down, and the other had dark-brown curls and eyes like glowing emeralds.

The soldiers hesitated, pointing their shaking swords, but the villagers accepted them with reverence and dropped to their knees, bowing low. He snarled and fought the impulse to call for their immediate slaughter. Holding back his rage was difficult, anger and envy gripped him. As the Master, he ruled only mindless soldiers. He longed to command the free people, desired such worship above all else. He coveted power like drunkards craved wine.

These children inspired devotion that should be bestowed upon him. He was a Master of the Order, and whether these fools understood it, the Order was the reason they had their worthless lives. Their only purpose, the only reason they existed, was to worship and obey, and yet they turned their back on their masters to follow these false idols. They would all regret their groveling display.

Clenching his fists, he stifled his tight, boiling rage. His breath whistled through his gritted teeth. He'd found them. This day was about more than his needs; it was about triumph and sacrifice. His shoulders dropped, and his jaw loosened. Victory rolled through him, raising every hair on his body and speeding his already rushing blood.

On the eve of his inauguration, the Grand Master revealed to him what he would be hunting, and the sisters had instantly become his obsession. Though all Masters desired the same result, his cravings had to be stronger, more powerful. They consumed him. Every moment, every breath he yearned for them. When he slept, they were his dreams. He vowed to succeed where others had failed.

Immediately after his Master's title was bestowed upon him, his crusade started, and for over two-thirds of his lifetime, he crossed borders, destroying any who stood in his way. He'd never stopped, never returned home. Countless had been sacrificed, but none of them were who he actually sought. And now, finally, after years of exhaustive questing, he'd achieved his greatest desire.

The sisters walked forward, past the quivering guards into the crowd. The villagers surged, circling them, shielding them, and pushing the soldiers back.

"Fools, they are not goddesses as you believe. They are evil abominations. Move away or face the soldiers."

The white-haired one, the tallest of the four, whispered to her frightened people. Her voice carried through the crowd, as gentle and soothing as the breeze. "Thank you, for your love and protection, but you must protect yourselves now. Leave this place, and do not return."

The last child remained hooded, but she stalked forward, leading her sisters with her hands curled into fists. Her hood couldn't quite hide the vibrant red, orange, and yellow strands beneath it.

Her black eyes, framed by those flaming locks, were hollow, but her monstrous expression was as vicious as any feral animal. "We are here for you, Master. We know what you have done."

His skin prickled, and shivers rolled through him.

"Permit these people to leave in peace, and we will spare you and come willingly."

The villagers shifted back, parting, allowing the girls to move forward, but a handful reached out, begging them not to go, to run. They stared straight ahead, through air that was heavy and thick. Sound was muffled and far away.

One child's eyes were cloudy, grey, and another had eyes as black as coal. The other two, their eyes gleamed like blue and green jewels. They stopped in front of the soldiers bordering the inn, and he shook his head, clearing the fog.

They are mine.

Stomach fluttering, he grinned again. Their confidence was so childlike, innocent, and misplaced. "Seize them."

Air crackled and sparked, wind surged and blew, driving the armed men back. The girls and the villagers behind them were still, their clothes barely rippling, but the soldiers couldn't fight past the gale force wind battering them back. Their cloaks snapped as they spun into each other, clanging shields and swords.

Blood sprayed in the wind, splattering his face and robes in crimson. Screams erupted from the din as their swords, still gripped in their hands and blown by the churning wind, swung into each other, slicing and severing without intention.

The Master raised his black-gloved fingers to his forehead and wiped away the warm drops. "Drop your weapons, you fools, and take them."

Metal clanged again, and the men lunged forward, struggling and stretching for what lay beyond their reach. Clearly, these children were monsters with great power. Their actions validated his crusade, here and now.

"You must leave. They will hurt you for sheltering us." The green-eyed girl with the brown hair pleaded with the people to disperse and seek safety. "This is how it must be. Please go. You will see us again."

The Master growled. The villagers hesitated, shaking their heads, but with his nod, the armed men parted, allowing them out. They shuffled away, their faces stunned and frightened. After the last group had disappeared in the last cart, the wind slowed and died.

The soldiers rushed forward and grabbed them, twisting their thin arms behind their backs. Only the black-eyed one struggled, jerking from the soldier's grip before he grasped her again with both hands.

Carnality rose in the Master. He wanted to take his time with them. He'd chased their shadows, crossing every border and boundary, following every false lead, every rumor they lived, for years. After such a lengthy pursuit, he longed to savor his achievement and linger over their deaths.

But they'd risen from the ground, and if they escaped the same way now, he would be the one hunted. The accounts of the sisters were true, and though they led him here, they were limited and inaccurate. These sisters were not born after the last sacrifice but twelve years ago at most. They possessed abilities never recorded before. The last successful sacrifice had been over fifty years ago and the sisters had not displayed such strength with wind and earth.

Any delay of the ritual was a risk. Their submissiveness aside, he feared them. Having seen it for himself, he had to admit their power.

He waved to the soldiers, and they dragged the girls to the four posts of the pyre and tied them there. The time had come. He would see their end in this, the greatest triumph of his life.

The soldiers advanced with lit torches, their approach intentionally slow, building fear with each step. The fire-haired child lifted her gaze to the flames, and her blank expression transformed into a vicious, snarling grin.

He tightened at her defiance before staggering back. Her eyes, previously black as coal, now flashed red and yellow against her pale face. His heart pounded in his ears. By disguising his stumble for a turn, he used the motion to hide his shock. Panic and fear were weakness. He couldn't show it. Even seeing hellfire in her eyes, he must remain composed and regal.

The torches sputtered and flashed, growing and blazing to the sky like beacons. He gasped, and she laughed at him. It was a child's laugh, sweet and playful, until she bared her teeth, and he recoiled again.

The soldiers dropped their torches onto the morning-wet ground, and they flared instantly, surging and rippling, engulfing their legs. Useless screams filled the air, and they rolled in the dirt, unable to smother the fire. Others ran to their burning brothers, throwing cloaks and blankets over them, but the shrouds exploded with more power and force. Wind blew strong and sharp, fanning the flames and pushing them toward the soldiers retreating for the inn.

No.

He had relished his victory too early.

Fire crawled along the ground and encircled the pyre, rising up in a great wall, fed by nothing and blazing ten feet high. The soldiers around the perimeter scattered, fleeing the scorching barricade.

Fear erupted into chaos. They would be useless against these witches. And they *were* demon-witches—he was there as witness. They commanded fire, wind, earth, and water; he had underestimated their power. He wanted credit for their deaths, but he would have to settle for the credit of their capture. He achieved all he could; others far more powerful than he would have to finish it.

On a silent command, the four black-cloaked shadows materialized and slid from the darkness behind him. The Master went to one knee and bowed low, refusing to stare too closely into the dark, faceless hoods.

There to complete the sacrifice, they drew their swords and sped toward the fire in unnatural synchronization. Their bodies blurred with speed as they charged, without breaking stride, through the searing wall.

The Master craned his head but hesitated to take even one step forward. Their fire licked out like fingers, spreading and gaping enough for him to catch glimpses of the deed. The wall lowered further as the burning figures advanced on their prey. Flames rolled over their cloaks while skeletal hands grasped each child by the throat. The fire barrier sparked and flared, surging once before it sputtered out into nothing.

As each girl struggled, their eyes wide, the Master gaped. His body clenched, and his stomach fluttered with glee. She who commanded fire jerked within the bony grip. Flames crawled up from her feet and covered her body, burning as fiercely as the beacons she'd just controlled.

The black-haired child was next. Her shape rolled and flowed. Her skin, if it was still skin, changed. It was reflective and the bright sunlight flashed in his eyes. Would she slip away?

The girl with green eyes lowered her head and with a grinding crack, her skin shimmered and hardened into an intricate statue. Wisps of her hair flew in the breeze and were caught at the moment she became stone.

Was she trapped within or had she become the sculpture?

The last child, the white-haired girl who commanded wind, hadn't changed. The cloaked face leaned closer, and she closed her eyes. For a moment, the Master feared she'd escaped, but she was there, only fading. He could see through her like smoke. She'd become vapor.

He was enthralled. He hadn't truly believed the stories; he hadn't fully understood, nor allowed himself to see that these children *were* themselves raw, elemental power. But in their final defense, they had each become fire, water, earth, and air.

The warriors released their grips and retreated a step, raising their broad, silver swords in unison.

The Master held his breath.

Together they drew their arms back to their limit, before swinging forward. The air hummed as the sharp blades gleamed and the purple-jeweled hilts sparkled and slid forward, slicing through the girls' shields.

The moment the swords pierced the elements, the girls regained their original forms, and four small heads lowered, chins to chests.

Eerie silence hung in the aftermath and the heavy air stilled as if the world held its breath. The four burning victors withdrew their weapons and sheathed them. Again, the Master bowed low but jumped, startled at the great crack that cut through the hush. The shabby buildings shook, the ground opened and as one, the victors dropped below.

They'd prevailed, and with their brilliant triumph, even his own consuming faith grew. Their power would increase, and the delicate balance continue. Finally, he'd return home to be praised and worshipped as a king, but first, he must hunt down and kill the traitorous villagers. His bloodlust was not sated.

~ * ~

Northern British Columbia, 27 years ago

Emma's farmhouse sat at the rear of the tree-lined property atop a sloping bank overlooking a small frozen lake. The full moon sat low and lit the snow, its blurred image reflected on the ice.

Inside, weak and throbbing, Emma faced the corner where a simple bassinet cradled her four tiny, newborn baby girls. They slept soundly only hours after their raucous entrance into the world, and she was grateful for the peace. *There would be no peace to come with four such little darlings.* She'd never been so proud or so exhausted in her life. *Thank goodness for Greta.*

Greta had transformed the living room into a makeshift bedroom when she reached her third trimester and the stairs became too difficult for her to climb. She'd placed the bed close beside the wood stove where it crackled and popped and the orange glow chased away the darkness. It burned around the clock, heating the small place and keeping the occupants warm and cozy in the harsh climate. The old-fashioned appliance was essential this far from civilization.

The nurse had accompanied Emma from London to aid her during her high-risk pregnancy. Her heavy stature and solid frame helped Greta care for her. Emma was young, too frail, and carrying quadruplets. She was only fifteen and terrified.

She'd never shared her reasons for running, and thankfully Greta hadn't asked. They'd arrived at the secluded location five months ago, and Greta had taken care of everything. Large and imposing, she now stood sentinel beside the window, casting long looks into the dark night.

Until she stiffened.

Emma caught the movement. "What is it?"

Greta didn't move. Her face was almost pressed against the glass but her muscles were rigid. Emma turned her head, also looking outside. Something moved…

He materialized from the shadows, striding toward the house. Four more figures followed behind, trailing him like black birds in formation. She froze. Their purposeful approach signaled dark, malevolent intentions. Bile burned her throat.

No.

Sighing, Greta faced her. "He is here, and they are with him. I'm so sorry."

She couldn't breathe; her heart hammered her chest. "No. How?" Her gaze swept back over to the bassinette. "He can't be." She shifted to sit up, but her body failed her. "What did you give me? I can't…" She peeled the covers back and started to roll.

Greta left the window to sit on the bed, pushing her back against the pillows. "Hush, Emma. The Master's here. What can we do?"

The Master? She stopped struggling, narrowing her eyes. "How do you know him?" Emma's anger swelled, overcoming her weakness and she glared at her nurse. "You...I trusted you. You were planted here?"

But as quickly as her anger came, it vanished, and she covered her mouth, choking on a broken sob.

Greta had played the caring friend to a tee, taking on a sister's affection for her, but she'd brought *him* here. She shifted her gaze to the door as it swung open, and there he stood in darkness as the wind whipped his black coat around him.

Emma's heart lurched and stuttered as the intruder entered with his face hidden in shadow. His four companions waited outside, standing on each side of the door like stone gargoyles.

She struggled, and Greta gripped Emma's arms tightly, shushing her. Tears spilled from her eyes with her body-clenching sobs. The young Master stared down at her daughters asleep in the bassinette. Though he was under twenty years old, she had never feared anything as much as she did him.

His four gargoyles strolled into the room, circling the bassinette, bending their heads low.

"Please, no." She fought Greta's iron grip. "You can't. Master, please."

Again, Greta shushed her pitiful pleas and bowed her head.

"No," she screamed. The shrill sound pierced her own ears.

"Air." The first word the Master spoke.

Her heart stopped. Shivers rose on her skin and a chill swept her body, freezing her blood. His voice would stop madness in its tracks and command obedience. It was low and cold, and conjured images of dungeons and graves.

One of his minions bent and blew strongly in each child's face. Her daughters woke. Three began crying, but one stared back with wide, unblinking eyes. The man picked her up.

"No, Greta stop him, please, help me."

Greta closed her eyes.

"Stop."

But the man turned with Emma's baby and left through the open door, blending into the night. Her body took the aching impact, and the weight on her chest crushed her.

"Fire."

Another bent forward, lighting a match. It flared, and he held it out, passing it in front of her crying girls. One stared at it with unblinking focus. He blew out the flame and tossed the still smoking match onto the floor. He picked her up, and they too vanished into the storm.

"Please, wait. Stop. You can't."

"Water."

A third man removed a flask from his cloak. He poured liquid into his cupped hand and sprinkled the water onto the two remaining babies' foreheads. One cried, and one didn't. He took the quiet one and left.

"Earth."

The last walked forward and lifted her crying daughter. He wiped the splash from her brow and tucked a small sprig of ivy under her chin. He pulled the blanket from the bassinette, wrapped her in it, and left the cottage without a backward glance.

No one would hear Emma's screams out here. No one who could help her. She'd lost them.

Greta still held Emma down, but as her last daughter was taken into the night, Greta's grip relaxed. Fear raced through Emma in such strong waves it covered her, muffling her racing mind and dragging her down with its weight.

The Master finally faced her. "Emma," he whispered, shaking his head. "This is how it has to be."

"You can't do this. Please, please, please don't do this. I'm begging you."

He glanced out the door to where his men had disappeared. "I warned you months ago… I wanted it to be easier for you, but you ran. I'm sorry." The Master bowed stiffly, and he too walked out into the fresh falling snow.

"I'll kill you for this!" Emma screamed and struggled again, but Greta forced her to lay still.

"No. You mustn't fight this, Emma. There's nothing you can do. They're gone."

Emma slumped back against the tear-soaked pillows, weak, sobbing. Greta left her side and closed the door before sidling back over to the window. The night was quiet and still again. There was nothing left to fear. There was no reason to hide. What Emma had dreaded for the last six months had come. Her daughters, her sweet babies were gone.

Greta returned, and Emma couldn't even meet her eyes to glare. Her chest tightened until she clawed at her throat. She couldn't catch her breath. Her churning stomach convulsed tightly. Her fingers slipped around her tear-soaked neck, and she yanked at her hair, pulling and twisting it.

Clasping at her scalp, she gripped her head, squeezing her eyes shut against the crushing pain.

Greta sat down beside her, patting her shoulder. "Stop that now. This will help you. It's for the best."

She grasped Emma's arm, yanked up her sleeve, and injected a needle into her arm.

"I'll find them, and you'll pay for this," Emma said before everything went dark.

Chapter One

Southern Colombia, 16 years later

Asha sat inside her tent, sweat beading on her forehead as she waited for her summons. It had taken days to trek through the jungle, each step too slow, with thick, wet foliage tangling and straining to obstruct every inch of their progress. She'd helped the men hacking at it with machetes in the relentless rain, venting her frustration, but her efforts did nothing for their pace. Being forced to cut through the thick jungle to avoid roadblocks and any heavily guarded side trails pissed her off. It wasn't worth it when they could have taken the roadblocks easily.

But stealth won out over speed, and they'd finally arrived after dark to set up camp five miles beyond the base's perimeter. Her rain-soured spirits sweetened as the sky cleared, and the insects chirped and buzzed like soothing music in the quiet jungle.

Father Sean opened the flap and crouched in. "Okay, they've returned. It's time to go. Remember, no survivors."

"Yes, sir." She brushed a loose lock of hair from her eyes and gave him a mock salute. He scowled at her and backed out, barking orders to the men. She grinned. It was so easy to antagonize him, especially before a mission. He was wound particularly tight tonight.

She crawled out and stood, stretching before pulling on her black, knit toque and tucking her ponytail up inside. Her hair tended to stand out even on the darkest night, but with a hat and dressed in black jeans and a black T-shirt she blended well.

Staring up, she took a deep breath as she studied the stars of the now clear, night sky. The stars always comforted her but in a melancholy way as if the distance was too great, and it prevented a full connection. They burned so brightly against the pitch, but combined with the jungle symphony, they were even more magnificent. Picking up the machine gun propped against her tent, she walked toward the trail. Eight of their hired guns slithered over to join her.

"Halt," Father Sean barked. "Not yet. You're not going with Asha. She'll do this phase alone."

Whenever Father Sean added new men to their team, they were surprised, if not shocked, by his reliance on her. She was his number one and their sexist minds balked at the idea she could do such an important, large-scale job alone.

Was it because she was a girl, or because she was sixteen? Probably both. But she didn't really care. She always worked alone; others were merely support, called in for clean up after her role was done.

On cue, eight pairs of eyes gave her the customary up and down evaluation. *Eww, gross.* She rolled her shoulders back, hiding her disgust, and returned their roving glances. She flashed her sassiest, most sarcastic wink and puckered her lips to blow a kiss.

"Asha, go."

She spun, smirking, and jogged into the jungle, jumping and dodging, cutting her way silently through the underbrush. The jungle thinned and her mind hummed as she approached her target. She slowed, coming upon the huge, stone wall. It rose before her and surrounded the rebel compound. Crouching low, she studied it without a clue how old it was. Ancient. It was definitely ancient. The rebels may have taken the structure, but they hadn't built it.

Crumbled rock littered the base; moss, and vines wove their way up the stone barricade. It had obviously faced its share of attacks over the years, but it remained strong and impenetrable. Regardless of its numerous scars, it endured. She liked that.

Until tonight...

She didn't like that. It was historical. The walls were twenty-feet thick, the diameter just under a mile. Guards walked high above, carrying machine guns and scanning the jungle for movement. She took note of where the jungle was dense and grew closest to the wall and then slipped back under cover as a guard passed on the upper level. The rough dirt road led to the only entrance, a huge, swinging gate large enough for trucks to enter.

She crept forward, drawing air deep into her lungs, and faced the gate, her machine gun resting heavy on her back between her shoulder blades. Her gaze followed the figure above. She drew her silencer-equipped pistol from her thigh holster. A muffled pop and the guard spun and fell a few feet to her right, dead before he hit the ground.

Quickly now.

She slipped the gun back as familiar tingling rolled through her. On her third breath, she called her power.

Bright orange flashed in the dark, and she grinned as delight bubbled inside her. She sent the flames, burning with unnatural ferocity, racing to the gate where they exploded then surged, engulfing the entrance. Instantly, the thick reinforced gate blackened and crumbled to ash, leaving a gaping hole. Someone shouted from inside the base, and she slipped back into the jungle and out of sight.

Her fire rolled like a tidal wave through the base while she waited safely outside, letting it do its work. The plans remained fresh in her head, and she could send the flames without looking.

She left her hiding spot and climbed through the burning gate to ensure all the guns and drugs, *and rebels* had been destroyed. From just inside, she scanned the entire layout. The four main buildings were burning ahead, just visible through the smoke. A muffled scream still echoed over the haze, and she clenched her fists, fighting to block out the horrifying sound. She dragged her feet forward.

Don't close your eyes; stay alert just a bit longer.

She finished off the remaining buildings by sending more trails racing along the ground. The flames hit their mark and exploded, lighting the jungle. It would be hours before the buzzing and ringing in her ears subsided completely. A lone rebel made a break and scurried along the wall before her fire swept up and overtook him.

She surveyed the compound, fighting to stay on her feet. Drained, her body was heavy, sluggish, and rubbery. Thankfully it was done. After the booms, the clean-up crew would already be heading her way. She turned to go, but a glint in the ash and soot caught her eye from one of the blackened jeeps beside her.

With a glance around and guilt creeping over her shoulders for her grave-robbing impulse, she pulled a sword from under its charred owner. Asha laughed aloud, gripping the golden handle, sparkling with diamonds and rubies. It depicted a fire-breathing dragon, beautifully crafted and winding around the hilt to protect the wielder's grip. The jewels were vivid fire, and though flashy and rather ridiculous, she loved it.

Testing the sword, she rolled it over, admiring the sparkle. It fit her hand but was far too big to wear around her waist. She'd never trained with a sword, but holding it, she was fiercer, stronger. Everyone carried guns these days, and though it didn't really make sense to use a sword, with this newfound beauty she didn't care. It called to her, like a natural extension of her arm, and she looked forward to using it. She was confident she'd master it after some dedicated practice.

One last glance across the compound for any rebels she'd have to finish off and another flash flickered. She squinted; she could see clearly through the smoke, but her eyes must be mistaken…wrong. Two small, charred bicycles leaned against monkey bars and a set of swings. One of those hollow metal structures that would wobble and jump the moment you swung three feet off the ground. They were black and charred with chips of red paint peeking out.

Her blood froze in her veins as she sprinted to the first building. She reached the door in seconds and kicked it in. A dark opening, smoke, and…

Overturned beds littered the rooms with burned bodies and broken machines amongst the blackened rubble. She gagged from the smell of cooked and burnt flesh.

A hospital?

Asha ran to the next building, kicking at the blackened wall. It crumbled inward revealing a scene from her most unimaginable nightmare. The bodies were much smaller there, children and infants, maybe thirty, crushed and burned.

I'm not seeing this. I didn't do this.

Not real. Their intelligence recon should have shown children, and the satellite photos would have shown the playground. Their sources had failed them. Shock clouded her vision turning it white, buzzing swelled in her ears. *No.*

The sound increased, expanding inside her head to near splitting. She gasped past her shallow breath, trying to get more air, but could only drag in thin wisps. Oh God, the panic was coming—the heavy weight squeezed her chest. She struggled to breathe.

I am a monster, slaughtering babies and children.

Her brain failed, short-circuiting and firing futilely inside her head. Rage and panic consumed her as the fire had consumed the compound. She didn't have to look down at her hands to know the flames were spreading, climbing up her arms and covering her entire body. Drained to the point of fainting, with her swelling panic came an adrenaline-fueled power boost.

A sliver of fear sliced through the chaos raging inside her. She hadn't lost control in years, and it would be bad…very bad.

Her heart pounded against her chest, and her vision spun. Power flooded her and built. Her fury flared inside like the roaring, jeweled dragon adorning her sword, but she couldn't contain it. Her rage clawed to be free. As she dropped her head back, the shock wave burst from her body, obliterating the compound to ash. Her vision spun, but she fought, clinging to consciousness.

No… Hold on.

Darkness closed into black, and she fell back into the ash-filled crater.

~ * ~

Ringing buzzed in Asha's ears, sounding so far away but

growing louder. Helicopter rotors coming closer. She groaned, rolling and grasping her throbbing head. A dart plunged into the ground an inch from her face, raising ash in a cloud. She jolted up, naked and dusted with gray soot. Even her boots had burned away. She squinted against the glaring sun.

How long had she been out? Where was she?

This couldn't be the jungle, not even scorched tree trunks remained on the blackened, flattened wasteland. She couldn't fully grasp the range. It resembled the aftermath of an atomic blast. All evidence of her crime had been erased.

What have you done?

Father Sean leaned out of his helicopter above, harnessed in and aiming his second shot. Heat bubbled, and she clenched her body until she shook. The weapon in his hand said it all. He was handling her.

No way, not this time.

With narrowed eyes and a teeth-baring snarl, she leapt to her feet. He'd used the tranquilizer before, but never when she wasn't in full panic mode. This was the aftermath, and he was familiar enough with her power to recognize when she was spent, yet he was still taking precautions.

She threw her hands into the air, her fingers stretching for her target and drawing her power. Fire shot out in a weak stream, but the helicopter veered away, and her flame failed to cover the distance. She tried again, but it traveled only half as far.

Please. She searched for a spark in helicopter's engine as it retreated.

"Come back, you coward!" She was out of juice. Her power was gone for the next hour or two.

She looked down at the sword, buried in ash, the rubies sparkling bright beneath the gray dust. Grasping it, Asha sprinted over the burned, blackened ground while scanning the horizon for the jungle. The blast perimeter was visible in the distance, and she pumped her legs harder. Their camp lay safe beyond but was littered with debris and covered in more ash.

Father Sean had taken the weapons but left their tents. Her hands still shook, and her stomach rolled as she yanked on jeans and another black hoodie. There was no way he would just sit back and allow her to escape. He would be after her even now. She craned her neck back, searching the trees for snipers waiting to contain her. It wouldn't be the first time.

With her gear on her back, she shook herself to clear her mind. *One step at a time. Stay focused on the next step, nothing more.* She urged her legs to move and jogged along the rough trail they'd carved out the night before.

Coming up on the military road, she ran parallel with it until she spotted the first roadblock.

The three boys were distracted, playing a card game with bullets and cigarettes for their currency. As boy soldiers do, they were dressed up like Rambo, complete with the tough-guy scowls only teens can master so well. But she could see those sad, devastated eyes, with no innocence left.

Goddammit, sometimes life was really unfair. She drew her gun and whispered curses for what she had to do then crept from the jungle. They continued their game as she took position. She cleared her throat, and they froze, all reaching for their forgotten guns.

"No!" Asha shouted halting them.

She gestured for them to sit and hold their hands in front of them. The scowls never left the boys' faces as she restrained them with plastic zip ties and covered their mouths with tape. Taking their guns and tossing them into the jeep, she climbed into the front seat. Keys hung from the ignition. *Perfect.*

The boys' eyes widened, and she turned her head just a moment too late. A man, most likely the boys' handler, lunged from the bushes.

Before she could draw her gun or even duck away, he'd grasped her by the hair and slammed her head into the steering wheel. Her nose crunched and broke as he smashed her face again. Blood meant nothing, but the blurring tears could get her killed in an instant. He yanked her head back again until her neck strained. Metal flashed before her. *Knife.*

He swung it around, and like the beat of a steady drum, time slowed on two counts. He was going to cut her throat. Still too drained to use her power, she wished her panic would rise and bring fire rushing back, but her emotions were never more calm or stable than during a fight. *Soldier mode.*

She thrust out her palm, and the knife clattered to the jeep's dash. Grasping the thick forearm still tangled in her hair, she jerked it forward and pulled his elbow down over her shoulder. The pleasing crack was followed by his muffled grunt and her release.

Time kicked back in but moving too fast now, like a runaway roller coaster, a spinning merry-go-round. She twisted and kicked out. Macabre shivers of glee tickled through her at the sound of more crunching bones when her feet connected with his face. Blood spurted from his nose, and he crumpled in a heap. She leapt from the jeep and landed on the ground before he could rise.

His knife gone, he aimed a pistol, but her boot clipped it,

knocking it away as he squeezed the trigger.

Too late. She jumped, stretching back into a handspring, dodging the bullet's unknown trajectory. Landing unscathed, she launched forward, her vision brimming red and teeth grinding, and kicked him in the balls. She spun, catching his face with a roundhouse kick, and he fell back.

She crouched and slammed his head into the ground. He was disgusting, repulsive, and evil, and she had no qualms about her actions. Putting scum like this to death was going to be a pleasure.

Warm blood splattered her face and poured through her fingers, but she carried on until she expelled her guilt and fury, and the roaring stopped and her vision cleared. She sat back for three panting breaths.

Back in the driver's seat, adrenaline pulsed. She shook and jerked but paused before reaching for the keys. She took the knife from the dash and tossed it beside the boy closest to her.

His brows rose over eyes as wide as sand dollars, and though his friends' expressions were hooded and suspicious, he could've been smiling under the tape covering his mouth. She gave him a wink, started the jeep, and sped down the dirt road.

Chapter Two

Southern Colombia, Present

Clay studied his target through his riflescope. *It wasn't possible.* His orders, as always, were clear. Take her out and return immediately. But how could it be that *she* was his target?

He relaxed his finger, sliding it off the trigger. First it was just a stir, the hairs on his arm standing up when she moved, and then it was visual confirmation through his rifle scope. Jerking away from the eyepiece, he scraped both hands through his hair, inadvertently slicking it back with the sweat forming on his scalp.

He placed his eye back against the scope and cleared his throat past the tingling in his chest. He'd never believed in fate or destiny, or any of that fluff, yet there she was—literally the woman of his dreams.

Dude, get a grip.

But it was she, and yet *how* could she be a real, living woman? She'd been cast as the lead in his most vivid dreams and nightmares. Now to see the living embodiment of her? *la Reina Guerrera*, the Warrior Queen, was a kink in the plan. He clenched his teeth.

In every dream, she was surrounded by chaos and fire. In jungles, deserts, cities, and towns, her black eyes would flash red, orange, and yellow with her panic and rage as suffocating as if they were his own. He'd run to her, his arms reaching out. But he'd always wake, sweat-soaked and panting, never knowing if he'd reached her in time.

Years ago, one particularly horrifying dream jolted him from sleep and sent him crashing to the floor. A shock wave had blasted and glowed with her in the center of the white light. He'd been jumpy for days.

Clay followed her movements as she climbed into a jeep and left the compound, leading four covered supply trucks into the thick jungle.

"Where are you going now, *Reina*?" He whispered the words, unscrewing and dismantling his gun and placing it back in its case. *Time to go.*

He secured the bag to the thick branch with a strap, scrambled down through the branches, and dropped to the ground. The landing was soft and quiet despite the height.

He needed to get inside that base before she returned. Clay sprinted silently through the jungle to where he'd hidden his jeep. Pulling a clipboard and papers out of the hidey-hole under the back seat, he selected a few and clipped them to the board. He secured a laminated badge to his khaki shirt and slapped a Red Cross magnet on the door of his jeep. Filled with thrumming energy and adrenaline, he jumped in and drove through the brush to the road leading to *la Reina's* compound.

He was acting rashly, but he had to see her up close, hear her voice, and confirm she was the real thing. The huge wall surrounded the compound, and he got out, slammed the door, and stretched yawning. He didn't have to wait long. A small door beside the main gate opened and a slight, young man emerged, his gun aimed at Clay's head. He narrowed his eyes but estimated the guard was at least twenty-five.

"What do you want?" he asked.

Clay pointed to his ID badge and held up his clipboard. "I have supplies for your hospital. We've heard of the work you're doing, and I am here to help." He spoke in nervous English though he was a fluent Spanish speaker.

Hell, he was fluent in French, Russian, German, Mandarin, and countless other languages. He learned long ago if he couldn't understand what people said, he couldn't fully trust them. He'd picked up a lot of valuable information when people presumed him a monolingual dullard. Intentionally stuttering and breaking the next words, he hesitated enough to get out, "Doctors Without Borders."

"Doctors Without Borders," the guard repeated, his eyes skewering Clay.

A second guard approached the jeep and went straight for the first aid kits and boxes of medicine. He unwrapped one and studied the stamped seals over the vials. The inspection must have pleased him because he grinned.

Clay itched to knock the gun away and put him down; instead, he smiled back at the stone-faced guard. The man took the clipboard and ID, patted Clay down one-handed then motioned him through the small side door.

Inside, the compound buzzed with disordered chaos as children played among chickens, guards, and even goats. It didn't appear to be the growing threat portrayed in the dossier. It was more of a commune than a military compound.

The hospital lay straight ahead, but he was led to the left, past a flourishing, fenced-off garden to a door opening into the wall. He managed one last glance around the bright, sunny base before the guard shoved him inside a small room. He was blind in the dark, but he smiled.

Pleased with his reception, since it wasn't overly friendly, nor overly rough, but perfectly suspicious as they should be. Someone in *la Reina Guerrera's* position would need to be cautious.

A crack under the door let a sliver of sunlight inside, and he could see the cell was equipped with a bucket and a hole in the ground. He dipped his finger in the liquid, sniffed then tasted it. The water was stagnant, but still thirst-quenching.

Sitting in the dark, Clay replayed his observations. He hadn't expected to find such an organized affair. He'd observed the base from his perch for two days, and finally today she'd appeared. She'd spoken to a few people, stayed less than an hour, and left again. He'd prepared for the usual camp of revolutionaries. Boys and men causing a ruckus and opposition to his bosses' nefarious interests. Not this…harmony.

Regardless of his orders, Clay would not act hastily.

He listened to the outside world for another two days from his dark cell. The guard brought stale bread, but good cheese and even fruit. He'd just finished his meal when the door opened again. He had to shield his eyes from the burning sunlight, but her quiet steps alerted him before he was swept away by her presence. His chest tightened, and his fingers twitched.

"Who are you and why are you here?" Her voice was lower than he imagined, gravelly, hoarse, but it only added weight to the heat thrumming through him.

Still standing in the open doorway, she was a silhouette, the light hiding her features in shadow.

"My name is Dr. Brent," he said. "Dr. Clay Brent. I'm with Doctors Without Borders."

She entered the room, and his stomach flipped. Her hair, her black eyes…her mouth. *Impossible.* It had to be a trick of the mind. Despite the distance and just a short glimpse, his gut had been right; he'd wished he was wrong.

"I don't buy it," she said. "We can't possibly be on their radar. How did you find us?"

Her voice caused goosebumps to run along his arms. "We've heard of you. I wanted to help. I took special leave and brought supplies."

"Yes, I saw them, thank you. I will accept your supplies, but you must leave." She paused, meeting his eyes for the first time. "I beg your pardon, you said you heard of us? How?"

"You don't need a doctor's services?" he asked.

"We have our own doctor," she said with admirable authority.

"I'm impressed," he said.

"Well, he's more of a healer than a doctor. Sometimes he gets stumped."

"What's wrong? I want to help. It's why I'm here."

"Regardless of the jeep and assorted paperwork we found, how do I know you are who you say you are?"

"Why else would I be here, other than to help? Ask me a question or have your healer test me."

"That won't be necessary, but I will quiz you."

Clay raised his eyebrows. "Do you have a medical background as well?"

"No, biology and a good memory. Name every bone and muscle in the human body, both sexes, and follow it up with a breakdown of the human circulatory system."

Clay stifled a laugh as he followed her instructions.

"Okay, that was good. Succinct…" She paused, rolling her eyes up to the low ceiling. "I wouldn't usually do this, but my friend is in severe pain, with a high fever. I wanted to take her to a real hospital, but the closest is a two-day drive, and now she is refusing to go."

He frowned at her. There were people, extremely shady people, plotting her death. She couldn't just waltz into a hospital with a sick friend. "Take me to her. I might be able to help."

"I don't know."

"I might be able to save her. If you do nothing, she could die." She paled, and he had her. "Please *Reina*."

She whipped her head around glaring. "Don't call me that," she snapped. "My name is Asha."

"Sorry…Asha." He was as genuine as he could be. She had to see that.

She studied him. Yep, he had her, and he wanted to help her. He had to kill her, but he truly wanted to help her first.

Uh oh.

"Okay, yeah sure, follow me. But don't underestimate me or this place. If you give me any reason to suspect you aren't being honest, I'll have Marco bury your bones where they'll never be found."

Not a particularly original threat, but Clay appreciated her effort at intimidation, and he nodded gravely.

Outside, the bright sun stung his eyes again, but he could see her better now. She had a confident walk, but still feminine. An interesting sword was strapped to her back, and he fought his spreading grin to no avail. It was too big to wear around her waist, so it lay between her shoulder blades in a leather backpack-style harness.

She was young, maybe twenty-five or so, yet she radiated the fierce strength of an ancient warrior. Power vibrated from her and she wore it naturally. Whether she liked it or not, her title was accurate. She was a warrior queen if he'd ever imagined one.

It was unbelievable. First, his target was young *and,* he reeled, *a girl.* Second, he'd seen her in his dreams, his dreams.

She held the door open for him, and he took the opportunity to study her face. Pretty, but hard and angry. She looked away.

Her hospital was small, clean, and surprisingly well equipped. Asha brushed aside the curtain and revealed a pale young woman, sweating and gripping a young boy's hand. Clay rushed to her side and Asha bent, whispering into the child's ear. He frowned but ran out.

Clay checked her pupils and touched around the patient's abdomen. Her scream was instant and metal flashed. He threw his hands into the air as the sword he'd just been admiring pricked his throat. He caught his breath. She was fierce all right.

He met Asha's glittering gaze across the bed. "I believe it's her appendix," he said. "It will rupture soon if it hasn't already."

She held the sword steady at his neck but glanced down, her eyes full of compassion. The anger and hardness vanished. "Are you sure?"

"Her fever, the abdominal pain. I won't know until I operate."

Asha lowered the sword. "Operate?"

"Yes, I must…right now. Do you have any anesthesia?"

She shook her head.

"Do you have a sanitized operating area?

"There." She pointed to the curtain.

"Grab one of the field kits I brought, hurry."

After sheathing her sword onto her back, she ran to the cabinet and brought back two. He picked up the young woman and spun, striding across the room to the curtained operating suite.

He laid her gently on the table. "Go, get your healer now."

Asha ran to the door and whispered to one of the two guards who took off. Coming back to the operating table, she went to work opening the kits and taking out the contents.

"Line up the syringes, IDs visible, scalpels, and suction too," Clay said, scrubbing his hands at the sink.

Among other things, he was a surgeon, but saving this woman wouldn't be easy.

He switched his mind off his reasons for being there and prepared for surgery. "What's her name?"

"Maria."

"Maria? Can you hear me?" She was unresponsive.

"What happening?" Asha shouted.

"She's unconscious." He yanked up her sleeve, rubbed the alcohol-soaked pad over her vein, and injected the tranquilizer. It was strong enough to last through the surgery.

A withered, dark-skinned man wearing nothing but a small pair of shorts shuffled into the hospital and bowed to Asha. "It's Maria, she needs an operation. You have to help Dr. Brent."

"Antibiotics, in an IV if you can," Clay said, lowering the scalpel and making a small incision. He clamped and sucked the blood away. It was there, but swollen and on the verge of rupturing.

"It's okay. It's still here, but it has to come out now. This is going to take some time."

~ * ~

Hours later, Asha returned to the hospital. Maria laid so pale on blood-soaked sheets. Asha rushed forward. Her friend looked dead.

Dr. Brent was at the sink with his back to her, scrubbing his hands again. "It's okay, she'll make it."

Asha dropped her head, Maria was breathing.

"It's a good thing I was here today, both for the surgery and the medicine. She would have died."

Warmth flooded Asha. "Thank you. I am so grateful for your help."

Maria lived because she'd gone against her initial judgment and trusted a stranger. When she'd returned from the village supply drop and her men told her about Dr. Brent, she'd planned to remove him. But Chi had waited at the gate and taken her to his mother.

She'd been so sick and weak. Boots, their healer, had looked worried. Asha had a choice—ask for help or do nothing. Caution kept her from going to him immediately, but Maria's fever peaked, and she made her choice.

"Why didn't you take her to the hospital when she first got sick?"

"I wasn't here," Asha said, her chest constricting. "How long will her recovery take?"

"She'll need bed rest for at least a week, but then she can take it from there. While she's still at risk of infection, the antibiotics will do the job. She'll have to take them for a few weeks."

Asha listened while studying him. A handsome doctor. According to the cliché, she should be swooning. He was tall and a bit too good-looking, and she'd never seen eyes that color green before. They were so bright in the cell earlier they'd almost lit the dark.

He had the predictable tousled brown hair and chiseled jaw, but she was no girly girl, and she wouldn't melt to mush because of a man's attractive shell. And regardless of his appearance, there was something off about him. His aura maybe? Not that she believed in that. But something…

"Why didn't someone else take her for help?"

She pursed her lips then said, "Yeah, I know, but they don't really trust outsiders. You met our healer, Boots. He takes care of almost everything around here."

"What?"

His smile glittered, and she gulped down a lump in her throat. "His name is Boots?"

"Yes, he never liked his boots. It's a long story. He's just a barefoot kind of guy."

"Okay…well, Boots was helpful but quiet."

"Yes, he's quiet," she said, her stomach dropping. "He can't speak because his tongue was cut out during interrogation."

Asha turned back to Maria, but a fierce grip clamped her arm. Electricity shot through her as the doctor swung her back around to face him.

His eyes were violent rage and she recoiled, but he dragged her back. "You cut out his tongue?"

She yanked back and kicked him in the ribs. He sailed into the sink, and she lunged forward, holding the sword tip against his throat again. She held it steady, but with a twist of her wrist, she cut a thin line and blood appeared under his chin. He froze.

"Me? You're accusing me of cutting out Boot's tongue?"

"I'm sorry, I'm sorry. Please don't kill me. Things are kind of rough down here…right? And you are *la Reina Guerrera* aren't you?"

"No, I'm not." She retreated a step, back sliding the sword back into its home. "It's stupid, but it's their name for me."

"The stories…"

Her stomach dropped. "Stories… that I cut out people's tongues?"

"Yes."

No.

"They say you cut the tongues from your subjects to ensure their silence."

Her knees buckled, and she held onto the sink for support. "That's not true," she whispered past her closing throat. It was difficult to swallow. "What else…do they say?"

"There are rumors that you're a ruthless warrior queen planning to overthrow the government. You're building a private army, and your brutal tactics force blind loyalty. The worst, I'm afraid, is that you have ranks of children in your army."

Crossing her arms over her stomach, she doubled over, taking deep breaths. "No, oh no…I was just trying to fix… How did you find us?"

"It wasn't that hard. I asked around."

Asha closed her eyes, her knees threatening to give out. "Who?"

"I don't know." He shrugged. "Some kid."

"I have to go. You have to go. Now."

"Wait Asha, hold on. It's crap. It's obviously government propaganda. The one rumor I do believe is that your people are loyal." He paused. "The ones I spoke with were definitely loyal."

He frowned, and for a fleeting moment he looked different, colder…angrier.

"If you heard those disgusting things, then why did you still come here?" She narrowed her eyes, picking up on the conflicting vibrations he was putting out.

"Because I learned of your clinic and suspected correctly, you might need supplies. I'm sorry. I didn't mean to accuse you of something so awful. I can't believe I did that." He rubbed the spot on his chest where she'd kicked him. "Really, I was just shocked that anyone could cut out a person's tongue."

Why was she buying this? "We're a long way from…where did you come from?"

"I grew up outside London, went to Harvard med and joined Doctors Without Borders last year. I was stationed in the village and arrived two weeks ago."

"Well, we need to get you back."

Just moments ago he'd been so angry, defending Boots. Her instincts told her nothing about him, but his concern for Boots appealed to her. She was more than grateful he'd saved Maria. Though she was only seven years older, she'd been a mother figure to her, Asha's best friend and main source of comfort.

"Sorry for kicking you." She frowned and glanced at the ceiling and away from his gaze.

"Sorry for grabbing you."

"I'd have done the same if I thought you'd committed such a crime." But she would've killed him the same way she had Boots's torturer.

Asha didn't have time for this; she was worried about those rumors. She'd broken her number one law to remain anonymous. Of course, as more and more people came to her, needed her, and eventually joined her, her risk of discovery had grown. Even with the extreme measures she'd taken to stay undercover, she'd blown it.

"I would like to help you, Asha. I mean it. I admit this is all out of my depth, but I can help."

She shook her head and looked up and away. Her stomach dropped. Again, she believed his words. *So, this is what a pretty face could do to a girl.* She wasn't totally clueless. She read books. He was a big man, confident and sure of his movements. Before she'd seen him cut Maria open, she'd been convinced he was military, and maybe he still could be.

So why was she buying the blue-blood doctor-with-a-heart-of-gold story? Her instincts, the ones she relied on, returned and came clearer now. They told her to trust him...*odd.* She was naturally suspicious, trusting was difficult, and his arrival was proof they were no longer safe. Despite all that, her instincts said he was okay.

Was this how attraction befuddled people and made them stupid? Her cheeks warmed, and her stomach fluttered. *Uh oh.* Foreign sensations and strange inner musings... *Focus.* She had preparations to make. They must disband and start filtering everyone back to the villages. She couldn't be a target, not with so many innocent people around her.

Her goal, her mission, had been restitution to help the people, protect them, but if the rumors were true, someone would come there eventually. "Dr. Brent, you have given me a lot to think about."

"Please, call me Clay, I can't imagine how you've come to your position, but it isn't safe. Loyalty will only last so long. Let me help you."

She ignored his sexist bafflement, but he was right. "I have no reason to trust you, but if you are willing to help, I can find use for you."

"Anything."

"I need to take care of a few things. If you could please gather the children. Make it a game. Twenty-five in total—eight toddlers. I'll send Chi along." She had to get the kids first and the seniors...then everyone else. It would take at least two trips to get them all out.

The air whooshed as the door swung shut, she was too lost in her plans to notice the doctor's departure. Sure, he may see this environment as strange, but it was her home and these people were her family. She loved them. She owed them.

Asha leaned over Maria, who was still sleeping. Chi needed her, and Asha needed her. Thank God, Clay had been here.

With Father Sean still at large, she couldn't pretend these people were safe with her. Of course, this would have to end. She wasn't a missionary or a charity. She robbed and killed evildoers, and those "fees" she'd paid to keep from making waves had obviously backfired.

South America drew its share of bottom-barrel scumbags, and she hunted them, sometimes for a price and sometimes just to exterminate vermin. If she ran out of targets, well there were places in Asia and Africa that would never disappoint.

Human traffickers were her main source of booty and in the last year, they were the only lure attractive enough to draw her from her base. The body count was usually as high as the take, and yes, she used a hefty portion of each to grease palms on all levels. More than one country's military had taken pride and recognition for her work.

Her hunting trips were always short, and she'd return home to care for her friends and keep her ear to the ground…she'd never picked up a whisper.

This had to be Father Sean's doing. He disappeared eleven years ago, and it was still her greatest mystery—well next to her ability to create fire, of course. But why hadn't he tried to find her?

She'd burned his compound, his buildings to ash and soot, and rebuilt it in memory of the refuge she destroyed. Father Sean never came for her. She searched but found no hint of him. Now all these years later, he was finally making a move, and the vicious rumors would only be the beginning.

Once she relocated everyone to safety, she would happily face him. Weight she wasn't even aware she carried vanished, and she sparked with energy. Asha kissed Maria on the forehead then rushed out.

~ * ~

Four days after Maria's surgery, Clay waited in the shadows as the last trucks and jeeps left Asha's compound. Yesterday, Chi and Maria had been on the first truck out. Clay prepared Maria for travel himself. Every child had gone with the first wave.

Now, Asha waved from the gate, displaying such an interesting contrast. She was both a sad, lonely, young woman waving goodbye to her friends and family and a warrior armed with a sword, machine gun, and holstered pistol.

He studied the outline of her figure; she also carried a smaller model in her calf holster. He found the oxymoron oddly attractive. She was the image of fierce vulnerability.

She'd managed the evacuation with expert skill. He'd joined the ranks, as one of her subjects following orders.

Her people had initially refused to go without her, but she spoke privately to her captains before the first phase of evacuation urging them to act. After explaining they were needed to protect the others from coming danger, they'd finally agreed. Now she was alone. She unhooked the rope and the huge gate swung shut. Dropping the barrier, Asha's shoulders slumped.

"Alone at last." He emerged from his hiding spot.

She spun around, her gun unholstered and up.

"Whoa. I didn't mean to scare you." He sauntered from the shadows, his chest out and his hands up.

"You were supposed to go yesterday with Maria," she stammered.

"She'll be fine."

"Dr. Brent, you must go on foot now."

"Yes, so you say, but I wanted to wait for you."

"Don't be ridiculous. Go."

"Why?" He walked toward her.

"It's not safe."

"Well, if it's so dangerous, you should probably come too."

"I will after I'm sure everything is all clear."

He stepped closer and stopped just in front of her, "Everything *is* all clear."

She was spooked.

"Hey Kid, what's wrong?"

Her eyes flashed, and his face itched, but he couldn't smile and provoke her while she had her gun pointed at him. She was on guard, alert, and he wouldn't push her.

"Don't call me kid," she snapped.

"Hey, whoa... I'm sorry. It's not a crack about your age, which is what, by the way?"

She didn't answer, just scowled with a squinted and suspicious gaze.

"It was your quick draw. Honestly, I've never seen anyone draw that fast." He paused waiting for a reaction. "Not that I've much experience with guns." He held up his hands. "I like old westerns, and I believe Billy the Kid would be impressed." Still no reaction. "Ma'am instead?" he drawled.

Her lips pursed. She was fighting a smile.

Phew.

She lowered the gun.

He could finish his assignment. He was already days behind, but standing before her, he couldn't do it yet. His work varied, and he carried out vile deeds, but he'd never struggled with it before now. Thanks to his special training, his questionable morals usually stayed on mute.

While waiting in his cell, Clay had used reality to put distance between the woman in his dreams and his target. She only resembled her.

Hell, it could be extreme deja vu. But any distance gained shattered the moment she'd walked in. No matter what, he would have trouble pulling the trigger.

From the moment he spied Asha through the scope, an invisible tether had stretched across the distance, and it tightened now, drawing Clay closer to her.

She stood her ground, and again he admired her courage. She didn't holster her gun, but there was almost no fear in her. The base they stood in was a testament to her accomplishments. No one could've risen to her position without facing strong opposition and intimidation tactics at the very least. People would've attempted to suppress her, but she'd flourished.

Until he'd arrived. He dropped his hands.

"Keep them up," she said.

Her voice was clear, even, and still that little bit raspy. Earlier he'd gone ballistic. He'd believed the worst, his outburst so transparent now. He literally leapt for a reason to end her in that moment, but she'd stopped him.

If she'd only been the person described in her dossier, it would be a bit easier…maybe. Something was wrong. It was clear she was strong and focused and very impressive, but he'd expected a ruthless mercenary and murderer.

There was no way she could do what he'd read, so either someone had set her up or they gave him incorrect information. He smelled a set-up. He lowered his hands again. She rolled her shoulders back and holstered her gun.

Standing before her, a slow grin across his lips as he studied her lips. His fingers itched to touch her.

Clay took immediate advantage and leaned forward grasping her arms before she could bolt, or rearm herself, and yanked her against him. It was a considerable risk considering how many weapons she carried on her person, but he took it anyway. *What happened to not pushing the girl with the guns and sword?*

He had to try. Closing his eyes, clenching against the possibility she might run him through, he bent his head. Electricity and heat blew through his body, the force jolting him and shifting him off balance.

Warm, soft lips, pounding heart and boiling blood was all he could grasp past the protestations in his head. He squeezed her arms; he was dizzy and struggling for control. She didn't fight his presumptuous assault. She stood rigid, her lips the only soft thing about her, but they opened on a small sigh, and her stiff muscles loosened.

With rhythmic fervor, they moaned together, and his blood

surged. He had to restrain his urgency to a hot simmer, but he craved more. She followed his pace, and he slipped his tongue in and explored her mouth. She sighed again.

Encouraged, he shifted closer against her, reaching up and taking her face in his hands. Why had he done it? Why had he given in? His mind raced, but he didn't care. The rush, his physical reaction was shaking his core and his control.

No. This couldn't happen...

He jerked his face away but squeezed her arms again. "Who are you?" His voice echoed in the empty compound. "What are you doing here?" This conflict unnerved him, yet he had a job to do.

Asha pulled away, but her fingers went to her lips as she studied him. "This is my home. What are *you* doing here?"

The boom cut through the night, shaking the jungle and echoing over their heads. Her head snapped around to the gate and she ran for the wall. She bounded up the steps and to the top, leaning over.

"No," she cried. "It's the convoy."

She threw her leg over the wall and jumped from sight.

"Asha, wait." Gunfire sounded in the distance. "Shit." Clay sprinted for the gate.

~ * ~

Drawing her gun, Asha raced down the road.

More shooting and now screams travelled across the distance; the convoy was under attack. She pushed her legs harder and surged ahead.

Approaching the ambush, she scanned and aimed. At least sixty armed men, dressed in combat black with night vision surrounded one of the burning trucks.

Shooting through the trees as she sprinted, six dropped, one for each bullet. But she was too late. They were gone, their bodies scattered everywhere. Her friends—dead. A massacre.

A red film blurred her vision, and she clamped her teeth, grinding them together. Her rage clawed at her control, building into a primal scream. Her nerves tingled. The monster tore at her to get out, and she obeyed. She opened the cage, and her power bubbled over.

Asha dropped her useless gun, hot air blowing around her. She called fire, and flames swirled between her fingers, rolling up her forearms. The remaining men spun around, guns pointed.

"You're so dead," she whispered, raising her arms.

A roaring, dancing inferno circled them and rose, catching the next wave of bullets in its burning wall. With her hands clasped together, the circle closed and the fire rolled, covering them. The living screamed and continued shooting, but the flames soon silenced them.

Clay burst through the brush gun in hand. "Asha?"

Her fire still burned, but they were all dead. She staggered, and she collapsed to the ground, her heavy head dropping. "What have I done? I was too late. If I had started the evacuation earlier…"

Wait.

Heat bubbled and boiled deep inside her again. She glared at the doctor, the gun gripped naturally in his hand. "This was you!" she screamed, standing. "Father Sean sent you."

She whipped around, sweeping Clay's legs out from under him and ripped the gun from his hand. Spinning it in her grasp, she aimed the muzzle at him. Where did he get a gun?

She looked up. Muffled helicopters in the distance were coming in fast. She was familiar with them. Rare and expensive, they were the latest in stealth technology. This wasn't political; there was too much money behind this operation. She searched the sky. Take down the choppers, remove the threat, and then question the doctor.

"I'm so sorry."

It was his tone more than his words that halted her. "What?" she snapped meeting his green eyes. They… glowed?

"I said I'm sorry."

Pain cracked across her skull, echoing through her head blinding her. Darkness instantly shut everything out.

Chapter Three

The ancient building's history was as dark as its obsidian walls. The shining, black-stone towers rose, stabbing at the bright sun. Nothing would grow on such a smooth, impenetrable surface. The Order's birthplace had endured since the beginning—imposing, frightening, and eternal.

Inside, the windowless hall remained dark, regardless of the hour. The building's labyrinthine halls and staircases led like veins and arteries to the Grand Chamber, the heart of the Order.

"Grand Master." Paul bowed. "Master Heath and Master Miles."

Heath sat beside his father on a raised dais at the front of the cavernous room. Four large candelabras cast eerie shadows against the back wall. His brother, Miles, sat stone-faced and silent on his father's right side.

"Masters, prepare to be shocked," Paul said, his voice thick with sarcasm, "but Benjamin has betrayed us." He nudged the tied-up man, gagged and cowering on the floor with his foot. "I followed him, searched his quarters, and found the evidence. He planned on meeting with an outsider."

Master Heath's curiosity, seldom piqued, jumped. They hadn't had a defector in years, not since he and Miles were in their mid-twenties. Heath glanced at his father.

His baldhead shining in the candlelight, the Grand Master narrowed his icy-blue eyes and glared at the man on the floor. "Remove his gag."

Benjamin choked and stifled a sob.

"Who were you meeting Benjamin?" Heath asked.

He twisted, staring up at the three men, stammering, "I…I don't know, Master. He kept his identity hidden…he contacted me…he claimed he had important information about the sisters. I believed it prudent to consult him…hear his information… I intended to bring it to you once I confirmed it. I was wrong. I should have come to you first." His answers stuttered and spilled in a jumble.

"He didn't get a chance to share anything of importance. I caught up with him in time."

"Thank you, Paul," Master Heath said, his voice calm. "What you apparently failed to remember Benjamin is that this is *our* battle, *our* business. It is what we must do, what we are destined to do. Our plans involve no one else. It is paramount, the cornerstone of our beliefs."

"Outsiders know nothing of the sisters." Miles's voice was hushed.

"Yes, Master this one did. He approached me."

"How?"

"He accosted me at a birth. The girls were not the ones we seek. I was leaving, and a man approached me, bumped me, and said 'I know what you are looking for, and I know where they are'."

Heath's heart raced. Sweat beaded his brow.

"I found the paper in his cell. An address in Rome and a number," Paul said.

"You may proceed," Heath said.

Paul's steps clicked and echoed across the black-stone floor to the shining armoire on the back wall. The piece blended into the surrounding walls but was large enough to hold all the tools he would need. It was the only piece of furniture in the room, aside from the Masters' table and chairs.

Benjamin squirmed on the floor. "No, wait. There have been signs. I meant no harm. Please. Please."

Master Miles stiffened beside the Grand Master, and Master Heath caught the subtle reaction.

"No harm?" The Grand Master gritted through bared teeth. "What if you'd succeeded? No one who's aware of us can survive. A chain of sacrifice for every soul's knowledge, their families, their friends, anyone it took to protect our anonymity. This is our way, yet you still risked our wrath." He paused then said, "I offer you a choice. Paul will proceed, and we'll let him have his fun, or you face the Four."

Protocol required either Paul or Shane, the Order's generals, to initiate the chain of sacrifice anyway. They couldn't guarantee Benjamin hadn't gotten something out there.

Paul opened the armoire, and the weapons flashed in the candlelight. From large cleavers to small scalpels and hooks, a vast array was strapped to the black-velvet background with more laid out on the shelves, each instrument catching the light with evil brilliance.

Benjamin sobbed again. "Paul… please, Paul." He rolled into a fetal position, moaning under his breath.

Heath inclined his head awaiting the first cut, and at Benjamin's scream, blood spattered across the spotless black stone and disappeared into the floor. A familiar scene, but the goosebumps rose anyway.

Heath glanced at his brother, watching the gruesome scene before them. The last scream ended abruptly, and a wisp of purple vapor floated up and disappeared into the stone. Paul's robes were covered in deep red splatter, but not a drop was on the floor.

Heath faced the Grand Master and his brother. "If you'll excuse me, Father…Miles, I assume you'll follow up with Benjamin's confidante and take care of it? I have to see Shane. He returned this morning."

The Grand Master and his firstborn nodded.

Heath rushed through the halls to his office. The files were already waiting on his desk. He opened the one on top and removed the hefty report. Shane knocked and leaned in the doorway.

"Come in."

He ducked under the crystal chandelier and bowed. Tall and willowy, Shane's frame was the opposite of short, stocky, pallid Paul.

Shane's dark skin shimmered under the light, his brown eyes lifting up. "I dropped off the files. I wanted to give you my report. There have been multiple scenes, all devastated by explosions with large craters left behind. The first happened fifteen years ago. I have discovered a fair more since then. I suggest you send someone to investigate further."

Master Heath flipped through the report.

"I suspect a cover-up. There has been no coverage of these events. The satellite photos were the most difficult to get and are the best lead we have."

"Good. That'll be all." When the door clicked shut behind Shane, Heath picked up the phone. "I want to see Clay the moment he returns."

He unrolled a laminated map, spreading it over the files. He had to fight to suppress the thrill rolling through him. It was too soon to celebrate.

~ * ~

Deep below in the Order dungeons, Clay carried Asha's limp body to the last cell. Thankfully, the others were empty for now. He gazed at her sleeping face, her dark lashes laying against her pale skin. He had to knock her out to take her from the jungle, but he regretted using the rock.

He'd failed in his mission. The retrieval team was sent to ensure he finished the job, so he'd played his only card. She was more valuable as a prisoner, and the Masters would want her alive. He had to use all his authority to keep them from killing her right there. After he'd loaded her into the chopper, he'd sedated her to keep her unconscious. She'd barely stirred during the flight.

The clean-up crew had shown no mercy to Asha's people, and somehow she'd destroyed them all. He'd searched through the carnage while she lay unconscious and the rest of the team swarmed. He'd held her, she wasn't carrying any grenades or bombs. Guns yes, but still, how? Maybe, she shot the truck's gas tank?

"Who is she?" His brother Aron leaned in through the open door and grinned.

Clay was still crouched beside Asha. He rose, but he couldn't tear his gaze away. "She was my target. Is my target?"

"Mm hmm, and she's here why?"

"Information," Clay said.

He faced Aron, who was taller than he was, but only slightly and not as bulky. His brother's black and silver-streaked hair was the color of angry storm clouds and so different from Clay's dark brown hair.

"Okay sure, but you'll have some explaining to do. I'm here to get you. Heath's looking for you."

"Yeah, I figured. Who sent the retrieval?"

"Paul. He's been impatient for your return as well."

"Okay, okay." Clay walked to the door, shoving Aron out.

He glanced back once; she was still sleeping. She'd be frightened when she woke up. He'd rush through his report and return as soon as he could. He had to convince her he'd brought her here to save her. But how could he protect her?

Locking the door, Aron followed Clay, whistling as they climbed the stone stairs leaving the dungeon. "It must've been an exciting mission."

Clay frowned, ignoring the rib. His mind buzzed; he had to come up with a feasible reason for not killing his target.

She was in trouble, yes, but what could he do about it? Nothing. She was here now, and he was responsible. He should have gotten her away when he had the chance. She would be killed unless he convinced Master Heath she had valuable information. Her followers were dead, and she was no longer a threat. His gut clenched. The Masters would never buy it.

She's dead, and you know it.

Clay was grateful the first convoy had made it safely to the village, but it didn't ease his crisis of conscience in the slightest. But at the very least, the children, most of their parents, and Boots and Maria were alive.

As they emerged on the main floor Aron's whistling changed

from its jolly tune to Beethoven's fifth symphony, doom and gloom, dun…dun…dun…dun.

Clay was in no mood for jokes. "Look Aron, I need to get this over with. I'll meet up with you guys later."

"Sure, of course."

Clay left him and rushed down the hall to Heath's office. He knocked and entered. "You sent for me, Master?"

"Yes Clay, good. Come in."

"My report—"

"It can wait. This is more important. Sit down."

~ * ~

Just hours later, Heath ran down to the dungeons, his strides sending his robe billowing behind him. He stopped at the cell door, holding the key to the lock, peeking through the window. He could see her asleep on the slab. *She's here.*

He spun and dashed back upstairs to tell his brother the shocking news. Heath found Miles in the Grand Chamber, the usual guards at the doors. "Success, Miles, success."

"Yes, I heard Clay returned, a little late perhaps, but I am pleased the mission was so successful." His brother spoke without looking up from his papers.

"More than you know. It's a miracle."

"A miracle? I would hardly qualify a discharged rebel regime as a miracle."

Heath swallowed and forced out a shallow chuckle. The regime change was nothing, just a small job to remove an obstacle and keep the flow of drugs and guns moving. The rebels led by *la Reina Guerrera* had interfered and slowed the flow, thus affecting their material gains. "Don't be absurd. That is not the miracle I am referring to, Miles. Clay found them."

He finally looked up. "Who?"

"Who do you think? The sisters. We should have confirmation soon. I've already sent a team to collect them."

Miles glanced at the guards by both doors. "You found the sisters? But there've been no signs. We've been searching."

"Not carefully enough, obviously. We have one here—fire. She's in the dungeon."

"I beg your pardon?" Miles's pale face was unreadable. "She's here? How?"

"Suspicious events were brought to my attention. I had to investigate, and what Benjamin said confirmed it. Clay did the rest."

"He *found* them?"

"Yes, *la Reina Guerrera* is *fire*, she's in the dungeon, and Clay brought her here himself."

"*He* brought her here?" He dropped his gaze. "Why didn't Clay kill her as ordered?"

"He said she was valuable. How true those words are," Heath said.

"Well, that explains it. If she is fire and he met her, he'd pick up her essence, and it would be easier to find the rest."

Heath swiveled his gaze to the guards. Obedience was required of all Order members regardless of their station, but chatter always occurred, and he had to be careful. "Miles are you all right? Do you know what this means?"

"Of course. This is fantastic news, Heath. But how did they elude us? How did we miss their birth?" Miles smiled. "Inform the Grand Master. Say nothing to anyone else until they are all within the walls. What does Clay know about this?"

"I can never be sure with Clay. After getting nothing for so long, he finally connected. He was as shocked as I was when he realized he'd brought one of them here."

~ * ~

Asha stirred in her rocky tomb. Her senses jittered. She opened her eyes and glanced at the door. There was a small window and a man staring in. His green eyes glowed clear across the room. Startled, she scrambled to her feet. The pounding in her head threatened her balance, but with each deep breath she pushed back the closing darkness until it passed.

Stay calm, don't explode, and deal with each event in sequence.

She counted to ten and tapped her leg with her thumb and forefinger before she opened her eyes and looked up again. Still he stared through the window, studying her.

Dr. Brent.

She'd been outside the base…he was there too, with a gun, apologizing. He watched her now, studied her. Her focus wavered, and she touched a lump, sticky with dried blood, on the back of her head. There was something more. The fuzzy vision, the tingling, rubbery legs—she recognized the symptoms. She'd been knocked out with a blow to her head and drugged.

The thick haze cleared. The attack on her people. He'd killed them, and she would kill him…right now. He opened the door and walked in. He appeared different, colder and harder than the doctor who'd betrayed her, but two things were obvious. She was correct in her first assessment: he was definitely military. And he'd locked her up on his base.

The room was noticeably fireproof. Even if it hadn't been, she couldn't risk a large explosion in an unfamiliar place. *Don't blow anything up without concrete intelligence about what it is first.*

Who knew what scary things they had there? She wouldn't risk nukes or chemical weapons or anything else she might find in a place that oozed evil as this place did. She would have to be fast.

Asha opened her anger, dropped her control, and drew her power. Get the fire hot enough, fast enough, and he wouldn't have a chance to alert anyone. Clenched against his inevitable screams she flipped open the doors of her constant control, but no tingle, no heat. *Wait, what?* She stared at his boots…nothing. With all her focus and strength, she urged it on…

Again, and again she tried, and nothing happened. Not even a hint of her power. Her fire was always there. It was a spark within her. Even after the times she'd blown her hottest and was drained for days, her power always flickered inside her. But this was different. It was gone.

Closing her eyes, she trembled. Why wouldn't the fire come? She opened her eyes. Clay stared at her. What's happening? She had never fully relied on her element; she needed to be good at what she did without fire. She'd worked in crowds and enclosed spaces as often as jungles and abandoned compounds. But fire was always part of her, there when she needed it. Her safety net, without it, she had far fewer options.

Her heart stuttered in her chest, and she collapsed, the pressure forcing her to gasp. Clay leaned forward, but she recoiled.

"Asha?"

She couldn't stop it. Panic raced through her full force, Bringing her knees to her chest, she screamed for release. Through her constricted chest, she could only manage a low, pitiful wail. Horror stories about labs and experiments rushed through her memory. Father Sean had threatened it often, and those threats were finally coming to fruition in his final revenge.

"I'm so sorry."

Clay's words penetrated through the ringing fury. Whenever she panicked, she risked causing serious damage, but without her power, that risk was gone. For the first time she accepted her terror, absorbed the weight, the heat, and the pressure.

She rolled it, churned it, and rechanneled it into rage. "Get out."

He left the room, locking the door. She rocked on the cell floor. *You're okay, you're okay.* She had to come up with a power-free plan. It would be tough, but her anger subsided enough to pull her scrambled thoughts together.

Clay scrambled through the dark forest, searching. He wasn't completely sure what he was hunting, but thundering urgency pushed him onward.

A ticking clock pounded in his head as time clicked forward faster and faster with his pounding heart. Where were the guys? Was he looking for them?

His legs tangled in vines that pulled him back. Heat pulsed beneath his feet, and he dropped to his knees, digging. The ground was hard, and his fingers grew bloody as he screamed. The imaginary clock sped on and his eyes were blurred, with sweat or tears he couldn't tell. He had to keep digging.

He opened the ground, but he was too slow. The box was big, a shoddy wooden casket, black and charred. The burned wood splintered and he pulled it apart. He was too late.

The skeleton burned with small flames running along blackened bones, but they blew out with the wind.

Clay sat up in his bed sweating and panting. *Shit.* Asha was in the dungeon, in a cell, and as long as she was, she was dead.

He left his room and crept down to the lowest level to the last cell on the end. No one was on duty because with their security they didn't need guards. But had there been a guard on duty, Clay would have been well within his rights and authority to be there.

He peered through the window. She was awake, sitting on the ground, her knees to her chin and her arms wrapped around them. His chest tightened.

He unlocked the cell, and she stiffened. "Asha?"

She turned her face. He barely recognized her. Her eyes were wide and her face was pale plus she was shaking.

"Something's wrong," she said. Her voice was a hoarse, whisper. She'd been screaming.

"I'm sorry...I don't..." He knelt beside her. His hands twitched, but he didn't touch her. Why hadn't he acted earlier? Taken her away? His arrival was enough to send her underground.

If he hadn't enjoyed himself so much and taken his mission seriously, he could have told her who he was and why he was there and convinced her to disappear. He could have lied to the Masters and told them he'd killed her. They trusted him enough to take his word, but that damn team had shown up and blown it all to hell.

Now she was here, barely resembling the warrior who'd taken and spun his own gun on him in the jungle, rendering him helpless. She was unbelievable. Just the memory made him smile. A tempest of fiery hair and temper, yet just two hours after leaving her, her transformation shocked him.

"Has anyone been here?" Clay asked.

A chill crept through his blood, twitching his muscles. If anyone had mistreated her, they would face a very unpleasant…

"Did anyone come in here while I was gone?" He didn't stop his hand as it reached out.

His fingers grazed her bare shoulder, and a shock ran through his body. Her skin was cold. She turned; her eyes were black. Clay jerked back as the chill in his blood turned to ice. Black pupils had covered the whites of her eyes.

"Asha?"

She looked terrifying. He had seen some weird things, but this was something he didn't understand.

She shook her head slowly.

He took her shoulders, turning her, and she crumpled as limp as a rag doll into his lap. "Hey, wake up."

She wasn't sleeping; her eyes were open.

He shook her. She didn't even blink. "Asha. Stop it, come on. Wake up." He wanted to slap her, but he hesitated. *It's not right. Do it.*

He tapped her cheek with his fingers. She didn't move.

Come on, she can take more than that. He opened his palm and slapped her. She didn't move.

He tried again harder. "Come on, wake up."

Her gasp resembled a drowning victim's first life-saving breath.

"Are you okay? What happened?" he asked.

Her open eyes were cloudy and gray while her black pupils spun and shrunk until her eyes were now completely white.

"Holy shit, what's happening? Asha?" Should he get one of the Masters? Hell no.

Clay turned back to the cell door. He had to do something, but her fingers on his face stopped him dead. She touched his face, and he clenched before looking down at her. Her eyes were still white, but she was smiling. Her smile was beautiful, and he was swept away.

Hold on. Why is she smiling?

Asha pulled his face down, and before he knew entirely what was happening she kissed him. Heat flooded him, and all rational ability escaped him. Her lips were warm, and her cheeks flushed. Her fingers stroked through his hair. He was kissing her, with his eyes closed.

You're toast, bro.

He drew back, and she released him. Aside from her eyes, her expression was serene and so out of place here in this prison.

She was still across his lap. "What's going on?"

"Your eyes."

"I don't belong here." Her voice was soft, gentle.

He lifted her and carried her to the metal slab. Her white eyes flickered and closed. She breathed deeply. She was asleep.

He couldn't help her. Futility swept over him, and his legs buckled. He'd just found her, and he was going to lose her.

Chapter Four

Ivy stepped off the late bus into frigid, soggy darkness. She'd worked way past closing at the veterinary clinic because Bubbles, the Parkers' two-year-old Siamese, had a nasty run-in with a raccoon. She'd needed stitches, but thankfully she was going to be okay.

Ivy dragged her heavy as lead feet as she staggered the few blocks from the bus stop to her house. Her trench coat may have kept the rain from soaking her through, but the dampness had already chilled her deep down, reaching her bones. It would take at least thirty minutes in a scalding tub to stop her shivering. Her drenched brown hair hung to her elbows, sticking to her face and jacket. She blinked her eyes and wiped the large drops from her forehead.

She never bothered with an umbrella. It was just another item to carry, and after growing up in Vancouver, she was more than used to the rain. But tonight, a shield from this downpour would've been worth it. She twisted the strands and squeezed the water out before tying them into a knot at her neck. It helped divert the rivulets streaming into her face. Good thing she rarely wore make-up or she'd look like poor Bubbles's sharp-clawed nemesis right now.

Increasing her pace, Ivy approached home, the sight already warming her. Her front garden grew lush and green and was definitely enjoying the torrential weather of the last three days. She'd start a fire, open the windows, and listen to it bounce on the roof while she soaked in the tub.

At her chipped, iron gate, she halted. Her welcoming two-story, white paradise with porch swing and gardens was dark and quiet inside. Silent, heavy waves pulsed from the house. She hesitated.

Someone's inside. Someone I don't know.

Hunched over, she crept up the stone walkway leading to the front porch. Her front door was open a crack. With her heart pounding and blood rushing, every instinct, all her training, screamed at her to walk away, leave the house, and call Father Bennett. But she couldn't.

Her suspicion spurred her forward. She dropped her bag silently on the front step, opening the door gently. With her hands up and fisted, she entered the dark house, ignoring the warning blasting through her, staying tense and alert. She grabbed her old field-hockey stick from her empty umbrella stand and held it like a club. The living room was dark, but she saw him, and her legs buckled.

No. Please no!

Father Bennett was slumped back on the couch. She stumbled forward on rubber legs but it was too late. The blood splattered on the wall behind him and his open, vacant eyes told her he was not asleep, or hurt, but much, much, worse. She automatically touched his wrist for his pulse…he was warm.

The blood dripped on the wall behind the couch. From the bullet hole between his eyes and the mess on the wall, it was obvious he was recently executed at close range.

Prickles tingled down her spine. Energy vibrated from the shadows behind her. Adrenaline surged, and she let her instincts take over. Spinning around, she swung her weapon, and the timing was perfect. She got the side of his face and the impact vibrated through the wooden stick down to her hands. His nose and cheekbone crunched from the impact.

She followed with a roundhouse kick and hit his forearm, shattering the bones and knocking the gun he'd just raised away. Her leg came down, and she used the momentum to swing her arm, punching him in the face before he'd recovered. Two more swings of the stick to his face and he finally staggered, but Christ, he was still on his feet.

Ivy rushed him, unleashing her fury. She gripped his shirt and belt and spun him from his disoriented stagger, sending him crashing through the glass doors into her backyard.

She jumped through the shattered door frame and dropped to her knees plunging her hands into the soggy grass. This man would suffer. She fed her rage and clawed her fingers deep into the soil.

The murderer got to his feet. His white teeth glittered in the dark.

You think you have me, don't you?

He strode toward her, and her anger and grief rose. Hot pulsing power exploded through her fingertips. The ground rippled from her hands like pond rings. The earth trembled and rolled beneath the assassin, liquefying.

He screamed, struggling as he was sucked down. He scratched and clawed, but the grass slipped through his clutching hands until he was gone. The earth swallowed him, and he was deep beneath the surface, an inconsistency within the soil and rock, his screams muffled as he fought. She linked her fingers together, and the earth responded, closing around the struggling shape until he was crushed to nothing.

With Ivy's hands still buried in the dirt, she collapsed, panting. After all the commotion, the police would be on their way. This was usually a quiet neighborhood. She couldn't be there when they arrived. It was their most important rule.

She withdrew her hands and stared at them. This day was always going to come. He'd warned her it would. And though it had always hurt her to do it, they'd prepared for it.

Don't cry. Get going.

Ivy took a calming breath and ran into the house. Father Bennett had been her advisor, teacher, father figure, and best friend, and she couldn't imagine her next step, let alone her life without him.

Vines and roots came through the broken glass doors. She smiled through the heart-crushing grief. The roots coiled around Father Bennett and carried him out to the yard, well away from where she'd crushed his killer. She followed while the foliage laid him gently on the grass. His face was peaceful even with the wound, and she would remember every detail.

The earth rolled and cradled him in a loving embrace, taking him down gradually, this process much gentler than before. Soil covered him, and he disappeared. A vine poked through the ground and circled the area. Ivy smiled at her namesake. She was pleased with the Earth's response to her benefactor.

Inside the circle, a sprout shot out. It uncurled, stretched, and thickened. In seconds, it grew into a beautiful, full-grown weeping willow. A breeze rustled the rope-like branches, and they danced. Sunflowers, gardenias, and rose bushes surrounded the tree unbidden in testament to her life-long teacher.

Ivy's body ached with heavy grief, and she stayed a moment in silent reflection before she rose. There would be time to grieve later after she was safely away.

Inside, she picked up her emergency pack filled with all the necessities a girl on the run would need. *Always be prepared.* Father Bennett's words echoed in her memory, and she saw him standing over her, his gentle face trying and failing to be stern with her.

At the front door, she paused and glanced back at her home, her sanctuary, now tainted. She wouldn't be returning. She took Father Bennett's briefcase, and urgency and adrenaline sent her running out the door, leaving her home for…where? Maybe she was less prepared for this day than she thought.

Without him, she had no idea where to go or what to do. The basics of stay away from the police and use fake IDs were covered, but now she had to start again, leave the city, and begin a new life.

She tossed her pack across her back and jumped down the steps. It was quiet, no sirens. Maybe she'd misjudged the noise level, or she'd misjudged her neighbors' concern for her, but either way she took off running out the gate to the old train tracks a few blocks away. Ivy had gone at a steady jog for more than half an hour before she stopped to rest at a small neighborhood park off the tracks.

She fumbled with the lock on Father Bennett's briefcase. *Where should I go?* Her stupid hands wouldn't stop shaking, and her chest ached, but there was more. Usually an even-tempered and grounded person, the flushing heat, the clenched, grinding jaw proved it…she was enraged.

His murder had been so coldblooded, and the murderer had stayed there…waiting. He was obviously a professional, and her power was the only explanation. Someone had discovered her. But who? How? Why?

Secrecy had been their only concern, their main focus; their safety depended on it. Something must've changed. She must've slipped up in some way, and she'd lost Father Bennett because of it.

The lock finally clicked, and inside the briefcase, was an old journal. Covered in worn, brown leather and filled with writing in his hand, it was full of accounts detailing her power and her studies. Why would he keep this for someone to find?

She flipped through the pages, reading entries dating back to when she was a child and used her gift without awareness or control. Her tense face relaxed, and she smiled as she read a passage.

> *At ten months old, Ivy likes to sit in her sandbox and entertain herself by creating sinkholes in the sand, sucking her toys down, then shooting them out and up into the air. The joy and laughter these games bring will encourage her to use her power when she needs it most. Her gift is strong and she can already manipulate both the earth, and the flora growing from it.*

Warmth flushed through her while reading the written words of a memory she didn't have. She could hear him speaking, and the heaviness returned. Whether smart or not, Father Bennett kept a diary, and she was grateful for the keepsake. She would read it whenever she needed him, and his words would connect them.

Flipping the pages, Ivy stopped at one with a folded corner. Her gaze stopped on a passage describing her power and how she used it. The words didn't quite make sense.

> *She already has the ability to find her sisters. At twelve-years old, soon after her parents' deaths, she first mentioned sensing*

water, fire, and air.

The book fumbled as her fingers shook.

Sisters?

Her head hummed, and a light switched on. Since her youth, she'd picked up vibrations from the earth. With her power, she had the ability to connect to the land, and while she learned to understand it, she discovered patterns and rhythms. As her power grew, her range spread to encompass each continent. She felt earthquakes, oil drills, and various anomalies, but there were also separate, distinct pulses of power.

Her heart soared—the flight all the more thrilling after coming from grief's lowest depths. The vibrations. They were her sisters. It made so much sense. She closed her eyes and searched for them now, water… air and… There was no fire.

Sisters. Finding them was her next step. If she was in danger, they could be too. Water was in Australia and Air was in Hong Kong. Where was fire?

Ivy unzipped the front pocket of her pack and slipped the diary deep inside. It caught on something, an envelope under the zippered flap. Inside was cash, a lot of cash—and a letter written by Father Bennett.

Don't cry.

My dearest Ivy,

If you find this letter and I am gone, I want you to know I am sorry, and I love you. You were as loved as any daughter could be, and I hope I did enough to keep you safe. The one regret I have is not being more honest with you, but I did it to protect you.

You have three sisters. You will need them now. You can find them. Their names are Avia, Asha, and Mere. You are quadruplets, separated on the day of your birth. You've always felt them. Do you remember?

Find them, and then find Master Miles. He is the only one you and your sisters can trust. Be safe, Ivy. I am so proud of you.
Father Bennett

Ivy had their names. She would start with Mere and work backward. But where was fire, where was Asha? Ivy would try to pick her up again, but an assassin had come after her tonight. She probed again and got nothing. Jumping up, she ran for the closest bus stop.

Chapter Five

In the Order's dank dungeon cell, Asha awoke on the slab. How did she get there? She'd been crying on the ground, defeated and terrified. How could she even have fallen asleep? The place's energy was off, dark and suffocating. Shame crept over her; she was acting like a pussy.

Father Sean would show himself, but being the coward he was, he hadn't yet. He'd managed somehow, to mute, or pause her power, and she had to admit however he'd done it, it was impressive. Without her power, they had a better chance of getting whatever they wanted from her.

The lock clicked. *Here we go.* A man in black robes opened the door and held out a tray. She would have tossed it in his face, but he beat her to it. He threw it like a Frisbee, and the food sailed through the air, splattering her as well as the stone walls. Before she could get to her feet he slipped out and locked her door again.

She wasn't sure what scared her more, black robes, or the white lab coats she'd expected. Unpleasant shivers of new fear crept over her skin.

Where am I?

Clay returned, and she watched him enter. His eyes were soft again, but hardened as he took in the mess. "What happened here?"

He must've assumed she'd had a tantrum and tossed her food on the flood like a toddler.

He stepped closer and reached out. She backed away.

Stand your ground.

But she couldn't and backed into the cold wall. The cold stone froze her skin through her clothes. She pushed away and slammed into Clay's body. His arms wrapped around her. She stiffened but didn't pull away.

What?

He lowered his lips to her ear and horrifying shivers rolled through her body.

"You scared me last night," he whispered.

His breath tickling her skin was the first warmth she'd felt since waking up there.

Last night? What happened last night?

He touched her cheek with his fingers and rubbed his forehead against hers. She closed her eyes and tried to ignore the heat and tingling spreading through her. His lips pressed against her cheek, and her heart pumped faster as he moved lower.

Stop.

He kissed her and electricity coursed through her. His lips were gentle, but the zap was strong.

Stop you fool.

She pushed back and swung. In his dazed stupor, she caught him unaware and cracked him hard on the jaw. She should have broken something, a tooth at least, but his head barely turned.

"What the hell are you doing?" she yelled.

He moved to the other side of the cell, and when he turned, he stood with his back against the wall. He stayed, and left, and then returned again, spending silent hours in her cell, fueling her rage. He wore his soldier persona when he entered, but it would fade over time and he'd be the handsome doctor again. His voice, stance, and eyes softened. He coaxed her to speak, to let him explain, but she ignored him.

It was her stupidity, her urges. *Jesus.* Whatever it was, it was her. *She* let down her guard. *She* fell for him when she knew better than to trust anyone.

~ * ~

Mere's favorite beach was crowded, even so early in the morning. An hour from Perth, her small, neighborly town was known for only two things: waves and hippies. She crouched, and the tide rolled in and crashed, frothing and foaming on the soft white sand. The sound, usually as soothing as any lullaby, was louder today, faster. The water was rough, urging her on—her perfect surf.

As she waxed her board, relishing the hot sun on her skin, she aimed for casual while swinging her hair over her shoulder and peeking at the cute lifeguard, sitting on his perch. She caught his eye and he winked, but the wave's rhythm drew her focus back to the water.

Thanks to the break's size, she would be alone out there, and she preferred it that way. She picked up her board and charged forward, gracefully jumping on when her toes hit the water. She glanced over her shoulder for a last gawk at the lifeguard. He'd risen on his perch and waved her back in. She winked and gave him a thumbs up.

Guys were usually surprised by her skill and ability on the big waves, even though some of the best surfers around there were chicks. She'd accuse him of sexism, except the water was extremely rough, and she was surprised he hadn't put up the red flag.

She turned back. He waved the flag over his head.

Oops. But I'm already here. I'll just ride one in.

She paddled out to the current, and it carried her effortlessly over the water to where the break was rolling. Trailing her left hand in the cool water, she connected to the current and it picked up speed, whipping her out even faster. The day was glorious, and she grinned.

Behind the break, she slid over the water faster than was natural, and in one swift, smooth motion, she turned her board and paddled with her first wave. She popped up into her surfer's stance, crouched low, and aligned her center of mass over the board. Shifting her weight to her heels, she slowed herself. Sliding across the water, she was as comfortable and carefree as she could get. She whooped with joy, riding through the pipe and trailing her fingers along the rolling wall. Tingles ran down her body through to her toes as she held the board steady.

She emerged into brilliant sunlight and steered the board sharply to the right. The board shot to the top of the crest, catching air and soaring over the wave as it passed. Her body stretched naturally and she dove deep into the water. Her leash, fastened around her ankle tugged her back and she did a somersault in the churning water. *What a day.* Laughing, she broke the surface and slid onto her board.

Distant cries echoed across the water from the beach, and she spun back. People yelled, jumping up and pointing.

She raised her arm to calm the lifeguard, but...*her wave*...her wave had crashed way too high up the beach and ten or twelve people splashed around frantically through the waist-high water. More were running forward to join them. The lifeguard sprinted for them.

She rolled off her board and sank underwater, forcing herself to be still and quiet. She held her breath, drowned out the sound of the huge break until the water was quiet and the noise from the beach a distant echo. *Block it out.* The waves spun, and the fish swam, but apart from the familiar ocean sounds, frantic movement about fifty feet away disturbed the flowing currents. She opened her eyes, searching underwater. There it was, a small shape being tossed and rolled in the surf. She reached out, and the current responded to her silent command and immediately, switched direction and carried the girl up.

Mere shot ahead, kicking her legs and reached her in seconds. Grasping the child's arms and breaking the surface, she dragged the young girl on top of her board. The surging ocean stilled as the water's surface smoothed till it looked like glass.

She whistled loudly, waving to the lifeguard on the beach. He was already running to his jet ski. Mere leaned over the girl's still body; her eyes were closed. Terror crushed Mere, and she gasped. So small and still, the girl's body was limp—she wasn't breathing.

Her heart pounded and the sea churned and frothed around the surfboard. *Damn it. Pull yourself together.* Mere pinched the girl's tiny nose with her fingers and blew air into her mouth. She gave her three breaths of air while using her legs to swim the surfboard-stretcher closer to shore.

Tears blurred her vision and spilled down her wet face as she counted three presses on the delicate chest and breathed into her mouth again. The jet ski was coming. She pushed on the girl's chest again, and the child jerked and sputtered. Small blue eyes blinked open, and Mere's body turned to jelly.

It was her fault. Her wave was too big and too powerful.

Idiot. Careless moron, you almost killed her.

The lifeguard's face relaxed, and Mere blinked away tears. "I think she'll be okay."

"Oh, my God, that was crazy. The wave—" He reached out for the coughing child, and Mere lifted her and placed her in his arms. "If you hadn't been there? Thank you, thank you. I have to get her to the beach." He held the girl tightly to his chest. "I'll be right back."

He cranked the craft around and sped to shore where the parents ran to meet their daughter. The hysterical mother took her baby, hugging her while Beach Rescue and EMTs arrived and guided them both to the truck.

Mere dropped her head.

Breathe, breathe, she's fine. Keep it together.

The water rolled again, slowly building its natural rhythm.

Mere shook herself and paddled back to the beach, catching the reverse current before the lifeguard could return for her. She ran to her towel. *Just get away before anyone notices you.* But of course she wasn't that lucky.

Several people approached her. "Good job. How did you find her? Thank God you were there."

She smiled. Her cheeks warmed, and she shrugged, embarrassed. "It was lucky. I'm sorry. I have to go. I'm late." She picked up her towel and board then jogged up the beach to the parking lot.

Her shift at the surf shop started in a couple of hours, but she had enough time to go home and change first. She didn't have any lessons booked today, but she was covering for Jess. Guiding her car onto the quiet beach road, she opened the windows to air out the stuffy car and the wind whipped her wet, black hair around her face as she sped home.

Now that she was in her car, away from the crowd, she floated as if sunshine poured through her body making her insides squishy. It was a tingling rush from saving the child. That poor, sweet baby…drowning. Her grin turned to tears.

It broke her heart to think about how scared she must have been at being so powerless under the rolling water.

As a teen lifeguard, she'd seen so many panicked and terrified faces in the water. She'd been born with the ability to swim and though she'd never feared water, she'd seen many others and their terror.

She shook her head. Don't go there.

Mere despised fear more than anything and witnessing a young child's trauma actually hurt her. She wiped away silent tears, thankful the girl was all right. So much for feelings of sunshine.

She pulled up to the house. Father Austen's gray, convertible Galaxy sat in the driveway, so she swung in behind it. She grinned; it was way too cool for him, but it sure gave him cred around these parts.

The small house sat across the road from the beach. It had been her parents, but the single-floor, hippy bungalow with peeling wallpaper inside, and chipped paint, chicken coop, and compost pile outside was hers now. The beach was perfect for swimming and playing and she'd loved it as a child. It didn't have a break, but she adored the quiet swimming cove. When she surfed, she could find big waves just around the point.

She hurried up the stairs and through the screen door into the kitchen. Father Austen was at the stove, kettle boiling, with his mug and tea bag ready on the counter. It was such a comforting and familiar scene. He smiled at her.

"Hey," she said, the guilt so clear in her tone. She had to tell him about the child. "I'm glad you're here."

"Uh oh, what have you done?" His smile froze, and his eyes darted behind her. His face went white.

"Are you okay, what—?" she asked, turning

He grasped her shoulders, gripping until she winced. "Listen to me. You must run. Grab your pack and go. Run and hide. Do not stop. Do not trust anyone except your sisters. Go, now." He took his gun from the kitchen drawer.

Her heart hammered, pounded too loud, too fast. She turned around, peering through the sliding glass door to the yard. There's nothing there. "But—"

He tossed her a second gun and she snatched it from the air with trembling hands. "Sisters?"

He hugged her, kissed her forehead, and shoved her to the door. "I am so sorry, I love you."

"No, Father, I can help." She looked again, but there was nothing in the yard. "I can help. What is it?

"No you have to run."

"What's happening," she screamed, squeezing her eyes shut.

"Go," he shouted.

And she obeyed. She was used to following his orders. Opening her eyes, she yanked her pack off the coat hook then ran as bullets cracked glass in the kitchen.

Father Austen fired back, saving her, giving her time, and she couldn't stop and jeopardize his sacrifice.

She slammed her crappy car into reverse, and her tires squealed as she flew from the driveway. When she was half a block away, her house exploded.

The scream echoed in her head, but she didn't make a sound. Her eyes were wide and her mouth gaping as she watched the fireball through her rearview mirror. Her home, the last family she had, dissolved into smoke and fire. Tears blurred her vision, but she pounded the gas to the floor, speeding away.

Is he dead?

Of course he is, stupid.

Her mind raced along with the whining motor. She couldn't risk going back. If he told her to run, she had to; if he could reunite with her, he would.

Was this it? Was this the day she prayed would never come? Mere yanked the steering wheel to the side and she barely got the door open before she heaved onto the dusty ground. Panting, she closed her eyes against the stinging tears and her spinning brain slammed to a stop.

Sisters.

She shut the door and peeled out, dust flying, toward the highway. With no plan, she decided to crash at a hotel near the airport. The Outback Hideaway, and though nowhere near the Outback, it was cheap and clean. She found her way to her room and set her pack on the saggy, queen-sized bed with the inevitable rusty floral print. She started to open the curtains but closed them again.

The TV was on a bureau across from the bed. It wasn't paradise, but it had air-conditioning and would do for now. But where should she start? Where should she go to find her sisters? Was she safe?

Her mind was a jumble. She paced, splintering with grief, afraid to think about Father Austen and open the floodgates.

She checked the bathroom and scoffed at the tiny bathtub. The cheaper the hotel, the worse the tub. But she needed water desperately; it would calm and soothe her enough to think more clearly. Her emotions raged, and she couldn't slow her pounding heart. Hot water trickled from the tap and she sighed.

She stripped and sat in the empty tub, letting the water fill up around her, warming her gradually. With every millimeter it climbed, her relief increased. The water reached the overflow drain under the faucet and she plugged it with her toe. The water crept up to the tub's rim, but because the tub was so shallow, it didn't even cover her halfway.

With her toe plugging the hole, water poured into the already full tub, threatening to rise over the tub's edge. It climbed higher, past the top but still holding the tub's rectangular shape. It rose to her chin, and she used her other foot to switch off the tap. She slid under the surface and lay submerged underwater, holding her breath and absorbing the heat and peace.

The hot water loosened her muscles and soaked into her bones. The muffled, echoing sounds soothed her, and before the water cooled, she got out and wrapped a small, scratchy towel around her body. The water still rose from the tub, holding the rectangular shape. She touched it and it vanished in a cloud of steam. She left the bathroom door open and walked out with the escaping cloud.

Dressed in faded, worn jeans and a Guns N' Roses T-shirt, she tossed her bikini and board shorts on top of her bag. She sat and groaned along with the bedsprings. She had to abandon everything. Find her sisters he'd said, but she had no clue how to start. Sisters. Excitement bubbled over the grief. Could it be true?

After a four cheese pizza and an even cheesier movie, someone knocked on her door. She bolted up and dove for her pack, clutching the gun.

Who gets visitors in a motel?

Weirdoes.

Another knock and this time a female's voice floated through the door. "Mere? I'm looking for Mere? I need to speak with you. My name is Ivy."

Mere put her eye up to the peephole. A young woman was outside. She backed up to get a better view. She had brown hair and piercing green eyes, but Mere had to brace her hands against the door as she leaned forward and her stomach dropped. The girl looked like her, very much like her—well, aside from the hair and eye color.

"I'm your sister. I must speak with you right away. I just flew in from Canada to find you."

Mere left the chain on and opened the door a crack. They were definitely related.

"Well, there's no doubt we're sisters," Ivy said.

Mere was speechless, staring into her sister's green eyes. It couldn't be true, but it couldn't be denied either. "Just a minute." She closed the door, slipped the gun back into her pack, and unhooked the chain. "Come in."

Mere opened the door wide. Ivy crossed the threshold and tossed her bag on the chair. Her eyes were so green, like a lush forest with light and dark flecks, and so bright they glowed. But behind their beauty, there was something deeper. She'd seen it in the faces of old sea captains around the pier. It seemed like hardness at first glance, and then loss, but mostly it was wisdom.

"My name is Ivy."

Mere couldn't deny Ivy was an identical copy of herself, but with brown hair and green eyes. But more than a physical resemblance, it was instinct, understanding, and before she could stop herself, with tears in her eyes, Mere hugged her.

Ivy's body was warm, slightly curvier than hers was, but it was the best hug she ever had. "Wow," they both said at the same time, breaking away. Their laughs were the same lilting giggles.

"It was good thinking, getting a place so close to the airport. We have to leave in a hurry."

"Where are we going? How did you find me? How did you even know about me? This is so unbelievable." She paused her rushing words. "Sorry, but I just discovered I had sisters a few hours ago when my guardian was murdered."

Ivy's head snapped around. "I found out about you yesterday. My guardian was shot and killed in my home."

Mere gasped, covering her mouth. "What happened?"

"I found his body. The killer was waiting for me, but I got him instead."

"Someone came to my house. They blew it up...I barely escaped. My guardian was inside, he saved me." Ice crawled through her blood, and her muscles clenched and froze. The crushing pressure spread from her extremities to her heart.

So, it wasn't random.

"It happened this morning." Mere wiped away new tears. "I'd just arrived home, and he was making tea. We were talking, then he told me to run." Her voice caught in her throat.

Ivy took her hand, squeezing it tightly. "I'm so sorry. Thank God you're all right. This confirms my fear that the others are in danger too."

"Others, how many?"

"Two, four in total," Ivy said. Her smile flickered then spread across her face, dazzling Mere.

How had she ever seen a glimmer of hardness in her?

"We're quadruplets. I found a letter Father Bennett wrote telling me about you and the others. We have to find them. I don't know where Asha is. I can't sense her, but Avia's in Hong Kong.

"Wait, you said Father Bennett? Both our guardians were priests?"

"We can talk about it on the plane, but we need to go now."

Chapter Six

Sitting in her cell, Asha met Clay's eyes. Again, they were gentle, friendly, but they were lying.

She had one road out of this dungeon, and he was standing in front of the door facing her. Whether he admitted it or not, whether he acted on it again or not, he was attracted to her. He was her get out of jail card; she just needed to ramp up her femme fatale identity. She'd played the part with worse than he was. Well, maybe not worse, but definitely less attractive.

She forced her voice to break and sound meek. "Where am I?"

His eyes widened. "Asha, the first convoy wasn't hit."

"Why did you do it?" she asked with a pitiful crack.

"I was ordered to take you out. You were on more radars than you realized. When I didn't return on time, they sent a second team. I wasn't informed they would do that. I thought I had time." He clenched his jaw. "I'm sorry."

He'd been sent to kill her. She'd been right to be wary, but she hadn't been cautious enough. *Play this right, Asha.* "So why am I here, Dr. Brent?"

A veil slid over his eyes, and his stone-faced expression was back.

Too direct. She wouldn't get anything that way. "Can I get a curtain for the window?"

"I will see what I can do." He opened the door.

But he couldn't leave when she was finally ready to play. If he left, she'd be alone in this dark, rocky crypt with no one to question and nothing but fear.

"Wait, Clay. Can you get me out of this tomb? Even for a few seconds? Please, I'll go crazy if I'm kept locked up in here. If you won't tell me anything, please let me breathe?" She choked on the word, fighting back her revulsion at her pitiful ploy. He didn't stop; he just kept moving out the door and locked it behind him.

~ * ~

Avia unclasped her antique silver barrette and shook out her waist-length, white hair. Leaning forward she stared at her brown eyes reflected in the mirror. She replayed the final notes of her last song in her head, repeatedly glancing to her locked door. She'd flown in to perform with the Hong Kong Philharmonic Orchestra as a special guest at the Hong Kong Cultural Centre and their performance had been flawless. She'd retreated to her dressing room as soon as the curtain dropped to wait out the others.

Finally, after all the thunderous noise, the excited musicians left the theater, shutting the alley door. She sighed in the peaceful quiet. She preferred to be alone after most performances and tonight was no different. At twenty-seven-years old, she was making a name as the best flutist in the world, but she shrank away from recognition and people in general.

She slid her finger over her eye and pulled the brown contact off, putting it in her case. She removed the other one out and blinked her light gray eyes at the mirror.

The performance had gone exceptionally well. The crowd's reaction had given her a momentary blast of pleasure, but when the curtain closed, the joy had vanished and she'd rushed in here. The tight quarters weren't ideal, but it was much better than a swarm of well-wishers and admirers. She just wasn't into people.

She played because she loved music, though she couldn't deny a small part of her enjoyed being the best. Music soothed her in a way nothing else could, and she'd worked hard. It was the one thing that shut off her spinning brain.

Avia took her trench coat from the hanger and buttoned it up over her dress. With her flute and sheet music cases under her arm, she left through the back door.

She paused at the threshold. A downpour of large, fat drops fell fast in the streetlight's glow. *Yuck.*

Avia sighed and left the sheltered doorway for the rainy night. Casting her eyes down at her sapphire heels, she shrugged. There'd be no saving her favorite shoes. Muddy splatter and puddle water covered them with every step she took toward the waiting limo. Her driver had agreed to wait back here because she'd need to make a quick exit. He was parked facing the street where the steady traffic flowed back and forth.

Ducking her head, she sloshed through the flooded lane to the car. The door opened and the driver exited with his back to her.

It wasn't Earl, her driver. This man's movements were too fast. She teetered on her heels, dropping her bags as the imposter spun.

I didn't see this coming.

A loud crack echoed across the alley, and instantly everything stuttered. Time ticked forward in slow motion, each raindrop splashing into undulating rings on the flooded ground. Her senses buzzed.

The bullet tore through the air leaving rolling waves in its wake. *No way.* She certainly was not going to be killed in a drenched Hong Kong alley.

She straightened, gathering all her power and the air in her lungs, and she blew it out. Forcing the bullet to stop, it hovered before her at eye level. She thrust out her palms as time regained its proper pace, and the bullet returned backward as fast as when the shot had been fired.

A wet crack and the man's head exploded in a bloody cloud, and his body crumpled.

There would be others. This wasn't random. Every nerve in her body screamed. Time to go. She picked up her bags and hurried to the limo. Crouching, she took the gun from the assailant's tight death grip and stepped over his body into the idling car.

Earl was slumped over in the passenger seat, a bullet hole in his left temple. Blood splattered all over the interior, along with brain and skull bits. The killer must have approached and shot him while he waited.

Her hand steady, she reached across the seats and opened the passenger door. The limp, bloody body fell, splashing onto the flooded ground and she pulled the door shut. She rolled down the blood-soaked passenger window and left it down, hiding the blatant evidence of a vicious crime.

She turned, gripping the seatbelt and froze, her chest squeezing until she gasped. Purple mist glowed outside her window, rising from the ground. Recoiling, her heart hammered against her chest, but she slammed the gearshift into drive, and punched the gas. The limo lurched from the alley, tires skidding on the wet pavement, and fishtailed into traffic. She avoided clipping a taxi, and raced on, escaping the cacophony of horns, squealing tires, and angry shouts she left in her wake.

One stop first. As a frequent visitor to the city for performances, Avia knew it well. She weaved through the creeping traffic to stop at the waterfront. Her hands were sticky with blood from the steering wheel, and she had to wipe them on her scarf, and then wipe her prints from the car before she went to the water's edge.

She opened the hidden pocket in her purse and pulled out her second passport and a wad of cash. She tossed her scarf, flute case, purse, and cell phone into the water. Her purse and flute sunk immediately. Two sheets of music, her own composition, floated on the surface as she spun and strode away.

Avia ditched the limo and walked until she hailed the first cab speeding by. On the way to the airport, the streetlights blurred as her mind whirred and clicked. She got nothing; she couldn't see why someone would be on to her now.

Inside the departure's terminal, the lights were bright and as crowded as everything else in Hong Kong. There was a flight to Zurich leaving in two hours and she bought a first class seat as Sarah Johnson with her passport's matching gold card. She hated to fly, but by this time tomorrow, she would be in peaceful isolation. There was just enough time to hit the new Chanel boutique and get a change of clothes and a new bag.

Leaving those bodies in the alley hadn't been smart, but she'd had no other feasible options. What else was she going to do? Dispose of them herself? The risk was far too high to involve the police, and so she'd reacted instinctively.

Of course, she'd be sought for questioning because she was Earl's last client, but they'd have to find her first and that wasn't going to happen. Her career was over, but she didn't really care. This day was always going to come.

After the flight and then driving three hours from Zurich, she arrived in darkness. The snow-covered, gravel driveway's steep rise hid the cabin from view but signaled her favorite place and her second most cherished secret. The property, one hundred and fifty acres below the mountain peak, was two hours off public roads. The house sat in the center of a large, open clearing bordered by tall pines.

She had to trek about a hundred feet through crisp snow in her new black boots. The stone cabin was a single floor and compact, resembling a gingerbread house with snow hanging from the roof like dollops of icing. Walking inside, she locked the door, punched on her security system, and went to the bedroom closet stocked with cabin clothing. She stripped off her clothes and slipped into gray sweatpants, a T-shirt, and a worn, oversized, gray cardigan. She finished the outfit with woolen socks and went back to the fireplace.

Once the fire was crackling and the cottage was warming up, she climbed into her bed, safe and secure. She fell asleep watching fresh snowflakes spin in the moonlight.

~ * ~

Asha's chest pounded as she ran, her legs aching, but she refused to slow her pace. Clay was right on her heels, his labored breathing not far behind. If she had to suffer, so would he.

The path through the woods was mostly shaded, but sunbeams

filtered through the canopy above, creating an ethereal strobe as she sped along the dirt trail, leaping over rocks and roots. The trees thinned into a clearing about half a kilometer ahead, and she sprinted toward the open meadow and bright early sunshine. Surging ahead and putting more distance between them, Asha exploded out into the open before skidding to a stop.

Clay doubled over beside her, panting. She was just as winded, her tank top sticking to her skin, but she'd won. She glanced around, noting the trail and the wall she could see in the distance. Still breathless, he stared up at her while she turned away, pulling her damp shirt away from her body and fanning herself.

The fresh air invigorated her, and a chance to run and burn the building energy that had no other outlet, cheered her. But despite her temporary relief, she continued to scan the area, studying the grounds and the layout. She wasn't on a typical military base; in fact, her location was even more mysterious seeing it from the outside.

The place was enormous, with a massive, shining black wall in the distance behind a wooded area. Her prison resembled some European cathedral, with ten times the usual space and pitch-black tower tiers poking the sky. She should have seen the architecture somewhere, like the Taj Mahal or Westminster Abbey. How did this place even exist? How was it not an international wonder?

She walked in a circle, catching her breath. Clay had come to her cell early and offered to take her out for a run if she promised to follow his orders. She'd been stunned he'd complied with her request sure it was the longest of shots. *So don't waste it.* This was her opportunity to find out where she was and search for clues.

The climate provided nothing. She could confidently scratch Central and South America, Asia, and Africa off the list, but that still left a lot of options.

He met her gaze, and she looked up and away. Busted. She pretended to ignore him, but her body burned with the weight of his gaze. She could overpower him. She had beaten men his size and bigger before, but something kept her from trying. Maybe his robust stature, or the intensity she'd just seen in his eyes, but she couldn't risk it…not yet.

He would relax, he would underestimate her, she would catch him off guard, and then she'd escape. She prayed she had time for him to relax.

"That was a good run," he said. "I haven't had a run like that in a while. You beat me."

Maybe it was happening already.

"You sound so shocked." She fought to keep the snarl off her face. "Because I'm a woman, right?" With a mental shake, she forced a teasing tone.

"No, because you're small. I never guessed you had such speed or stamina. You're faster than you look."

"Sexist," Asha snapped, but then forced a smile. *Retract claws, or you won't get anywhere.* "Ha, ha." Her laugh was wooden, so obviously phony. "I love it when men underestimate me. It's quite gratifying, proving them wrong." She giggled, faking again.

His smile lit his stupid eyes. "Kid, I could never underestimate you. My esteem for you has no bounds. Remember, I saw your operation." His smile wavered and fell.

She gagged. He might as well have punched her in the gut.

"Shit, sorry." He raised his hands, but she flinched back.

Don't go crazy, this is working.

He'd been more relaxed than before, and she'd managed what seemed impossible. She was out of her cage. *Keep going.*

"I have to take you back. You can't be missed."

"Where am I, Clay?"

"The Order."

She'd never heard of it. "What's the Order?"

He didn't answer. He was closing off.

"Clay, please tell me, why did you bring me here?"

"It's time to go." He spun back to the trail and motioned for her to walk ahead.

Try again, he's loosening up. "I could escape," she said lightly, going for flirty as she passed him close enough that she brushed his body. Electricity prickled through her.

Clay stepped closer, his fingers resting on the tranquilizer gun strapped to his waist. "You wouldn't get two feet before I'd be forced to dart you."

Asha glanced down and frowned. "I was kidding. Sheesh."

She backed away and walked along the trail, her back burning at his presence so close behind her.

While locked up, other than meal drops by random shrouded guards and Clay, she'd been left alone and she wasn't sure if she should be relieved at the neglect or terrified of what could be building. Something must be coming. She wouldn't be here if it weren't.

She paused at the tree line to the open grounds and stopped him by placing her hand on his arm. A strange zing pulsed through her and she stepped closer to him. He backed up, his eyes locked on hers. Inching forward again, she closed the gap and lifted her face to his. He broke eye contact, searching behind her. What was he looking at? She turned, but he gripped her upper arms and yanked her against him.

She wrenched back, but before she could spin out of his grasp, he crushed her lips with his mouth and her knees buckled.

My God, Asha, more clichés.

His lips were firm, hot, in control of the kiss. She was swept away as stars danced behind her closed eyes. Her stomach dropped to the ground, and though her body was weak, she bubbled with energy.

Ringing filled her head and drowned out anything coherent enough to grasp, but she had to fight against her surging response. It was her turn to force her eyes open and scan behind him.

But he was scorching her. She burned even hotter than the last time. If she had her power, Clay would be no more than piled ash.

He shifted lower, holding her tighter, kissing her chin, her jaw, down her neck.

She gasped…she flickered. It was her spark. She could feel it, so weak, stunted. It was like trying to catch a fading dream. It was there, but it wasn't. She grasped for it as he kissed her. But as quickly as it came, it vanished and she was cold and powerless again. *Get a grip. It's now or never.* Hard and fast, she lifted her knee connecting with a man's greatest weakness and a girl's best option.

He grunted, doubling over. Yanking back, she tore away sprinting for the trail back to the clearing and the wall she'd seen.

He was up and behind her in an instant, speeding up the hill, but the path…roots and rocks forced her to stumble. She darted off the trail, into the thick trees. With her smaller size, she should be able to lose him. His body heat pumped in waves from right behind her before he gripped her shoulder. His forward momentum was a weapon against him, and she dropped, crouching, and clutched his arm, twisting it off her shoulder and launched him over her head. He crashed into a thick tree trunk with a thud and another grunt.

"Asha," he growled.

Shivers rolled over her scalp and down to her feet. Before he could get up, she bolted again, but within four steps he tackled her from behind. Her forehead slammed into a rock, half-buried and covered in moss.

Her vision swirled and unconsciousness pulsed at her with pounding pain. Clay dragged her toward him and flipped her onto her back. She kicked out, but he threw his leg over hers, pinning her. Her heart thrumming along with her head, heat raced from her core and out her skin.

He leaned forward, and his cold anger skewered her. She fisted her hands together over her head and with all her strength, slammed him in the chest.

He winced and exhaled loudly. He took her hands, pinning them over her head. "Are you hurt?"

She glared. "You kiss me, then you tackle me?"

He glared back. "You were about to kiss me."

"Oh really? So I was *asking* for it?"

He frowned at her. "What? No."

His face twisted with confusion and anger. "I shouldn't have done that or said that. I'm sorry, but I told you, you had to behave. If anyone sees you out—"

"What?" she shouted, her façade slipping away. "Tell me what's going to happen? What is this place? What happened to the trail? I'm going crazy, confused. I have to get out of here. This place is suffocating me. I can barely breathe." She pushed at him with tears burning her eyes. *Don't you fucking dare, Asha.*

If one tear escaped she'd be done for. Clenching her body into iron and grinding her jaw, she forced the tears back with her eyes squeezed shut. "Get off me!"

Clay scowled. "Come on." He yanked her up with him and she shot out her left fist catching his jaw. Her hand crunched, and she yelped. His head snapped around with the impact, but he didn't release her.

He glared down at her and sighed. "I didn't want to do this, Asha."

She didn't hear the muffled shot past the pain in her throbbing hand, but the dart hit her in the stomach at close range and sunk deep.

"Asshole," was all she managed to get out, but his arms caught her before she hit the ground.

Chapter Seven

Avia rolled over in her cozy bed. Even with the assassination attempt looming, she could compartmentalize, prioritize, and as always, stay calm. But she couldn't lounge in her warm cocoon all day.

She had to get up so she crawled out of bed and bolted through the chilly living room where she stoked the embers in the fireplace and added two hefty logs and crumpled paper. Prepping the coffee maker, she counted each drip until there was enough to fill her mug, before sitting on the couch and sipping the delicious brew.

How could someone have discovered her? She'd been careful.

She spent the morning searching for news about the alley shooting. Nothing, not a hint. Two violent fatalities in downtown Hong Kong should have made the wire at least.

Casting her suspicions aside, she went to work building her disappearance. The other bodies would be enough for authorities to suspect she'd met a foul end. No contact with her manager, a blood splattered limo, she'd never returned to her hotel. They wouldn't even need her body.

Later, two glasses into her bottle of wine, Avia stirred the marinara sauce she'd heated from her pantry for dinner. Moving to the sink, she snapped her head to the window and dropped the steaming colander of cooked pasta. A whirring engine and crunching tires indicated a car was coming up her driveway. She'd left her alarm off after getting the last load of wood from the pile against the house, intending to go back out before eating dinner. A careless mistake.

She took her gun from the drawer in her bedroom bedside table, switched off the cabin lights, and ran back to the window. Moving the lacy curtain aside, she peered out, watching until headlights cut the darkness. She couldn't see clearly inside the car, but there were two people, the driver and a passenger. No one could find this place. She'd made sure of it, but after the events leading her here, she had to be ready for anything.

The gun was cold and heavy in her hand. She'd bought it as a precaution and had never fired it. Flipping it over, she had to search for the safety switch.

Face them. You are Sarah Johnson. They have no way of knowing otherwise.

She opened the front door and the crisp air filled her lungs and came out in soft puffs. The driver and passenger doors opened at once, and she raised her gun.

Two women poked their heads from the car.

"No trespassing. Get out of here. Now!" she shouted and they hesitated, ducking back down.

"Avia?"

They knew her name.

Wind blew, rustling through the trees bordering her clearing.

"Hold it." Avia raised her gun again. "My name is Sarah. What do you want?"

They raised arms in surrender, but the passenger walked forward smiling. "It's definitely her," she said to the driver.

One cautious, one not. "How did you find this place?"

"Wait, Mere." The driver spoke, but the passenger had already stepped into the light cast from the open door.

Avia gazed at her face. Her heart lurched and stuttered before racing at an unhealthy speed. Why hadn't she seen this? She squeezed her eyes shut and opened them again.

"We're your sisters," the driver said.

She moved into the light beside the one she called Mere. Aside from their hair and eyes, and a slight difference in body shape they appeared almost identical. Almost identical? She wasn't making sense.

"We have so much to explain, but before we do, we need to go somewhere safe."

"I'm not going anywhere."

"Please, Avia," Mere said. "You're in danger, we're all in danger. We're your sisters—look at us. How can you deny it?" She lowered her hands and flipped her palms face up.

Water spouted in a geyser from each one. Avia's gaze followed it into the sky as it froze into ice. The large chunks fell back and Mere raised her hands again, melting the ice into steam.

"I'm Mere. My power is water. Ivy's is earth."

Ivy faced the bordering pine trees, and they swayed in the now still night. Creaking and rustling they swung forward, bowing until the tops rested on the snow.

Avia lowered the gun. "All right, you have my attention. Come in."

The trees swung back up to stand straight and still.

"Wait." Mere hesitated. "I think we should move. We could be in danger here. We were both attacked in our homes."

"I was attacked too, last night in Hong Kong, and like I said, you're welcome to come in, but I'm not going anywhere."

Mere and Ivy returned to the car to get their bags.

"How did you find me?" Avia had gone through a broker famous for keeping his clients' anonymity. Paid cash to keep it secret, taken extra measures to ensure there was no paper trail.

"I located both you and Mere with my power. I can sense your energy anywhere. Yours was a bit more difficult, your energy is fainter. Perhaps it's your air power. I've always sensed you, all of you, but I had no idea what it was, or what it could mean. They were only energy pulses, one for each of you, corresponding to your element. I am Earth, but there were pulses of water, air, and fire. I can sense people's energy anyway, especially if I've met them before, but with you and Mere, your element stood out. I guess you could say your power boosted your energy, and of course, we've been linked since birth. I just didn't know you existed. Once I was aware of it—pop, there you were. Well no, actually, it wasn't that instant or that easy, but you get it."

Avia admitted it was a useful gift.

Mere grinned. "I still can't believe it all."

"You were in Australia," Ivy continued turning to Mere. "And although there's a lot of power in the water there, you were stronger. You were a light, leading me right to your hotel."

Ivy turned back to Avia. "You were in Hong Kong, but I lost your energy for a while. I worried because the connection was new to me, but then I picked you up again in Switzerland, and we had time to change plans and come here. But we still have one more sister to find. Her name is Asha."

"Let me guess, Asha is the fire element." Avia let them pass into her home. "We are safe here. No one knows about this place." She studied Ivy's green eyes, "Well, other than you. I want to hear everything."

Mere went across to the room and caressed the river-rock fireplace. "Wow, this place is beautiful. It's like a spread from *Home and Garden.* Cozy cabin chic. I hope it isn't rude to ask, but what is it you do for a living?"

"Of course it isn't rude. I am a flutist."

"You must be fantastic," Mere said.

"I'm okay."

She laughed but stopped the moment their eyes met.

"It's the only place I can truly relax, so you can understand my caution." Avia placed the gun on the counter. "Can I get you something to drink? Hot tea maybe? I'm sure you've had a long, tiring trip." They both nodded.

Avia paused, holding the kettle, her back to the sisters she hadn't seen since her childhood daydreams. They weren't just a silly fantasy.

She put the kettle down and took an unopened bottle of wine from the counter and held it up. They grinned, and the tension in the room eased. They took the offered wine glasses and sat on the couch by the fireplace.

"The information I have is pieced together from Father Bennett's diary and a letter he left for me," Ivy said. "I'm thankful for the information, or I'd be completely in the dark. Both Mere and I had guardians. Priests. Hers was named Father Austen and mine was Father Bennett."

"I haven't spoken to Father James in years," Avia said, frowning. "We parted after my twelfth birthday. I've been mostly on my own since I turned sixteen."

"You had one too then?"

"Yes."

"Could that be the plan?" Mere asked. "To kill our protectors and leave us vulnerable?"

"We're not vulnerable. I'm not, and as I witnessed, neither are you," Avia said.

"Yes, but if you were away from your handler... Father James was it?" Ivy asked.

Avia nodded.

"You were attacked, not him?"

"Did you really doubt we were the targets?" Avia asked.

"No, I guess not," she said.

"Where is Asha? She is our priority."

Ivy frowned. "I don't know. When I try to connect, I can't feel her. I couldn't feel any of you while I was on the plane, but I haven't picked her up since I found out about you. I first sensed both of you two days ago. I don't want to think it, but whoever came after us may have found her."

"You think she's dead?"

Mere covered her mouth. "What?"

"Possibly." Ivy frowned. "I don't know why else I could locate you two so quickly and feel nothing of her."

"But you don't know for sure?" Avia asked.

Ivy shook her head and removed a book from her bag. She

opened it to a page near the back. "According to Father Bennett's diary and his letter, we shouldn't trust anyone other than each other and someone called Master Miles."

"I have a problem with anyone who goes by Master anything," Mere said.

Ivy smiled. "Yeah, good point."

Avia agreed. She'd had enough of priests and authority figures in general, and Mere was correct. Master was not a title associated with benevolence. She sipped her wine and cleared her throat.

"So, if we trust the source, then we have to find Asha and Master Miles." Avia poured more wine into each glass. "We need to find out who sent those hits and why."

"We didn't even know of each other, yet someone else did?" Mere asked.

"And they found us," Avia said. "Look at the timing. They were coordinated hits."

Mere nodded. "I've always been very secretive, and I'm sure all of you were as well."

"Perhaps we can find this Master Miles and ask him about it," Avia said.

Chapter Eight

Asha shook off the druggy haze and sat up in her dungeon cell again. *Shit.* She jumped from the metal slab and paced her cage, her mind racing while she struggled to hold the reins on her temper.

You blew it. She'd had the opportunity to escape, and she'd failed. Clay had stopped her. That damn dart. That kiss… Heat flushed through her again.

Her flirtatious ploy began as planned, and then she'd approached him without realizing it. It wasn't until he broke eye contact that the pseudo-trance broke.

This place. That man. Reaching out, Asha touched the mirror-like, black-stone walls. She snatched her hand away. The wall was clammy, cold. Nausea rolled in her stomach and her mouth filled with saliva. She was trapped within these strange walls and it was getting difficult to breathe. Like being smothered, the air was too thick or her throat too narrow.

She tapped her leg, keeping her breathing even. The place was darker and more frightening than any of the labs or prisons she feared, and she expected the worst was yet to come.

Face it, you're caught. And was it really any less than she deserved? *You're a monster. It's the truth and you've always known that.* She'd killed so many people; many of them had been innocent. It was those innocent lives she'd taken—their faces haunting her. With her power, how could she not be dangerous? Something to fear? She was fire, and fire was pure destruction. She laid back down on the cold metal slab.

Her family—her mother, father, and little sister were the very first to suffer because of her fire. It happened over fifteen years ago, yet the memory hadn't faded with time. It was still so clear, too vivid…

A few days before her twelfth birthday, she walked into school with her head bowed, afraid to return after the day before. She suffered from severe and chronic panic attacks, and she had to force herself to take deep breaths before walking into her daily torment.

Advanced in her studies, Asha was a twelve-year old freshman in high school, and the majority of the students who shared classes with her didn't appreciate her presence. She was smart and, as a result, the other kids tormented her. Because she wasn't cool, because she wasn't their age, and because she wasn't on their level, they made her life miserable. It wasn't fair. They picked on her because she was smarter than the rest of them.

Dressed in her dorky jean overalls, she wore a dark toque on her head, even though it was a hot, sunny day. The hat didn't quite cover all her weird red, yellow, and orange hair even though she had tucked it up inside.

God, she'd hated her hair and paired with her black, almond-shaped eyes, she was unusual looking. Hell, she looked flat out strange. When she dyed her hair, the color never lasted more than a single wash, so she'd given up and resorted to hats.

Of all her classmates, Sharon was her biggest problem. She was the mean one, and although Asha had worked hard to fly under her radar, Sharon instantly disliked her.

"I don't like you," Sharon had said one day in the hallway.

Asha ignored it and carried on. Apparently, it had been a mistake. Perhaps if she had cowered and apologized for her existence, it would have been better, but—maybe not. Needless to say, aided by her pack of girlfriends, the teasing had become full-fledged bullying.

Just the day before, she'd had a bad panic attack in English class and had run from the classroom to hoots and laughter from her callous classmates.

Mr. Archer found her sitting against the lockers with her head between her knees, panting and holding her chest. "Asha, what is it?"

She couldn't respond. She'd been sure she was having a heart attack and was going to die. Her kind teacher had taken her elbow and half-carried her to the nurse's office.

She'd been mortified and spent the afternoon ignoring the taunts from her classmates until she could finally head home. After such humiliation the day before, she avoided the halls after lunch, and took a short cut through the pool to her science class. Her nostrils tickled from the strong chlorine odor as she edged around the large pool where the swim team usually practiced. Sharon, Catherine, and Tina sat high on the bleacher's top level, watching her.

"Hey, Asha," Sharon's voice echoed against the walls.

Asha froze, the quintessential deer in headlights.

Sharon walked down from the bleachers with confident strides. "You are such a psycho, you know. Nice display in class yesterday."

She sidestepped Sharon, but the older girl grasped her arm, and spun her to the pool's edge. Asha's blood-curdling scream tore her throat, and Sharon grinned as Asha kicked out and fought. She was so much smaller than the older girl and before she could get away, Tina and Catherine rushed over and helped Sharon shove her into the pool.

Asha had no time to scream or even take a breath before she fell. The cold silence immediately surrounded her and pushed her down. Terror filled her as she kicked out, reaching for anything she could get her hands on. Her vision darkened to black and she couldn't breathe. It was different from her panic attacks rearing without reason. This terror was from a very legitimate cause.

Water terrified her because she'd never learned to swim. It was just too cold and wet, and now she sunk, flailing and fighting, to the bottom. Terrified certainty overwhelmed her—she was going to die. Her heart stuttered and thudded. She wasn't ready to go. *Fight.*

Her feet eventually touched the bottom, and she managed to get her bearings. Her panic subsided, and with all her strength, she pushed off and shot up through the water. She broke the surface, and took the air in with deep gulping breaths, splashing and dog paddling to the edge.

She pulled herself from the pool and rolled over, soaking wet and panting. The girls were gone. They had left her there. They had pushed her in and left her to drown.

Fury rolled through her and built to a red rage. It bubbled and fought loose. She had a quick temper, and once triggered it was difficult to contain it, and she was so tired of trying. She bent to pick up the books she'd dropped, and still steaming she hurried to her science class.

She walked in late, said nothing to anyone, and took her seat. Sharon, Catherine, and Tina giggled like idiots, and her anger fought free.

Asha met Sharon's eyes. The other two had their heads bent in laughter, and Sharon flinched. It was her flinch that was blamed later, when her Bunsen burner flared out and ignited her hair like a torch. Sharon's straw-like blonde hair caught, and she screamed. Mr. McIntosh ran over, swift for someone his age, throwing a student's sweatshirt over her head and smothering the flames. She was hysterical, screaming and crying, and when he removed the shirt, her face blazed bright red.

Mr. McIntosh helped her up and guided her out as the classroom erupted in noise. Among the din, Asha was the only student still sitting and the only student smiling.

Sharon didn't return to school for the next week. Asha was thrilled, but the science class camping trip to the coast was coming up and Sharon would be back in time to attend.

The school camping trip, with hiking, and canoeing was supposed to be a bonus to the curriculum's work assignments. The students studied the local eco-system's flora and fauna and wrote reports for their class. She hated school, and she dreaded the trip with the older kids, but Asha couldn't avoid it.

Her parents didn't understand how scary school could be or how stressful it was to be different. She had to go, but she definitely wouldn't go canoeing. Getting to the campsite by boat would be difficult enough.

On the first night, they hiked to the beach to set up their tents safely beyond the high-tide line. All the wired and excited students relished being away from their parents and enjoyed the freedom. Asha read in her tent while the students sat around the campfire on the beach, toasting marshmallows.

She had to admit, it had been fun. Caught up in the exercise from hiking and exploring on her own, she could appreciate the beach, and even the ocean's wonder and beauty.

The students were grouped up with their friends sharing various tents, but Asha had one to herself. She preferred to be alone and she refused to be paired up with someone the way teachers liked to do. She'd told Mr. McIntosh she'd bring her own tent and she wouldn't share. He didn't argue.

Long after Mr. McIntosh and Mrs. Young doused the campfire and the campers retreated to their tents, Asha woke up shivering in her sleeping bag. She groped around in the dark for her sweatshirt, as her full bladder urged her go out into the cold, wet night. She shuffled to the front flap, slipping on her boots. By moonlight, she stumbled along the trail to the campsite bathrooms hating the cold, wet air.

Approaching the restrooms, muffled voices floated from off the trail, deeper in the forest. She stopped to listen. It was Sharon, Tina, and Catherine.

Asha couldn't run into them. She had seen Sharon from a distance; her face had healed and her hair was shorter. It killed her to admit it but it, didn't look so bad. It was probably why she was back because the burn was healing, and of course, she had gotten sympathy attention in droves all day.

Asha considered going back, avoiding them completely, but she really had to use the bathroom and she wasn't a 'squat in the cold, wet bushes' kind of girl. Slipping off the trail, she took a big detour and arrived at the washrooms from the rear. After using the facilities, she left the same way she had come. She crept along in the dark toward the beach and the tents when suddenly, Sharon slid out from the shadows.

"Hey, Asha, what are you doing out here?"

"I was just going back to my tent."

Tina and Catherine followed, joining Sharon on the trail. They blocked Asha's path. "Don't go back yet. I want to talk to you."

Asha gave an unconvincing smile. "I'm really cold. I have to go back."

Tina sidled closer. "What's wrong with you? God, you're such a loser."

"It's okay." Sharon's voice was low and chilling. "She doesn't have to stay."

Catherine blocked her path, a vodka bottle in her hand. "Here, stop being such a wuss and have some."

Asha backed away, but Tina slid around and shoved her from behind. Asha spun around, surprised, facing the petite blonde.

"You know, we were just talking about you." Tina jabbed her finger into Asha's chest.

Why couldn't they leave her alone and let her go to her tent? Why was she their number one target? What had she ever done to them? Oh, yeah. Sharon's face, but they didn't know she had done it.

Asha was tired of being on alert, and she was tired of taking it, especially since she could fight back so easily. How dare they constantly try to intimidate her? Bursting with sudden temper, she decided she'd had enough.

She walked forward, staring up at the taller girls with fury in her eyes. "What are you guys going to do? Fight me? Beat me up? Come on," she scoffed. "You already tried to drown me. You don't scare me anymore. You're bullies and you're pathetic."

Her voice was strong and clear, unlike the butterflies fluttering in her stomach. The shock on their faces spoke volumes. She laughed aloud and turned back.

Before she could take two steps, some boys from her class sauntered up the trail.

"Boo!" Tom and his friends approached the girls, all cocky grins, and drunken swagger.

Asha rolled her eyes.

He smiled at her. "What are you doing here?"

Before she could respond, blinding pain exploded through her head. There was a dull, thudding sound as the bottle hit her from behind. Darkness flashed, and glimmering stars floated in her vision, but she stayed upright swaying on rubbery legs.

They all laughed. The boys too. Someone shoved Asha from behind, and she fell forward onto her hands and knees, splashing into a deep mud puddle. The mud ran down her face. Mud or blood, she wasn't sure.

The throbbing in her head kept her from getting up as she fought spinning darkness and unconsciousness. Trying not to pass out, she clenched her fists in the puddle. Rage rolled through her, steady now, no longer the flashing heat, but building slowly, heavily.

"Tom, why would you talk to her?" Sharon's voice sounded like an echo from far away, but it surrounded her.

"My God. What did you do? Seriously Sharon, you could've killed her," he shouted back.

"Relax. Look, she's getting up," she said sweetly. "She's fine. Let's go." The laughing continued all around her. She dragged Tom away and the others followed along behind them.

Their laughter and chatter faded as they made their way deeper into the forest. Asha was humiliated and hurt. Rage and hatred boiled inside her and something snapped.

Her hands warmed and started tingling. Steam rose from the water and bubbles formed around her fists. The puddle rolled and boiled around her skin tickling her. She relished each tiny bubble running over her hands, through her fingers, and up past her wrists.

Searing heat burst from her core and blew out through her skin in a rush. Her fury was like a living thing, escaping her body and overcoming her control. She didn't want to fight it. Instead, she opened up to it, letting it out.

Asha's hands clenched as powerful shocks surged through them. A loud boom echoed from the beach, snapping her from her vengeance fantasy of Sharon burning slowly and painfully. She sat back, yanking her hands from the puddle. They were on fire. She doubled over and screamed as blinding white-hot pain raced through her body. Another boom in the distance and as quickly as it had come, the pain vanished. Her hands were normal pink skin again.

Screams came from the campsite, and she swung around toward the beach. She could see the light glowing, and she connected to a raging fire, burning in the distance. She jumped up and took off sprinting toward the campsite and her classmates.

The beach was in chaos. The campfire, just wet ash before, had become a raging inferno, shooting flames impossibly high up into the sky. Three tents were burning and flames stretched from the campfire to the trees bordering the beach. The students were huddled by the water, as far away from the flames as they could get while pale Mrs. Young frantically counted the students.

Asha ran up to them.

"There you are," Mrs. Young shouted. She pointed her bony,

trembling finger. "Get over here."

Mr. McIntosh approached, clearly distressed. "The burning tents belong to Sharon, Tina, Catherine, Tom, Troy, Calvin, and John. They weren't inside, they're missing, but Asha's gone too."

"She's here," Mrs. Young said. "But where are the other students?"

"I saw them in the forest. They were past the washrooms. All of them." Asha couldn't catch her breath. Her hands tingled again, and she stuffed them in her pockets, just in case.

The crackling flames grew louder, the fire was spreading. The flames bent, though there was no wind, they stretched for the trees, and they flared like matchsticks, shooting sparks high into the air. The campfire, the fire's source, sputtered out, but the forest kept burning. It spread through the trees, moving at an unnatural pace away from the sand and shore. Rolling along the forest floor like carpet, it rippled up the trees in its path.

Mr. McIntosh burst into action, running up the beach toward the fire.

"Don't be an idiot," Mrs. Young screamed after him.

Asha stood rooted to the beach, taking in the beauty of the raging destruction. Unblinking she watched and swelled with each crackle and burst. It wanted to grow and move, and she grinned as she encouraged it forward. Power flooded her and it was the greatest high she could imagine, except…she wanted more.

"What a psycho."

She heard the whispered voice through her catatonia. She blinked and looked at the students. A group huddled close by stared at her with disgust.

"Hey pyro, did you start this?"

How did they know? Asha sprinted across the sand after her teacher. Mrs. Young yelled at her to stop. She kept going.

She caught up with Mr. McIntosh just as the flames broke and a gap opened, spreading wide and large enough for them to run through. As they ran farther into the forest, the path stayed open and clear before them, like the biblical Red Sea.

They approached a break ahead. "They went that way," she yelled.

He spun around still in motion and hit a low-hanging branch going full speed and his head snapped back with the impact.

She dropped beside him.

He was out cold, a huge gash on his forehead. The forest burned all around them, the smoke building up in the thick woods, and if she couldn't get him out, he would suffocate.

She could hear faint screaming in the distance—the missing students—her tormentors. The fire had spread everywhere except around her and her teacher. She had to do something fast, but she couldn't leave Mr. McIntosh or he would die. He had been so heroic, running into a forest fire to save his students.

Soothing warmth touched her. She could save them all. Stillness overtook her racing mind and rolled through her as the rage had earlier. She lifted her arms to the sky. Breathing deeply, with all the focus and concentration she possessed, she lowered her arms. Strong, hot, tingling power flowed through her. She grinned with joy as the flames responded, shrinking and withdrawing from around them. She ran down the trail to the students, the flames sputtering and disappearing as she ran past.

"Help!" Tom huddled with the others on a large gathering of boulders and rock. They all coughed, shaking, surrounded by a flaming circle.

Asha paused outside the circle for a moment, watching them, and then she burst forward. The flames parted and she landed inside the circle. *Show off.* She had to smile at the awe on their faces. It gave her such intense satisfaction. The flames disappeared as she walked toward them.

"Come on. Let's go. Mr. McIntosh is over there, and he's unconscious and hurt. I can't carry him alone." To his credit, Tom got up immediately with John, and the girls followed.

"Sharon, get up." Clearly, in shock, Sharon shook her head and mumbled incoherently.

"Tom, pick her up. We have to go." The girls were practically catatonic, but at least they moved. Sharon leaned away from Tom, refusing to budge.

Oh yay, more fun. Asha bent, staring into Sharon's vacant eyes, and slapped her across the face. She wasn't gentle.

Outrage flashed through Sharon's eyes and focused on Asha. Tom yanked her up and together, they hurried down the path to Mr. McIntosh, still unconscious on the trail. Troy took his arms and Calvin and John took his legs. The paunchy, balding teacher was heavy for the young boys, so Catherine and Tina pitched in to help carry him back along the trail to the beach.

Mrs. Young ran up to them completely frantic while they laid Mr. McIntosh on the sand. "What happened? Is he dead?" Poor Mrs. Young.

Asha shook her head. "No. He hit his head, but he's breathing. The fresh air will help him."

Mrs. Young bent and slumped in relief when she saw his chest rise and fall in a steady rhythm. "And you." She spun toward the dazed students. "You weren't in your tents. Where were you?"

Asha stood away from the students grouped by the water as the sun rose in the smoky sky. They stared and whispered. They could think she started the fire for all she cared, as long as they thought she used matches.

The adrenaline coursing through her made her stomach roll. She needed to process what had happened and she desperately needed to get home and report to Father Sean.

Mr. McIntosh was airlifted to the hospital, and two police officers took her home after the evacuation by Lake Police. Someone from the school had called, informing and assuring the parents all the students were safe.

"I'm fine, everyone is fine," Asha said walking into her mom's warm, sweet-smelling embrace. "I'm sorry," she whispered.

Her mother patted her head and shoved her inside. "Thank you officers, the school informed us of everything."

"You're welcome, ma'am. According to Mrs. Young, your daughter was a hero."

"I'm sure she was," she said shutting the door and turning her devastated expression to Asha, "but she can also be too reckless."

Her mother's stern expression caused her stomach to flip. She hated upsetting her, but as the freak she was, it was a constant occurrence.

Asha slumped back. She was home; yet after all the adrenaline, her stomach continued to toss and roll. Her dad sat on the couch with Father Sean. They'd want a debriefing, an explanation, but she wasn't ready to give it.

"I need a shower first." She ran up the winding staircase to her room. Pausing, she waited for the nausea to pass and then picked up her fluffy, red robe and went into the bathroom.

The hot water ran in dirty streaks down her body. The soapsuds blackened as she scrubbed ash from her skin and hair. Her classmates' terrified screams still echoed in her head, and she ground her teeth.

Leaving the bathroom clean but numb, Asha overheard Father Sean instructing her family in hushed tones in the living room. She headed back to her room, the plush cream carpeting, cushioning her feet. Her queen-sized bed, complete with her dark purple duvet and overwhelming pillow pile waited for her. It was her zone, and she flopped down burrowing in.

Father Sean knocked once before walking in. Why couldn't she enjoy her denial a bit longer? Why couldn't she sleep and clear her head before she was forced to rehash what had happened and explain what she couldn't explain?

"Tell me everything."

Trying to distance herself from her words, she described the night's events; how she snapped when Sharon and her friends had pushed her too far. They'd left her in the forest, battered and bruised, and in her desire for revenge, her temper had surged, igniting the forest.

She told him of the searing pain and how her fire covered her hands but didn't burn. Her power had acted alone, and when the pain faded, she was eventually able to control and finally contain the fire. His eyes stayed wide through the entire story.

She sat up. After saying the words aloud, the events sunk in. Closing her eyes, she choked on the pounding in her chest, Asha tapped her thigh. *Not now, stay calm.*

Her eight-year-old sister, Millicent, was downstairs talking with their mother and father. The sound soothed her and slowed her building panic.

"Your family knows of course, but no one else. No one can ever find out about you."

"They knew. One of them asked me if I started the fire."

"They can't possibly know. They may suspect you started it, but they will never guess your power."

"But it was so big—the forest. It was too much. People almost died."

Father Sean backed away holding his hands out. "Relax Asha, you're fine. Everyone is safe. You must calm down, or you could cause another accident."

Her power had always allowed her to fuel or shrink fire, but it took intense concentration and focus, and so far, the effects had been minimal.

"Asha," he snapped. "If you calm down, I'll explain. You were born with this gift, and it can be very dangerous. *You* can be very dangerous, but I can keep you and everyone else safe."

She hugged her knees to her chest, fighting to slow her breathing. What was he saying? She was too shaken to follow his words. Her rage had taken over. Her power had acted alone. *And I liked it.*

Joy and glee had filled her as the fire consumed her, and that freaked her out the most. The exhilarating, seductive new sensations had thrummed through her while lives were at risk and the world around her burned. An unnerving reaction at the very least. Sociopathic was probably more accurate.

"I told your parents I will take over your education. You can't risk being around others for a while. Your power is volatile right now, and you could inadvertently trigger more destruction." His voice held an edge. "You must leave your family for their safety. They are at great risk being near you."

Asha shook her head. "No, I need them. I'll go somewhere temporarily until we can work something out, but I won't leave them. I would never hurt them."

"I know it will be hard, but you must protect the ones you love. Until we make sure your power is under your control, you need to be isolated."

He was right. She couldn't put them in danger. "Okay, but just until I'm under control."

"Good girl." He handed her a pill. "Take this. It will help you sleep."

She took the pill and swallowed it, praying for darkness.

"We'll pack when I get back. I have arrangements to make." He left the room, and Asha finally slipped under the covers.

~ * ~

Then

"Asha, help! Help!" Sharon's voice screamed; her hollow eyes staring from her charred black skeleton and reaching for her.

Asha recoiled, but the skull and bones transformed in a spinning dreamy mist into her mother burning and then to her sister Millicent.

She jerked up. Everything was red, orange, and burning. She fell back against the pillow, sluggish and weak, unable to hold herself up. Fire filled the room. Flames rolled over the bed covering her and sliding along her skin. Her family screamed from down the hall.

No.

Fighting the sedative's effects, she dragged herself off the bed, making it to her feet and stumbled through the flames to the door. Her rubber legs gave out before she could reach the knob. Her heart pounded in her ears, drowning out the sound of the fire's hungry breath. She struggled to her feet again, and her weak legs held.

She kicked the door, and it splintered into sparks and ash. Jumping through, she screamed for her mom, but the fire engulfed the entire house. There was nothing but red flames. She faced her parents' room, but a loud creak stopped her short.

As she raised her arms, her heart stopped. She was too late. The floor splintered, the house collapsed, and Asha fell with the crumbling floor into burning hell.

There was nothing to grasp and nowhere to jump. The flames

flared up, and her vision narrowed to a pinprick. She'd killed them all.

An explosion split her ears the second before her head hit the ground, and darkness took her. She lost consciousness as she prayed the fire would take her too.

Someone prodded her, and she sat up, naked inside a large black crater, ash floating and piled everywhere.

Her neighbor, Mrs. Stark was there sobbing, trying to hug her close. Asha's family was gone, her home was gone, not even the basement remained. Other than black soot, the neighbors' houses were damage free.

"Oh, my dear…where did you come from? You shouldn't have gone inside. It exploded. There's nothing left." She waved and backed away as two firefighters came running toward her. "Finally, the fire department is here."

Guilt crushed her like a cannonball, and she panted from the force, falling back. Mom, Dad, and Milly…poor, sweet Milly.

They'd been good people, loving, adoptive parents—the best an orphan could ask for. And when their miracle daughter, Milly, had come along, Asha had not been replaced. Her parents' love and care continued unchanged.

She was aware of the usual horror stories surrounding foster care and adoption. It was a crapshoot and rarely was the child a winner. And she'd repaid their generosity by killing them. She had to stifle her urge to scream.

Finally, getting her on the gurney and shutting the doors, the paramedic covered her with a blanket, shushing her soothingly. At the hospital, they questioned her, poked and prodded, but she barely moved and said nothing.

Father Sean arrived while they examined her and spoke with the doctor who told him she was unhurt except for a slight concussion and shock. Her doctor raised eyebrows when Father Sean started quoting scripture and speaking about miracles. But she was released into his care with instructions to watch her.

When they were alone he stared with his usual clenched lip and narrowed eyes. "What have you done, Asha?"

Her mouth opened at the force of his accusation, but no sound came out.

He bent over her and whispered, "We must play this right. We will get you somewhere safe before the police can arrest you, somewhere you can't hurt anyone else."

Asha couldn't respond. Her eyes were blurry with tears as she choked on her guilt.

They left San Francisco in silence while she stared blankly out the window. She stared at the full moon, sitting low and huge in the dark sky. She barely blinked. Her eyes locked on the lunar display throughout the journey. She'd always loved the moon.

Hours later, they arrived at a gated property with a driveway and barbed-wire fencing. It was an abandoned industrial site with five or six outbuildings. Father Sean led Asha to the largest, and she followed with her head bowed.

Inside, they walked down the concrete hallway to another door, but it resembled the front door of a home, complete with a doorknocker and fake plants. She followed Father Sean inside, to a luxurious living room complete with a grand piano. She'd never been to Father Sean's house and it was unexpected.

He indicated the pristine white couch, and she sat. "If you can start a fire in your sleep, we are going to have to be very careful. You must obey me, following my every command."

She was so numb, so far away.

"Asha, you should've been able to stop it." His eyes could barely restrain his anger. "This was a critical test and you failed. I am very concerned by your lack of control. We have a lot of work ahead."

Grief stricken, Asha sat with her hands in her lap, and her head bowed. She raised her red, swollen eyes to his. "I was asleep. I woke up, and the entire house was burning. I tried to stop the flames, but I couldn't."

"Not a valid excuse. You could have stopped it if you had enough power. Like I said, we have a lot of work to do." He smiled and continued callously, "But chin up now. You're fine, you were inside the house, and you didn't burn. You survived."

He paused and poured a drink from a rolling bar cart, loaded with assorted bottles sitting by the grand piano. "I have always helped guide you, but now I am also responsible for you. You killed your family, and I saved you from suffering the penalties. You're aware of what you're capable of now, even against your will."

His eyes glimmered, and he couldn't quite keep his tone even. "If the authorities find out about you, they will imprison you for your crimes or worse, they will want to study you like a rat in a lab."

Nothing terrified her more. Yes, she was different, but she didn't deserve that. She was still a living person.

"But what happened?" she asked, finally succumbing to her sobs. "How did it start?"

"I told you, it was a test and now that I've seen the damage you can do, it will only get worse. Unless you are removed from the public, trained, and taught how to use your gift correctly, you will undoubtedly cause more death and destruction. I know you don't believe me now, but there are positive uses for such gifts. Your parents trusted me. We will continue our training and eventually you will be able to live an ordinary life.

"You just came into your power and it is stronger than ever before. You must use it, or it will burn you and come out against your will. Emotion can fuel your fire, but I will help you. We will use your power to help people. We will try to make up for the damage you've already caused. We will do it together."

He gave her a basement room of concrete and steel to sleep in. Fireproof, in case she had another accident. He assured her it was only a precaution, and once she mastered control, she'd be allowed to move upstairs into one of the real bedrooms.

Ever since the day she burned her family alive, the monster slept dormant under her rigid control, until the times she called it forth. She had spent a year imprisoned with Father Sean, honing her power before they moved to South America. And ever since the morning Father Sean flew away in his helicopter, she worked to make amends.

~ * ~

Then

Asha opened her eyes. She was in a dark stone cave, her arms wrapped around a man who held her close. His embrace was warm and safe. She wore a heavy, black cloak over her body. Where was she?

"Do it, do it now," the man whispered in her ear.

Her body shivered, and she raised her eyes, but shadows hid his face. She hesitated. She didn't want to, but it was the only way they could be together.

"Do it now."

She jumped at her lover's sharp tone, but she sensed his urgency. The three women were bound and huddled on the ground, burlap bags over their heads.

Her desire for him was overwhelming, and these women were their last obstacle. She was sorry. She didn't know who they were or what they'd done, but she was a warrior and warriors didn't balk at killing.

The lit torch flickered behind her on the wall, and she held out her hand. Flames jumped to her outstretched fingers. Fire covered her hand, and she rolled it over and over like a snowball. The red, orange, and yellow flames fused together into a perfect sphere, and she paused.

She held the fireball up to her face and took a deep breath, gathering her focus. It rose, hovering above her hand, and as she pushed her palm out, it shot toward the huddled women on the ground. They burst into flames before her, and she built the fire as hot as she could to end it faster. She didn't want to see them suffer.

It was time to claim her prize. She faced her lover, and he lunged forward, stabbing the sword she hadn't seen him draw through her chest.

Gasping out, Asha jerked awake, shaking on the small metal slab, soaked in sweat and grasping her chest. Just a nightmare. She wiped the sweat from her forehead and sucked in a deep breath.

Today was the day. She would escape or die trying. She paced back and forth. Her only option was to wait and see where the opportunity presented itself, and then do what she needed to, to get out. If she had to fight Clay she would, but she'd have to disarm him of that blasted dart gun first.

The wall to her right cracked and cracked again. She searched the shadows and movement rippled in the dark. Suddenly, a searing bolt hit her chest with such force she flew back slamming into the wall and dropping to the slab. Her skull split and she screamed, grasping it. Light flashed in the dark and shocked through her body, burning in pulsing torture. Her skin was splitting open. She struggled to scream, anything to release her pain, but she couldn't open her mouth past her gritted teeth.

The tests…the experiments.

She couldn't breathe. There was no air. She clawed her throat, gasping for breath. She was going to die. Stars appeared in front of her eyes, and she dropped her hands. Cool air rushed over her face and her throat opened. She managed to gasp a tiny, shallow breath, but the shocks burned her again.

Four cloaked figures emerged from the shadows moving as one and her vision darkened to black. She struggled, but her arms were restrained. She opened her eyes and they were blasted with morning sunlight.

Her arms were tied behind a post and three women were tied beside her. They were all dying with swords piercing their hearts. Darkness again and another vision, her power useless as she burned, and a sword stabbed her.

She coughed blood, and the scene shifted, changing again. Hundreds of scenes flashed by speeding forward like slides on a projector. She couldn't catch everything, but with each sight, her terror increased from the horrifying visions of sacrifice and torture committed by faceless cloaked figures. Every sword thrust sliced her, every burn cooked her, and every shock jolted her.

Asha had never suffered fear or pain like it. The ground beneath her vanished and she fell. It was impossible, but she was falling, the dark so deep it weighed on her, pushing her down faster. Air rushed by her ears as she plunged on. She was going to die, and it was the only thing she desired. To stop the terror and pain she was ready to go, needed to go. She prayed for death's release.

Splashing into icy water, Asha sunk down into the frigid darkness. She couldn't move her body; she couldn't swim. She hung, frozen and breathless under the black suffocating depth.

Fear filled her, organs strained, and she gave up. But instead of water, sweet air flooded her lungs. Her eyes snapped open, and she was alone in her cell.

She took a breath and cried out. The skin on her arms was torn open. She had indeed split, and the wound ran from under her feet, up both her legs, arms, and torso, over her shoulders and up her neck. Wincing with shaking fingers, Asha touched her scalp, and her fingers came away bloody.

The sharp pain thrummed through her, cutting like a thousand hot knives. But those images—the pain and fear from being murdered a thousand times. Unable to control her jerking body, she cursed her fear. *Use it. You must get out of here.*

~ * ~

Now

The lock clicked on the cell door, and she jumped. A man entered dressed in black robes; she stumbled back, but he held up his hand.

"My name is Alex. There is nothing to fear from me, my dear. I am here at Master Miles's request." He was middle-aged but stooped with small, slanted blue eyes. "You are leaving here today."

Was it a trick?

He handed her a stack of folded black clothing and dropped boots at her feet. "Put these on and try to hide your shape. Keep quiet and try to blend in. You must go as one of the soldiers. You'll be taken off the grounds. Escape the moment you land. Don't come back."

The monk turned his back and with a lot of wincing, she dressed in thick, black, baggy pants. She put the second bulletproof vest he'd brought over the first and added the jacket over both. The boots were close enough to her size. Her wounds would give her more difficulty while running than the boots. She finished the uniform with a balaclava and helmet, flipping down the tinted visor.

The man checked her over. "It should do, but you're short."

He left the cell, and Asha followed, her mind numb and her body screaming through the silent halls and out to glorious, fresh air. Every step pulled her torn skin, and she couldn't stifle the small gasp, but her escort didn't hesitate.

Was this actually happening?

Of course not. It had to be a ruse. She was more likely on her death march than an escape to freedom. But then why the outfit?

He escorted her through the forest to a runway with a waiting jet, the engine already running. The door opened, and Clay shuffled down the steps. Stumbling forward, she gasped at the forceful jar on her wounds, clamped her mouth shut and lowered her eyes.

The robed man, her savior or quite possibly her executioner — she wasn't entirely sure yet—whispered to Clay, inclining his head toward her.

Aside from the helmet and balaclava, he was dressed in matching combat attire. She was being handed off to Clay. She didn't understand. He'd dragged her here, darted her the day before…tortured her?

Despite all that, her heart jumped and stupidly, her dashed hopes flickered with his presence. Could this really be her luck? Was he helping her? The day she planned to escape was the same day it was managed for her? The robed man turned and marched off, and though still shaky she walked to Clay.

"You're coming with us," he said. "Stay close to me and keep quiet. Orders from the top. You're part of the team." He wouldn't meet her eyes. He was angry, fiercer than she'd ever seen him. She couldn't speculate as to why. He'd brought her in, and now he was taking her out. Please let him be taking her out. She climbed the steps and entered the plane.

Clay followed, shutting the door. "Okay. Let's go," he shouted to the pilot up front.

Who were these people? She stood inside what looked like a sleek private jet on the outside, but completely militarized inside. She counted two more men, also in combat gear, plus the pilot. The plane took off, and the grip on her heart and stomach loosened.

"Clay? What is this? What are you doing?" The speaker was young with cold gray eyes and dark hair.

Clay ignored him. "The targets are in a small house in the Alps. We will go in from the trees and destroy the house without engaging the targets. They are at the top of our list and intel says they are extremely dangerous."

Frowning, she listened.

"These targets are unpredictable, and they may be expecting us, so be quick and cautious. Paul is point on this one, and he's already there with his team waiting for us."

"Who is she?" asked the blue-eyed soldier.

So she didn't pull off her disguise after all.

"A recruit with special skills. Asha, these are my brothers, Aron and Rio. Cole is flying the plane."

"Clay?"

"Yes, Aron?"

"We didn't expect this addition. Who cleared it?"

Clay scowled. "Christ Aron, relax. Master Miles sent her."

"Strange," Rio said studying her. "Since when does the Master concern himself with staffing issues?"

Asha barely acknowledged their discussion; her body still throbbed and burned. She would run as soon as she could. She'd go underground, and she might never come back up.

"Trust me, guys, she'll be fine."

Yeah, she could handle herself, but she was hurt, and she would need to get past the pain in order to escape these guys.

Clay rose. "Okay, we have to work together. There are multiple targets. We need everyone on cue."

Chapter Nine

Asha's seatbelt jarred her wounds as the jet landed in a small snow-covered meadow with minimal skid. She kept the wince from her face and looked out the window at the rising sun lighting the gray sky.

She trailed Clay and his brothers out of the plane and into the woods. Over a hundred soldiers waited, silent and eerily still just inside the trees. Rio and Aron stepped in front of Asha, blocking the soldiers' view of her.

Clay led them uphill through the forest, and she walked with them for over an hour. They arrived at a clearing and stopped. Asha winced again as she crouched behind Clay's brothers and peered out between the trees to a small cabin ahead.

The sunbeams through the forest lit the picturesque setting. A snow-covered road ran parallel to their trail through the forest. A nondescript white car was parked in the driveway, and smoke curled from the chimney. She backed up, slipping away from Clay, but she kept her eyes on the adorable stone cabin and the carved front door.

He sent hand signals to the soldiers, and they spread out in two lines along the border. He was distracted, checking over the men as they took position. His brothers studied the cabin. Asha kept moving away.

She found it rather odd to track 'most wanted' villains to such serene and lovely surroundings, but she understood better than most that appearances meant nothing. She'd found scum in the most beautiful places, as well as the expected slums and undergrounds.

Someone, she assumed it was Paul since he was on point, called the order from the other end of the line, and a rocket squealed and launched toward the cabin. It struck the roof, and the ground shook. The house exploded in flames.

After being without her power, Asha had to fight the urge to control it and spur it on. The fire burned hot and contained, and the connection swept over her. She was back. Hypnotized she reached out to touch it, just for a moment to reassure herself

"She has power."

The voice was low, the pilot. The only one of Clay's brothers who hadn't spoken earlier. *Oh, shit. Wait...how?*

"I know," he snapped.

He knows? Asha scanned the field. *Just go now.* The battle chaos was her only chance for cover. The ground shook again, harder this time.

Clay swiveled to his brother. "Rio?"

"It's not me."

Forget cover, go now.

With a crack and rumble, the ground surrounding the cabin broke apart and water burst from the earth. It sprayed as strong as any fire hose up and over the cabin. The pounding force was like a waterfall in reverse, and the flames sputtered and died.

She had never seen anything like it, an enormous water fountain extinguishing fire burning that hot. The cabin door, charred and still smoking, flew off its hinges and onto the flooded grass.

Three figures darted out into the early morning glare. Asha took off her helmet and slouchy hood, but her eyes weren't playing tricks. She could see them clearly, even across the distance, and her stomach dropped. They stopped short, facing an army with guns raised. *No.*

"Fire."

"Stop!" Her scream was too late; the soldiers fired. She didn't have time to act. They were sitting ducks. She prepared for their thrashing bodies, but like a swarm of hovering locusts, the bullets stopped in mid-air and dropped.

What? She couldn't get her mind around the scene unfolding before her. She'd lost control of her body. Her muscles wouldn't move.

"Hold your fire," Clay shouted, but the soldiers continued shooting.

His brothers were the only ones not attacking. They had to be as shocked by the falling bullets as she was. She couldn't blame them. She was as still and as useless as a rock, unable to move or act, only watch in growing disbelief. Three young women stood against an army.

"Asha," yelled one of the girls. Her eyes were even brighter green than Clay's. "We're your sisters. We've been looking for you."

Sisters? Black hair and blue eyes fired a small pistol dropping two soldiers. Green eyes stomped her foot, and the ground lurched. The snow rolled like a wave across the ground toward the soldiers. Stones and boulders erupted in front of them, stacking magically into a huge wall blocking the offensive. Asha shook her head.

"I'm Ivy, and this is Avia and Mere. You belong with us, but we have to get out of here."

Asha's feet finally moved, one step then another, but a deafening crack echoed from behind her, and she spun back. The wall, cracking and splitting, opened to reveal Clay behind it, his shaking hand outstretched.

He pushed through the shattered wall, and his brothers climbed over the debris after him. Soldiers followed, halting in side-by-side formation.

They opened fire once again, but black hair and blue eyes… Mere, shot back, emptying the clip. After she threw the useless gun at the enemy, it sailed into the air and hit one of their targets, knocking him to the ground. She whooped and clapped her hands. They were facing an army out in the open, but they were giving them a fight.

"Thanks for the boost, Avia," Mere shouted, a grin clear on her face. She was enjoying herself.

Avia, her white-haired sister, threw her hands out, and the air waved and glimmered in front of her. The bullets stopped again and dropped silently. It'd been her. Somehow, Avia continued to block the soldiers' constant fire. Beside her, Mere raised her arms as water swelled from the ground. She lowered her hands in front of her face. The geyser bent, sending thunderous pressure against the line.

Water battered at the soldiers, and they fell and slammed into each other. The water sprayed and flooded the ground.

The geyser had caused the break she needed, and Asha took advantage of the lapse. Sprinting toward her sisters, she sent one of her smaller fireballs at the soldiers. The men still standing swung their guns to her and opened fire again.

Clay yelled as she ran, and the ground lurched again, so violently it knocked her off her feet. Soldiers fired wildly, with their fingers still on the triggers as they fell. Thankfully they did more damage to each other than to her.

The moment she hit the cold, wet ground, she sprang up, sprinting again for her sisters. Clay commanded the men to stop. But back on their feet, the soldiers held their positions, firing as before. Asha made it to them just as Avia went to her knees.

"I'm draining," she said.

Asha scanned her enemy. They had lost a few soldiers, but there were still so many left. Her confusion had spiraled into anger and now peaked into rage. She sent flames racing along the ground with her left hand, and more fireballs from her right, taking out three or four at the same time.

The field rippled again, and mud and water gathered and formed an enormous wave coming from the opposite side. It crested, and met the fire, extinguishing it just before it reached the line. Steam billowed and rolled back across the field toward them.

Raging, frantic, screamed commands came from the trees behind the soldiers.

Asha hurled more fire at them as the bullets kept coming. She hesitated a moment. Clay would die if she went any further…but he was with them.

She shook her head. *What's wrong with you?* He'd captured her, killed her friends, and he was fighting on the side of those trying to kill her. They'd already tortured her, and it was a miracle she'd survived it. Now it was her turn to hurt him back.

Doubt and fury battled within her. He'd seduced her into caring for him, and he was the enemy. He'd been part of a massacre killing her friends, he'd kidnapped her, and he'd been her jailer in that horrible place. Why did she need to keep reminding herself of those things?

The dream of the man in the cave returned like a warning she must heed. She couldn't trust him, and even though she'd always understood that, she was behaving as if she'd forgotten. Filled with fresh strength, she sent another blanket of fire but this one rose effortlessly into a wall toward him.

"Stop," Clay yelled in the distance.

The fire sped forward. Wind pushed and slowed the flames, more water rose again to meet it, but couldn't stop it completely. Her fire engulfed their right flank, and thirty soldiers fell burning.

The remaining soldiers kept firing. A familiar squeal rose above the din. *Christ.*

"Rocket," she cried, warning her sisters and swept her hand in front of her.

The rolling fire sped back toward the line. But the rocket was already coming, and she couldn't stop it. She braced, but nothing happened. It got eerily quiet. She opened her eyes and blinked and blinked again. Her eyes couldn't be seeing what was right there before them.

A massive wall had risen silently between the two sides, but the wall was made of water, stretching across the field, clear and still as glass and at least fifty meters thick. She could see the rocket floating within, defused and immobile.

Even the soldiers had stopped shooting and stared. It was Mere, Asha's grinning, clapping sister, who'd called it and held it, her arms outstretched in the thick, pulsing silence.

The water started to move and swirl, frothing inside the wall, "I can't…guys. I can't hold it, get ready."

The wall dropped soaking into the field, and Ivy sent the ground rolling and knocked the men off their feet again. Mere swayed, falling, as a shot rang out in the silence and fresh blood sprayed across the soggy grass.

"No," Ivy screamed. She lunged and dropped beside Mere.

Avia's shield came up, catching the new onslaught, but a second too late. One bullet had gotten through and hit Mere in the shoulder.

Buzzing pounded in Asha's ears. Her vision tinted red, her pain and fear forgotten and replaced by fury. It rolled, building until she feared she might blow the whole place away and kill her newfound sisters in the process.

A dirty root, wide as a baseball bat, surged from the ground across the field and whipped in the air curling and winding until it hovered, pointing at the soldiers. Snapping forward as fast as a cobra's attack, it speared Mere's shooter through the chest, lifting him into the air. He struggled and fought, his arms and legs flailing as he slid down the long root, like a bead on a thread. Ivy guided it on with her finger, and it shot through the line, impaling the soldiers one by one and sewing them together.

It was gruesome, but effective, and it distracted her from her spinning frenzy, letting her focus on the battle at hand. Clay plunged his hands into the mud as the root sped toward him and his brothers.

"Clay, look out," Asha screamed, now warning her enemy.

Ivy lowered her hand, and the branch fell at his feet. Soldiers still twitched and squirmed on the branch like fish on a line.

Avia threw her hands out, and the remaining soldiers blew back into the trees.

Ivy laid both hands over Mere's shoulder applying pressure to stop her bleeding.

Mere gasped and opened her eyes. "Ouch," she whispered, her voice hoarse.

"Hold on," Ivy said.

She shoved her right hand into the ground and drew out bright green and red weeds, squeezing them into mush. She then lifted her hand. The blood had slowed enough for her to spread the weeds over the wounds. She took three long thin vines poking from the ground beside her and laid them over Mere's shoulder.

She tilted her head toward Ivy with a questioning look, but she jumped as the vines stretched and wrapped over her shoulder and under her arm like a bandage.

"Too tight?" Ivy asked. She stood, reaching out to Mere.

Asha caught her breath.

Mere shook her head, "It's perfect." With her hand on her

shoulder and Ivy's help, Mere got to her feet, testing the vine bandage. "Amazing, thank you."

Asha turned back to the trees, Clay had flown back with the rest, but came sprinting out, running toward them. She shifted forward, compelled like a magnet to go to him.

"No, don't," Avia yelled.

Her sister's voice stopped Asha and shook her from her trance.

He charged.

What on earth was she doing? He was the enemy, and she moved toward him like a ship to a siren.

"Take her!"

The command was shouted from the trees. Clay reached out, but light shimmered between them knocking him back. It was Avia's shield, and he battered at it like an angry bee bouncing off a window but still fighting to get through. He was going to capture Asha again and take her back.

Ivy grasped her hand, towing her over to Mere and Avia. "Hurry, we need to hold hands," she said.

Avia's shield fell.

Clay kept coming.

"It will be okay. I promise," Ivy said. The earth opened up beneath their feet, and they dropped below ground.

Chapter Ten

Only moments before Asha had been in a field with a picturesque cottage transformed into a war zone, now they were underground in a cave after transporting to another place.

"What happened? Where are we?" Avia whispered, breathing heavily.

"I'm sorry," Ivy said. "I had to get us out of there. I used a sinkhole. Things were out of control. Sorry, I'm sure it was a shock."

Asha couldn't catch her breath. They were safe, but for how long?

Mere sat down and laid back, pale and panting. "I'm okay. It's the shoulder. It's nothing. I was lucky."

Ivy bent over Mere and moved the vines aside to study her wound. "Nothing? Have you ever been shot before?"

"No, but I heal fast, and it barely hurts. What did you do?"

"It's poppy and ginger, and pressure."

Asha tapped her leg, counting. "I don't understand. What's happening? How could I have three sisters?"

Heavy, suffocating dread crept past the anxiety and gripped her. It wasn't quite like her panic attacks. This was much worse. Solid weight crushed her chest, and she couldn't take a breath.

"Are you all right?" Ivy asked. Her voice echoed and faded.

Asha shook her head and collapsed to one knee, stretching her neck back, and opening her mouth to suck the thinning air.

Ivy knelt beside her. "What's going on?"

Avia's body was as still as a statue, her ghostly hair fluttering lightly and her eyes closed. Her body clenched so tightly her lips were pursed and white.

Asha took gasping, labored breaths and managed to point behind Ivy.

Ivy spun, lifted her arms over her head, and the rock and soil around them shifted and rolled.

"Stop it, Avia," Ivy shouted.

The cave expanded and grew, spreading into a huge cavern. Once a small cave just large enough for the four of them to stand in, it had grown bigger than two football stadiums stacked one on top of the other.

Her eyes opened, and they were swirling, gray, and stormy.

"You're taking their air, you're killing them," Ivy shouted.

A hole crumbled and cracked open above, and sunlight beamed in lighting the darkness. Avia stood under it and stared up at the opening. Her eyes stopped spinning.

Mere gasped, and Asha coughed, drawing in air. She leapt up onto shaky legs and glared at Avia. Air shimmered, and a trail of fire raced along the ground following the path of her eyes. It hit an invisible barrier, and wind from nowhere blew the flames back. Her temper flared, and she urged them on. The fire rose effortlessly into a wall, but Avia blew it back again.

"Stop," Ivy cried.

The ringing in Asha's head and the pounding in her chest drowned her out.

Water splashed from above, soaking her as a huge, thick, *Jack and the Beanstalk* vine burst from the ground and wrapped around her pinning her arms.

Cold. Sputtering, she took a deep breath and glared at Avia again. "Are you trying to kill us?" *Calm down.*

Everyone but Mere was soaking wet.

"I'm sorry." Avia's voice was flat. "I didn't realize what I was doing."

The vine loosened and dropped Asha to her feet. She watched it retreat into the cave floor with her subsiding anger. "I'm sorry too," she conceded. "I shouldn't have attacked you."

Her combat training had kicked in without thinking, and she'd gone after her sister. Granted they were new to her, but still… She was wound so tight one wrong move, one wrong touch, and she would snap.

"What happened up there?" Mere asked. "Obviously they're the ones after us, but who were those men? The ones with power. They're like us." She paused before continuing, her voice shaky. "Could they be related to us?"

"I hope not," Asha mumbled under her breath.

"Sorry?" Ivy asked.

"Nothing," she said, looking up and pretending to inspect the cavern.

Avia was still wide-eyed. "We need to get out of here. They may have retreated, but they'll return."

Ivy confirmed the army had indeed withdrawn, and she touched the rock wall. The cavern shivered, shifting once again. Large rocks jutted from the wall creating a rough staircase along the cavern edge leading to the hole at the top.

"That's handy," Asha said, impressed. With three powerful sisters, she was no longer alone, but their enemies were four men with similar power, and Clay was one of them.

Stop. Get over it. So he was on the other side? *You're a warrior; you can handle this.* But… Why couldn't she shake him? It was as if she carried him with her even now. She needed her head in the game. Everything in her world had drastically changed, and her moony feelings were not only a dangerous distraction, they were completely wrong. She'd warned him of danger, and she'd almost gone with him. He could be the most threatening enemy she'd ever faced. She had to do something about that.

One by one, they headed back up to the surface to take care of Mere and figure out what was happening. Asha couldn't shake the sliver of insanity, a flickering idea she grasped illogically. Clay helped her escape, and he didn't attack her or her sisters during the battle.

~ * ~

Asha was gone. They'd disappeared.

"Where did they go? Find them," Paul shouted, marching up to Clay.

He flushed with restrained rage. "I don't know."

Paul leaned closer. "Where are they?"

Clay stared at the ground, calling his earth power, searching but there was nothing. Not even a glimmer of fire. He struggled to pick up her energy, but it was gone. "I can't sense them."

"Your lies won't convince the Masters." His voice had lowered, but the ferocity was still there. "How did the prisoner come to be on this mission then escape?"

Clay didn't answer.

"The Grand Master will kill you for this."

He glanced at his brothers. They all stared back at him. Cole had fire power, but he couldn't do what Asha could do. Clay could barely comprehend the amount of power she had. The amount all four girls had was staggering. They had much more than he and his brothers.

This morning Heath gave orders for them to join Paul's team and remove the threat. The threat Clay had identified and tracked. Since he was a teenager, Heath had him looking for others like them and it had become Clay's own obsession. It was foretold that they would face others with the same powers, and he and his brothers would be killed.

So he'd searched as the Masters had trained him to. He'd never succeeded. It was his most coveted and unreachable goal—until he'd returned with Asha, and Heath sent for him.

Cole had tried again, preparing for the usual disappointment and connected to the earth, reaching for the elements. But he connected to fire instantly. It wasn't him. It was her, deep in the dungeons below, and like little lights switching on he saw the others. Earth and water and just a hint of air, they were in Canada, Australia, and Hong Kong. He'd finally found them.

"Clay?" Aron asked.

"Not now," he snapped.

"Back to the Order," Paul growled. They hiked back to the jet.

~ * ~

Back on the surface and away from the cavern, Avia drew in deep breaths. Asha climbed out and turned back. She blinked repeatedly and bent over the hole, gasping. Mere followed. Ivy walked up the same stairs they had all used, but the ground rose with her. The soil and rock rolled and churned, filling the hole behind her. *Wow.*

Avia led them a short distance to the cabin. The burned front door was still on the ground near the entrance. Water dripped from the ceiling inside, and she went to the bedroom and changed her clothes. Ivy helped Mere lay on the couch.

Ivy with her casual navy-blue sweater and jeans was radiant. She had gorgeous loose, wavy auburn hair with so many highlights it was the color of fall leaves, changing as it moved. Her flashing eyes were as green as freshly sprouted grass.

Avia returned and started packing. Her hair was not the white of age but white, like lightning. It shone like moonlight and paired with her gray, stormy eyes, she was strikingly beautiful in an unusual way. In black skinny jeans and her gray cashmere sweater, she was impeccable down to her shining, black-heeled boots. She was stunning, and Asha doubted she'd been teased about her mystical white hair as a kid, as they'd teased Asha about her crazy orange and red locks. There was something about Avia, a presence that screamed don't mess with me. It would take a ballsy kid to pick on her, and bullies were cowards by nature.

Mere was slightly smaller, and her hair was black, shoulder length, and wavy. But her eyes were the lightest blue Asha had ever seen, and yet during the fight, they had been so much darker. Mere was tough, enthusiastic and joyful, even with a hole in her shoulder and practically suffocating in the cave. She wore a blue hoody, Guns 'n Roses T-shirt, and jeans. *I bet she could rock a bikini like no one else.*

Mere caught Asha's gaze. "So, we should probably discuss what the hell is going on? Apparently, we've discovered the source of the attacks, but who were those guys and why were you with them? Oh yeah, and why are they trying to kill us?"

Mere's wound was already healing. So it wasn't a side effect from Asha's fire but must be a shared gift amongst sisters. She recovered from her wounds faster than was natural and even though her body still ached, the skin on her arms appeared as wounds healed after weeks instead of mere hours. *Hours?*

How could it only be hours since that horror?

"I am as in the dark as you are. They call themselves the Order. Or the place is the Order, I'm not sure," she said.

"Order of what?"

"Nothing, just the Order, I think."

Ivy frowned. "Days ago we didn't have a clue about each other, but this Order did, and they tried to kill us. Our guardians are either dead or missing. Father Bennett, my guardian is dead, and Mere's we assume is dead. Avia's is missing."

"Mine's missing too," Asha said, gazing into Ivy's gentle green eyes. "I haven't seen him since he left me in South America eleven years ago. I thought all of this had to be his doing, but I'm having doubts now. Whatever is going on here—it's out of his league."

They stared at her.

"You thought your guardian was trying to kill you with an army?" Mere asked.

"It's a long story."

"How did they find you?" Ivy asked.

"I was on my own, doing my own thing, and this doctor shows up. He saved my best friend and helped me enough to gain a smidge of trust. But he caught me off guard, knocked me out, and kidnapped me." Asha didn't want to tell them about the torture, or what she'd seen as she didn't understand it herself.

"I woke up in a very creepy place. I'm not sure where. Whoever they are, they have their own army or security force and as you saw, decent resources to back them up. The place was huge and dark. I've never heard of it or spoken to anyone else who's come across anything like it, and I should have. It's too big, and they're organized, powerful." She paused then said, "I couldn't use my power inside the buildings or anywhere on the grounds. That's never happened to me."

"Strange," Ivy said.

"I was kept in a cell, like in an actual dungeon. It was crazy."

Outrage flashed across Ivy and Mere's faces.

"But then this morning I was told I was leaving. I was dressed as you see, smuggled aboard, and told to escape at my first opportunity."

Asha should tell them about the torture and visions, but she was still trying to process it all. They already understood they were in trouble. Should she terrify them too?

"I couldn't sense you," Ivy said. "I thought we lost you, that maybe they found you. You say you were powerless? That could be why I couldn't find you. Without your power, you wouldn't stand out from any other person."

"It was a fortress. Clay, the one with the earth gift—"

Mere giggled. "Ah ha, I get it. Earth? Clay? Huh, that's pretty funny."

Asha frowned. She hadn't made that connection. "I didn't know he had power until the fight when he broke that wall. He was the one who captured me."

"But then he also saved your life," Mere said.

"Pardon?"

When Asha thought about it, she realized Mere was right. The tremor had given Asha the opportunity to get away from them and join her sisters. It had knocked the men off their feet too, stopping their offensive short. Her relief that he had been there to help her, battled against her rage at his purpose and his allegiance. She didn't know what to believe, but he'd tried to take her back.

"I'm ashamed to admit he tricked me." Her cheeks heated, and her stomach dropped. "He introduced the others as his brothers. So yeah, I guess they're like us."

Where were these feelings coming from? How could she have trusted him even for a second? It was her own stupidity shifting her so off-balance.

She was smarter, harder than the type who fell for romantic delusions. "I'm lucky I got away."

You're an idiot. Asha kept certain confessions to herself because she didn't want them to judge her. She'd just found them.

"Speaking of getting away," Avia said quietly. "You said someone helped you—someone on the inside?"

She hadn't delved too deeply into her fortuitous escape, but having seen the Order's true force, power, and reach, she was grateful for his help. However he managed it, he had reunited her with her sisters. "Clay mentioned his name. Alex, I think. He was sent by Master Miles. Apparently the order to remove me came from the top." But the top of what?

Ivy, Mere, and even Avia stiffened.

"Master Miles?" Ivy asked. "He was there? With them? Did you see him?"

"No, I never saw him, and I only heard his name once. Why? Who is he? You all look so—"

"According to Father Bennett, Master Miles was the one who separated us, apparently to protect us. He'd be the one with answers. If he got you out, we have someone helping us from the inside."

Asha wasn't sure about someone called Master Miles, or any of the rest of it, but something huge was going on and her battle instincts were revved up.

"Guys, we're in some serious trouble here," Asha said.

And not my usual kind.

Ivy agreed. "Someone wants us dead, but why?"

Asha was at war with herself. She still reeled from Clay's betrayal, but she was under his spell. It had to be a drug or hypnosis, or something they did to her in that place. Wary of her instincts for the first time, she looked at her sisters. It was her job to protect them now. They needed her to be strong and ruthless. She had to be prepared to kill him if she faced him again. She choked and went rigid. But she didn't want to kill him.

"Exactly," Mere said. "If those men are like us, why would they want to kill us?"

How was she going to kill him?

"Asha?"

Quickly, burn him to a crisp before you have a chance to think about it. The thought made her ill.

"Asha?" Ivy asked.

"Sorry, what? Oh, I don't know who they are. Perhaps they're threatened by our power. We are stronger than they are. They had to work together. They needed each other."

"We can't speculate on how strong their powers are," Ivy said.

"Did you notice though, how the man with water power never called water?" Mere asked. "He only controlled the flooded water that was already there. And did you feel that boost in your power? I've never been able to create such a big wall, and it was effortless. It didn't last, but it appeared instantly."

Both Ivy and Avia agreed. Asha's fire had never burned so intensely, and her reaction in the cave? To say it was an overreaction was being kind. The power had come so effortlessly, even after the battle had drained her.

"It makes sense our power would work well together," Ivy said.

"We should go," Avia's quiet voice was cool, detached, and

slightly robotic.

They left the house through the back with their bags and walked along the gravel path to a large wooden shed behind the tree line. Avia opened the doors, revealing a flashy SUV hybrid.

"Cool car," Mere said.

Avia went to the ground under the front passenger wheel and pulled up a flap of floor and revealed a hidden panel.

"What's that?" Asha asked.

Avia's voice floated from beneath the car. "We'll need resources. And with a force like theirs, we should stick with cash."

"That's a good idea, Avia, but…"

Avia dragged a huge duffle bag out from under the car and when she unzipped it Asha gasped. Ivy and Mere rushed up to look over her shoulder. It was like a scene from a drug dealing drama.

Avia reached in and pulled out stacks of cash. "Before you ask, my family was wealthy, and I have my own money. I keep it as cash because it's safer."

"Unless your house burns down," Asha mumbled.

"Yes, you're right. But as they say with eggs and baskets."

"Are you saying these aren't all your eggs?" Mere's eyes widened.

Avia handed two stacks to Mere, but she shook her head. Asha was reluctant too. "Take it. We're going to need it."

"I have my own," Mere said.

"This will just be more. Please."

Asha stepped forward and took it. "Thank you. You're right. We'll need to hide, and we'll need to travel. I'd be lost without cash."

Avia nodded, and Ivy and Mere took the money she offered. She gave them each five stacks and zipped up the bag, storing it back under the shed floor.

Avia brushed off her clothes, and they all got inside the truck. She drove past the house and across the scorched and flooded clearing toward the road, leaving the ruined rental car in the driveway.

"Oh, dear," Mere said. "I don't suppose we can return it like that?"

Asha twisted in her seat glancing back at Mere. Avia checked the rear-view and smiled.

"What?" Mere asked. "With GPS they'll find it eventually."

Asha smiled. Could Mere really be so sweet? Fear and bullet wound aside, her concern was genuinely endearing.

After coming around a hairpin corner halfway down the mountain, Avia stopped the car. There was a roadblock about two hundred yards ahead. Two fire trucks, a police car, and ambulance blocked the road.

"Who are these people?" she mumbled.

One of the firefighters glared across the distance. Asha jumped from the car sprinting toward the blockade. The firefighter darted behind the rig. *Oh no, you don't.*

She swept her hand across the front of her body. Fire rolled from her hands like a flamethrower crossing the distance, covering both the men and vehicles. Despite their protective clothing, the flames washed over them, burning their curling, smoking bodies like dried leaves.

Both Mere and Ivy jumped out of the car, screaming at her, but it was too late.

Ivy ran up to her, "What've you done?"

"They're not firefighters. Trust me, they're the bad guys. I recognized one of them from the Order—he likes to throw food. This," she gestured around her, "is all a ruse. They're wearing costumes. Who knows where they got these vehicles? Like I said they have formidable resources."

A bullet flew between their heads and struck Avia's windshield. Asha spun around and shot a fireball through the fire engine's windshield, shattering the glass and hitting the gunman hiding within.

Mere jumped back inside the car, and Asha ran through the burning blockade. The flames sputtered out as she approached.

No bodies. She hadn't burned her fire that hot, but with her sisters, her power was much stronger now. She would have to resume her control training as soon as possible. Asha seized an armful of guns from the backseat of the smoking police car.

Thrusting them at Ivy, she grabbed the rest. "I can confidently say at this point, we'll need all the guns we can get."

"What happened to the bodies?" Ivy asked.

"Burned to ash," Asha said looking at the ground. Purple-tinted smoke moved in wisps around her feet. "It happens."

Avia pulled the car alongside, and Asha got in, tossing the guns into the back.

"Ivy?" Avia said through the open window. "We should move."

Ivy went around the car and placed the guns carefully in the back before getting in the truck and doing up her seatbelt.

Avia drove around the roadblock and continued on the road down the mountain. "I have another place about an hour from here," she said. "We can go there for now."

Asha turned back in her seat again, scowling. She blew hot and focused fire at the smoking wreckage. A bright white flash burned fast and contained, erasing the blockade and leaving a scorched black stain on the road.

~ * ~

As Clay suspected, the ride back to the Order was extremely tense. He explained to his brothers that he'd only followed orders, yet their stony faces showed their distrust.

At the very least they had the edge with their plane. They would beat the others back by more than an hour. He would need every minute of that time to save his ass.

Alex had said Asha's removal was on Master Miles's command, and although odd and unprecedented, Clay hadn't questioned it for obvious reasons. He wanted to get her away from the dungeons and the death sentence that came with residence there. At a loss as to how Clay could help her, Alex provided the answer.

During the battle Clay was about to lose her, so he'd reached out, and that damn force field had blocked him. He wasn't sure what he planned to do once he had her, but he was prepared to help her in any way she needed. In that moment he was willing to take her and leave his brothers, leave the Order…anything to save her, convince her he was trustworthy and to be with her.

But she misunderstood his actions, and her expression had chilled him. He panicked and pummelled the barrier even harder, but before he could make it through she'd vanished with the others.

The others. Asha didn't know them. They were her sisters, but it was as if they'd never met. Her reaction couldn't have been an act. Her shock was genuine; he would have bet his life on it. How could she have managed to balance her fire all these years without her sisters?

Remembering Cole's struggle with his power, Clay's esteem for Asha grew. If it hadn't been for his brothers' ability to work together and help each other, Cole's power would have consumed him. How had she survived, let alone stayed hidden, without her sisters?

This all had to be a mistake. They couldn't be the prophesized enemies. There had to be some misunderstanding. The moment she'd crossed sides, he vowed he would never risk her safety by taking her back to the Order. He couldn't have harmed her now, even if he'd been commanded to. He'd fallen instantly for the dark-eyed firecracker, and now after seeing her power, he would have smiled at the apt description if he wasn't so worried.

The Masters had adopted him and his brothers as babies, and they owed everything to the Order. But they were threatened and constantly reminded that if they weren't strong enough they would lose it all. The Order's primary focus was to maintain balance, but it was always described in the vague language and metaphors of religion. He paid little attention to the teachings, but now after what he'd seen, he questioned their deeper meanings.

They'd been educated, given special training, no expense spared. The Order gave them everything, except for a traditional upbringing.

Why was he ordered to take Asha to her sisters before killing them? It didn't add up. Clay needed more information, and once inside the Order's walls, he searched for the Master. If he were on the grounds, he'd find him and ask the questions swirling in his head.

He located him immediately and ran down to the dungeons on the lowest level and stalked to the very last cell. Heath and Shane were inside with him.

Clay sensed them, but he couldn't hear them through the black wall. *What the hell is going on?*

~ * ~

Heath studied his brother's faraway eyes, his dark expression somber as usual. Miles's betrayal was undeniable. "You are accused and punished for your betrayal. What could have swayed you from your purpose? You were to be Grand Master."

Miles sat chained to the floor staring at the black wall. He was bloody and beaten.

"How could you do this to us, to the Order, to Father, and your legacy? What have you done, Miles?"

Miles stared back blankly.

"Benjamin was right, there *were* signs, and you've been covering them up. You let us torture and kill one of our own." Heath leaned in closer. "It was always you—you were *the one*, the scary one, the loyal one. How could you betray us?"

Silence.

"It's plain on your face, you are no longer with us. You've abandoned us, and Father will kill you."

Silence.

"He will kill you."

Miles shook his head. "You're right. I've changed. Almost thirty years ago."

"How could you help her escape?"

"I kept up the façade by working in the field and covering up what I could, but they are Emma's daughters. They are Emma's."

Emma?

"Why didn't you tell me that?" he shouted. He couldn't hide his shock. "Where is she?"

"She's dead." The words were no more than a whisper. "She

died after childbirth. She went into hiding because she knew we would come."

Heath stared into Miles's battered and bloody face and swallowed. He'd kept so much from him, "Dead?" He couldn't believe it. "Did you kill her?"

"No, never."

Heath glared at him, anger swelling. "They are yours."

"I don't know for sure, but I've protected them as if they were. I couldn't hand them over to the Four. Mine or not, they were Emma's babies, and she loved them."

"Stop. You can't justify your betrayal to me," Heath snapped. "You hid them." He paused and took a breath to calm his rolling stomach. "You have explained why you might have hesitated for a moment, but your duty? You should have come to me. You've exposed yourself and put us all in danger."

Heath studied his brother, the most dedicated to their cause—the one in line to sit the throne. How could he have taken this risk? "I can't help you, you're on your own, and like I said, Father will kill you."

"So be it."

"So be it? After all your scheming, it was for nothing. It's too late. We found them. You sacrificed yourself for nothing. The Grand Master is on the hunt and soon the Four will be too."

Miles's head dropped to his chest. "No."

"Yes. You've lost, and now you'll die." Heath sighed, tilted his head to Shane, and ushered him out of the cell locking the door behind him.

~ * ~

Clay waited until Heath and Shane had left the dungeons. He peered through the small window and touched the stone wall beside the door. Even as it cracked and crumbled it opened.

Once he passed through into the darkness, the scent of dank, dirty rooms and something sickly sweet hit him. Both men stared at each other, Clay furious, but Miles looked defeated.

Clay's hands were clenched in fists at his sides, but he took in Miles's battered face and frowned.

How could Master Heath treat his brother like such filth? "Why?"

Miles shook his head. "It didn't take them long to realize she was gone. It took less time for them to realize it was me."

"Why did you send me after her in Colombia, and then break her out? They'll kill *me* for this." Clay studied the Master's face.

"I didn't know she was *la Reina Guerrera*. None of us did. She was just a minor problem. It's why we sent you alone. The fact she turned out to be one of the sisters we seek is a monumental forfeit to the destiny I am trying to prevent, or if you prefer, it's a bloody awful coincidence."

"I don't understand." Clay rubbed the back of his neck and scowled. What are you saying?"

"You didn't kill her then?"

"No, of course not. She got away."

"Good."

"Master, what's happening?"

"You and your brothers knew there would be others like you. They would rise in power and take you and the Order down."

Clay nodded.

"What you don't know is the sisters are the originals. Sisters with power have lived throughout history, since the beginning. You and your brothers? You're new."

"I beg your pardon."

"You know of the prophesy. It was discovered by a nutcase alchemist who lived hundreds of years ago, and we haven't put stock in it in decades. But we used it to push you and your brothers. We needed you to find the sisters, and we needed you all to be stronger than they were. It was imperative. But we have always hunted the sisters. The balance and harmony of man and earth depend upon it."

"You hunted them?"

"Until twenty-seven years ago. I knew when the sisters with elemental power were born. I had advance warning. I separated them and hid them from the Order."

"Why?"

"To protect them. Killing them is the Order's most important duty, and if I hadn't hidden them, they would have been murdered in their cribs, or worse, kept in the dungeons and tortured until they reached their full power."

Clay clenched his fists again. "The Order would have *killed* them? Helpless babies?" He wanted to scoff at the absurdity, but Master Miles's expression was dark and telling.

"They weren't going to remain helpless."

"Why are you helping them? If killing them is *our* duty." He shuddered with revulsion at such evil. "Then why?"

"That isn't important right now. Heath will send a team after Asha's sisters. They'll be on their way now. You and your brothers must find them first."

Clay stared at him. "What do you mean? We were just there."

Miles narrowed his eyes. "What?"

"We failed our objective, I am happy to say. Asha joined her sisters. But I can't find them. They escaped, and Paul is on the warpath. He wants me dead—"

"They're together? You were supposed to get her away on the first trip out."

"Going after her sisters was the first mission out. Heath had me tracking them. If they are your greatest goal, then of course he would send us after them as soon as I found them. I was ordered to kill them."

"They must stay apart."

"They were apart," Clay barked. "Their whole lives. Asha didn't know them. What did you expect? She saw her sisters facing us, defending themselves, and she joined them. They're sisters." His anger burst out. "Do you remember how it was for Cole?"

"The Four will be able to trace them." Miles's eyes were fierce.

"The Four?" Clay asked, scoffing. "Right, the ghosts of the Order's past?"

"You don't know anything. Do you really think you have all the information? You know better than that. You've been specifically kept in the dark."

Clay's fingers itched to draw his gun and shoot the Master. He flexed his fingers to relieve the desire.

"The Order's sole purpose is to find the sisters and take their power through sacrifice. We do it for the Four. The Order serves *them*. The Four are the true hunters, and we are nothing more than their hounds. They will find them. You must take your brothers and get to them first. Separate them and protect them. They *must* live."

Repulsed, Clay gagged as invisible pressure squeezed his chest. The Four?

"Apart the Four can't track them." There was an edge to the Master's voice. "That is why I separated them. If they are together, they will be found, and the Four will kill them."

Shame and fear rushed over him. Asha was in danger.

"What are you waiting for?" Master Miles shouted.

Clay was taken aback by the force in his voice, considering his condition.

"Go now. Find them, separate them, and keep them safe."

Clay left the cell running. He had to find Asha; he'd brought her into this evil nightmare. But first he had to explain to his brothers what he'd learned. How would they take it? Would they understand? Would his brothers follow him?

The Grand Master would kill him for helping Asha escape, but if he pleaded with Heath to spare his brothers...would he?

Doubtful…they were kind of a set.

How would Clay find Asha now that he couldn't sense her anymore? A voice inside urged him to move.

He would have to get Master Miles out too. He was in bad shape, and the Grand Master would definitely execute him. Even at Master Miles's level, a betrayer was a betrayer.

Clay would just tell his brothers what happened and why they had to leave their home. They would be well aware that if they succeeded in escaping, the Order would come after them full force. But it was a necessary risk. He was dead if he stayed.

He burst into the wing of the building he and his brothers shared. Rio and Aron were drinking beer in the kitchen and speaking in hushed voices. They swung around at his harried entrance.

"Clay what the hell's going on?" Rio asked.

"Grab the essentials. We have to leave now, go underground. We're not safe here anymore. I'm going after the sisters. We're on the wrong side."

"You can't be serious. What do you mean wrong side?" Rio asked.

"If we stay here, I am dead. I don't have time to explain. We have to leave before Paul gives his report. He's probably getting back right now. Asha escaped on my watch."

"What were you doing bringing her along in the first place?' Rio asked.

"I will tell you once we are away, but there's no time. Trust me. You'll agree it was the right thing. It's appalling, almost too disgusting to believe."

"He's right, Rio. He screwed up, but he's made his decision," Aron said quietly. "Look, he's already out the door."

"If we leave, they'll come after us. Are we prepared for that?" Rio asked.

Clay glanced at Rio, his more cynical brother. "I am," he said.

"Okay, then." Rio shrugged. "You're obviously up the creek. Let's go."

Cole walked into the room.

"Cole?" Clay asked.

"I heard you, and yes, let's go."

"Guys, hit the armory on your way out. Stock-up and I'll meet you outside the walls on the north side." He tossed a bag to Cole. "This one, too. Hurry, I'm not sure we have much time."

"Where are you going?" Rio asked.

"I have to get Master Miles."

Chapter Eleven

Clay waited until Shane left Miles's cell before he opened the wall and slipped through it. The Master's head rolled back as if he were too tired to hold it up.

He knelt at Miles's feet and unlocked the chains at his ankles, then his wrists, and shook him awake.

Miles's eyes sharpened, and he pinned Clay with his dark gaze. "Clay?"

"Come on. We're leaving.

"I'll slow you down. Just go."

Clay ignored him. "You can't stay here. They'll kill you. We'll find the sisters, but I need your help." He pulled him to his feet. "I can't find them alone."

"As long as they're united you won't. Their elements are balanced together. Their individual power can't stand out. It's the same for you and your brothers. You can't be detected if you are together." His eyes rolled back into his head, and he lost consciousness.

Clay caught him and half-dragged him through the wall. The corridor was clear. He picked the Master up and rushed down the dark hallway. Running up the stairs with Miles over his shoulder, Clay broke through the last wall into fresh air. The sunlight blasted and blinded him after the darkness of the halls. He sprinted across the open grounds to the perimeter wall.

It resembled obsidian stone but was much tougher. It was his biggest challenge growing up, and he'd spent countless hours building his power against it. Right now, he needed to be the strongest he'd ever been.

Sweat beaded, he clenched his teeth and held out his shaking arm. He pushed once, and then again. Bringing his power in desperately and visualizing the wall breaking open, it finally cracked. As he touched the cold stone, the wall shuddered and opened, and he slid through with the Master, making it past the Order's final boundary.

Rio and Cole leaned against a sleek black BMW parked ahead

in the shadow of the wall. Aron waited inside with the engine running.

When Clay stumbled through the wall with Miles, Cole and Rio ran forward to help.

"Jesus," Rio said, taking the Master's arm over his shoulder and carrying him to the car and into the backseat. "What the hell happened to him?"

"How did you get out?" Clay asked.

"We said we were going to the pub. You were giving your report, and you were going to meet us there later," Rio said. "It was easy, considering that whatever this is, is going on." He gestured at the unconscious Master. "What's happening?"

Cole got in on the other side of the car to hold the Master up. Clay climbed into the front passenger seat, and Aron threw the car into gear and sped over the fields to the road.

"Come on, spill," Rio said from the backseat.

"Like I said guys, it's bad." Clay told his brothers everything Miles said.

They were silent until Aron spoke. "Okay…yeah, you made the right choice."

"Are we all in agreement then?" They were, and though Clay was sure they would be, he was still relieved he hadn't forced them into something they didn't want.

But what now? Asha was with her sisters, and he couldn't find them. But the Four would…

How can I draw them out? He had to get Miles somewhere safe—somewhere he could heal. *The cabin in Switzerland where you lost her.*

Miles was weak with blood loss, and the twelve-hour drive would be rough, but it was their only option. It was the best place to start, and maybe in the meantime, the girls would separate long enough for him to locate at least one of them.

~ * ~

The sisters had arrived at a duplicate cottage. Asha was stunned by the replica. Why would someone have two?

"Why do you have a copy-cabin?" Mere asked, echoing Asha's inner voice. "It's exactly the same."

"I like to have backups."

That was weird.

Inside, Asha scanned the open layout, same as the previous cabin. The kitchen opened into a large living and dining room area on the right. Two bedrooms sat across from the kitchen and living room with a small bathroom in between. There was a small nook to the right of the master bedroom with a backdoor exit and a mudroom porch outside. It was the perfect setup with enough room, but cozy and cute.

"May I?" she asked.

Avia nodded, and Asha snapped her fingers at the fireplace. Fire burst to life from the cold logs resting inside.

No one spoke. The crackling fire was the only sound.

"Asha?" Ivy asked.

"Yes?" She clearly had something on her mind.

"Can you tell me about Father Sean, your guardian, and how he trained you? At the cabin, and there on the road, you didn't hesitate even for a moment. You knew they were the enemy, and you acted so quickly."

Her soldier identity out of the closet for her sisters to see.

Asha glanced at Ivy's face, and the desire to unburden her heart to them overwhelmed her. "I started combat training pretty early—just after I turned twelve. I worked for him and protected him. I had a rough transition into my full power. I killed my parents and my younger sister. It was an accident but…"

She told them about the class camping trip and her test, everything else up until her last mission with Father Sean at the orphanage. Her guilt prevented her from confessing all the details of what she had done for her guardian, and what she did for herself— hunting scumbags. She couldn't share her chosen occupation. It was obvious she wasn't like her sisters. Though they all fought well in battle, they were too soft. Ivy's root was the one exception.

Finishing her story, she was weak and tired from keeping her emotions under control, yet she was also lighter somehow.

Avia and Ivy stared at each other, and Mere studied the floor as tension built into thick, heavy air between them.

Panic clenched Asha's heart. "You're not scared of me are you?" She didn't think she could take it if they feared her. "I know I can be unpredictable and violent, but it's been years since I've lost control," she lied.

"We're all unpredictable and capable of losing control especially when our power was fluctuating. That's not it. It was something you said. You didn't kill your family. I can see you carry a lot of guilt, but it's time to let it go."

"I can't. Could you? Could you let it go if you were responsible for killing your parents and your little sister?"

Ivy knelt before her with her head bowed before she looked up. She had tears in her eyes. "Our powers can't manifest in our sleep or our nightmares."

Asha shook her head.

"You must be conscious to use your power. It's always been that way for me."

"And me," Mere said.

"And me," Avia concurred.

"What do you mean?" Asha jumped up, her heart pounding again. "What are you saying?" The fire surged in the fireplace. "I didn't kill my family?"

"No, not in your sleep. You didn't start that fire."

Asha's cheeks burned. "Father Sean. I told him I wouldn't leave my family, but then I agreed. There would be no reason for him to…" The fire in the hearth burned blue and white burning up the chimney. Avia glanced at it then to Mere.

"Asha," Ivy said. "You can't use your power in your sleep, but you can in anger."

"He killed my family. He blamed me and used my guilt." Sometimes Asha's penchant for darkness frightened her, but not this time.

Fantasies of pain and torture floated through her mind. She'd make him hurt, and the more he suffered, the happier she would be. She couldn't wait to get her hands on him.

Mere snapped her fingers, and steam billowed from the fireplace. Hot steam rolled over Asha, shaking her from her vengeful visions.

Her heartbeat returned to normal. One day she would have her revenge, and oh, how sweet it would be. But right now, she couldn't change the past, and it wasn't all about her. *Temper, temper Asha.* She closed her eyes, sighed deeply, tapping her leg. After a ten count, she opened them.

"I'm sorry." The news was both revealing and shocking, and yet she still managed to shut down her anger and shed it like clothing.

Her soldier identity snapped back into place and her training kicked in. She could compartmentalize her grief and anger and still feed her rage underneath, building her strength and her power. But yes, sometimes her temper could get her into trouble.

Avia handed Asha a mug of tea. She took a sip before clenching down and grinding her teeth.

~ * ~

Master Heath sat with his father in the Grand Chamber, studying the files Shane put together on the sisters. He was tense, and he'd glanced over to his father more than once in the last two minutes. He couldn't tell him about Miles's betrayal yet. He would wait until the team returned with the sisters. Pair the bad news about the betrayal with the good news of the sisters' capture and wish for a miracle of mercy. The plan was falling apart. Emma's daughters? Miles's daughters?

Paul strode into the Grand Chamber and bowed low. "Disaster. We lost them. The sisters are united, and they are much stronger than we anticipated. They took out over two-thirds of our force."

"I beg your pardon. United? We have one here in the dungeon," the Grand Master growled.

Heath cringed. His father's anger had a way of turning him into a sniveling five-year-old, but he couldn't hide from this. His brother was on his own now.

Paul flinched and bowed. "Grand Master, the prisoner was at the battle. Clay smuggled her on his transport. He must know more than we thought. They were useless. They couldn't land a blow against the enemy."

Heath faced his father, but the Grand Master's face flashed so white, Heath instantly reached out in aid. But he recoiled, wincing as his father's face flushed to blazing fuchsia. He was going to explode.

Sweat beaded on his forehead. "Father?"

The Grand Master shook. Heath reached out again, but his father dropped his head and drew a raspy, phlegm-coated breath. "If they are together, the Four will know soon enough. It is no longer in our hands."

The old man picked up the dagger in front of him and sighed, spinning it in his hand. He threw it with such force and accuracy it stabbed deep in Paul's right eye. His body quivered a moment before he fell to the floor twitching.

Heath recovered quickly. His father's fits of temper were often violent and bloody, but Paul had taken the fire. The Grand Master would be slightly calmer now. "Paul was valuable, Father. Loyal. You've heard that saying about the messenger?"

The Grand Master shrugged. "He failed us. It's done."

"Yes sir."

"Clay betrayed us. How much does he know?"

"It wasn't just Clay. It was Miles. Clay removed the girl on Miles's command. He is the one who betrayed us. He engineered the prisoner's escape, and we can assume the brothers know everything."

"Kill Miles and bring Clay to me."

Heath flinched again and studied his father. "Sir, he is still your son and my brother."

"You no longer have a brother. Miles betrayed us, and you know very well what we do with traitors. If we don't, the Four will when they discover what he's done."

"He freed her because the sisters are his. They're his daughters."

Heath couldn't protect Miles from this, and he couldn't save Clay or the brothers. He had betrayed them for one of the sisters, a risk Heath foresaw years ago.

The brothers' wing was empty. They were gone. He'd been too easy on them, and now they too had betrayed them. They would search of course, but how could they find or fight them? They were the strategy and strength of the Order's arsenal.

The cell door swung open revealing an empty cell with chains on the ground. Miles was gone too.

Heath took a deep breath and counted to three before he regained his composure. Fear of the consequences shuddered through him, chilling his blood. The Four would be informed soon, and they would take over, but as he hurried up to the Grand Chamber, he admitted part of him was relieved by his brother's escape.

If Miles hadn't separated the sisters, they would have found and killed them years ago. But instead Miles, almost as dark and frightening as their father, appeared to have a heart and hid the girls from them.

And now? No one had ever betrayed the Order like this.

The door to the Grand Chamber crashed against the wall, the sound halting Master Heath in his tracks. He scurried against the wall, in the shadows of a large statue. Time slowed. His skin prickled, and he held his breath. In his desperation to stay hidden, he dared not blink, cursing his loud pounding heart.

The four black-robed figures—their features hidden as always— glided out the door and down the hall. Adrenaline flowed into nausea as he expelled his breath. Leaning against the wall, he clutched his chest. His heart still beat too fast.

The Four exited the building, and he was free to move again, but he couldn't. He waited, staying another moment to regain his composure.

He had more bad news to deliver. Heath pushed away from the wall and entered the Grand Chamber. The Grand Master, the most powerful, fearsome man, who could still trigger Heath's cold sweats and gaping wordless responses, was slumped back, cowering on his throne like a frail old man. Pale and wide-eyed, his father was terrified, and for the first time in his life, Heath saw his father's age and understood he was mortal, even vulnerable.

"They are on the hunt. They know of Miles's betrayal. I told them everything. They will deal with him after they deal with the sisters."

"He's gone. The brothers are gone too. They took him."

Color poured back into his father's skin. Rage replaced the fear, so evident on his face a moment ago. "Find them, Heath. Kill them all.

We must fix this, or we're dead."

~ * ~

Over twelve hours passed before Clay recognized the same quiet road they had flown over earlier. The dirt road led them to the stone cabin sitting charred on the field. The last place he'd seen her, his only lead, and his only hope. *Empty*. Of course, she'd be moving. She was too smart to hang around.

Aron parked near the front door, laying burnt on the lawn, and Cole and Rio helped Miles inside. Other than the water damage, inside the cabin was intact. For the second time today, Clay was relieved the mission had failed.

Rio and Cole carried the Master into one of the bedrooms and returned to the living room. Cole stacked wood in the fireplace and clicked his lighter, blowing the flame toward the logs.

"Now what?" Rio asked.

"Okay, you're not going to like this, but I have to leave. The Master said for the earth sister to see us, we have to be apart. Asha may trust me enough to come, but only if I'm alone and away from the Order. I don't know how else to find them."

Rio frowned. "You're not going alone. They pack some serious juice bro, and after what you've done, she's going to be pissed."

He had that right. She might even kill him, but Clay had to try.

Cole agreed with Rio, but Aron disagreed. "It's our best plan and the only way we can find them. They might get suspicious if they see anyone other than Clay. They don't know the rest of us."

"I'll be back as soon as I can."

"Wait." Aron stopped him. "You need to rest. We all do. Wait and set out in the morning."

Clay didn't want to wait. The longer he waited, the closer the Four could get to her.

"You have nowhere to go," Aron continued. "You're going blind. By all means if you pick something up go, but in the meantime rest."

He nodded to Aron. "Okay, but just a few hours. The Master was adamant we find them quickly."

Clay was exhausted, and he did need to think things through. He'd taken in a lot, and he was raging with the Master's revelations. Facing Asha again would require his wits and his strength.

The next morning Clay prepared to set out. "Give me until tomorrow morning, but if you haven't heard from me, take Miles somewhere safe, and I'll find you."

He took his pack and left the house. He drew in a deep breath of crisp mountain air and glanced up at early morning sun. "Okay, Asha. I'm coming for you." Clay headed up the mountain. He'd have some explaining to do, but he needed to find her first.

Chapter Twelve

Asha was in the shower when Ivy knocked and walked into the bathroom. She shut off the water, opened the curtain, and frowned at Ivy's unhappy expression. "What is it? What's wrong?"

Ivy handed her a towel and sat on the closed toilet. "During the fight, you warned Clay—when the root was heading for him."

"Yes, so? What about him?" She looked away from Ivy's inquisitive look. Asha regretted her impulsive warning to the enemy. Her sisters were picking up on the issues she couldn't hide.

"I picked up his energy. I can sense him. There was nothing before, but a moment ago he was there. The three others—water, air, and fire—are either at or near the first cabin. But Clay is definitely away from them and moving this way on foot. They've found us again, and they're too close. We have to move."

Asha burned. He was coming for her. She couldn't let him take her back, but if she could get her hands on him, she could take her revenge. *No, you won't...wait. Yes, you will. You have to.*

She looked at Ivy. "It's probably a trap, but there is a chance we could learn more from him. Maybe I should investigate. Now that I have my power back, I can take him. I'll go, check it out, and report back."

Ivy shook her head.

"Trust me, Ivy. I can take care of this myself. Tell me where he is."

Ivy stared at her for a moment. "It's too risky."

"I have unfinished business with him. I know I can't trust him, but I have to go, and if I'm wrong, I won't be responsible for dragging you guys in with me."

"We need to stick together. If you must go, we all go together, and we go prepared for the worst. This affects us all, and we're stronger together. You aren't going alone." Ivy's eyes were kind but firm.

"I have to see him."

"Why?"

"I can't explain it. I'm sorry."

"Try. You can tell me."

"I think I'm in love with him."

Ivy's mouth dropped open.

What? Oh my God. How could she say that? Asha raised her hands. "Not love, no, I didn't mean that. But there is something about him I don't understand. I am drawn to him."

"You need to tell the others."

Asha nodded, shame sweeping over her again.

Ivy took her hand. "Hey, it's okay. It may not be a bad thing. Love is wonderful."

Not if he was your enemy. Asha snorted but smiled at her sister's kind and supportive words. If the roles were reversed, she'd be slapping Ivy back to sense.

She left the bathroom so Asha could get dressed. Avia lent Asha a pair of dark jeans and a black sweater, much too chic for her, but she kind of liked how girly she looked in it. She was a thug by nature. The beautiful clothes were strange on her.

"Oh Asha, you look great," Mere said.

Asha smiled. "They're Avia's. Thanks by the way."

Avia nodded from the kitchen. Ivy sat on the couch with Mere in the living room. Everyone appeared at ease, but how could they be?

One step at a time. Deal with Clay. What did he want? Asha's mind wandered to the kiss that knocked her off her feet. She'd been thinking of him too much, and she had to force her mind from kisses to plans for vengeance.

"There's been a development," she said. "Ivy said Clay is close. We need answers, so I think we should go get them."

Ivy was correct. Going after him with her sisters as backup would be smarter. After all, it was more than obvious Asha couldn't trust her actions or emotions when it came to Clay. She had proven that by walking to him on the field, just because he called. *Be honest with them.*

"This is really embarrassing, but I have to tell you now, before we go any further. I had this instant connection to him, and I don't say that lightly. I can honestly say I've never connected to a man like that. He was interesting, fascinating, and an exceptional liar.

"Even though he was my kidnapper and my jailer, I was attracted to him. I had to keep reminding myself who he was. I wanted to believe him, tell him everything—my whole life story. It was an odd compulsion I had to fight, and I can tell you guys that's not me. I'm not like that."

"We can't trust him," Mere said. "I don't think we should trust anyone but each other."

"I agree," Ivy said. "But there *was* something about those men.

I believe Clay saved your life during the fight and if he is separating from his brothers, he might guess that I can locate him. We have similar gifts. Perhaps we share that one too. He might be coming for you. Or he could be sending a signal."

"I want answers. We have to find out what he knows and what his intentions are." In her head it was so clear. Find him and kill him. That was why she was going. But was it really? She didn't know. If she told them she desired revenge, would they still support her?

"What do you think?" Ivy asked Avia.

She leaned back against the counter, holding her mug with both hands, "I think we should go, but we should be prepared for a trap. Ivy, you'll have warning if it's an ambush. Right? We'll have time to escape."

Asha appreciated Avia's support.

"Okay," Mere said. "If you all agree it's a good idea—"

"I didn't say it was a good idea," Avia said, her eyes serious.

"I'll know if there's anyone with him, and right now he's not with his brothers."

"Okay, good," Asha said. "let's go."

Ivy drove Avia's truck this time, while Asha stared out the window. He was close. Her body clenched, and her stomach fluttered. *Stop it. Be strong. He's the enemy.*

They'd been driving for under an hour when Ivy pulled over. "We should walk from here. Clay left his brothers at your cabin and went up. He was heading right for us." She pointed into the thick trees. "If we cut through here, we can cut him off."

Asha got out and breathed in cold fresh morning air. They walked through the forest for fifteen minutes.

"Over there, he's through those trees," Ivy said.

Asha peered ahead. There he was.

He raised his hands a second later. "Asha."

Her heart leapt and she could feel a stupid grin stretching her stupid face. *Stop. Don't be an idiot.*

She choked. She couldn't do it. Seeing him in the flesh, all her deadly intentions vanished. Her feelings frightened her more than the army they'd faced. She couldn't cave to attraction or whatever it was driving her crazy.

But with a rush of rage at her impotence, and her weakness for him, her doubt was all she needed to spur her anger on and bring her back to who she was.

Before he could take a step, her fury surged, and she threw a fireball to explode at his feet.

"Wait!" he shouted.

"Let's hear him out," Ivy said.

Anger and now fear bubbled deep within Asha, but she met Ivy's eyes, secretly grateful for the out she offered. *You're acting like a psycho.*

Asha had been too rash, and she couldn't kill him yet. It would be a regrettable, spiteful reaction, and they came for information. "Okay, talk."

"My brothers and I left the Order. We want to help you."

"Do you think I'm stupid? You were trying to kill us."

"I know how it must look, and I don't blame you for being cautious—"

"Cautious? I'm going to kill you."

"Come on Kid, just hear me out. I came here alone hoping you would come, and you will understand once I explain. Master Miles is with my brothers. He's the one who got you out. He sent me to find you, to warn you."

Energy shifted behind her.

"I should believe you?" she asked.

"I can take you to him. He told me he was the one who separated you just after you were born. He said it was to protect you. You are in terrible danger. You have no idea. Please, we want to help."

Asha faced her sisters, shaking her head, but they nodded.

Avia walked closer to Clay and stared at him before speaking. "Follow the road from the cabin down to the third fork, turn right then head straight up. You'll find our cabin at the end of the road. You'll come across some obstacles blocking the road, but I'm sure you can handle it. Bring your brothers and Miles."

"What? You guys, we can't just trust them." Asha's stomach rolled.

They were going for this, and it was her fault. Her need for revenge or something else entirely had brought her sisters into this meeting, and now Clay was playing the same game with them as he had with her. He used that trustworthy, charming facade to con them as he had her.

Avia walked back past Asha. "We should listen to them first and question Master Miles. They have information we need," she whispered.

"Fine." Asha stormed off.

Ivy, Mere, and Avia followed her back into the forest.

"So, I'll just go back and get them, and see you later, then?" he called.

Asha didn't answer and neither did her sisters.

Chapter Thirteen

The sisters drove back to Avia's place to await Clay, Master Miles, and his brothers. Even though Asha was still reluctant, the others wanted to hear Clay out. They trusted he had enough information to warrant the risk. It was how Asha convinced them to let her go after him in the first place, so what did she expect?

They arrived back at the cabin and hurried inside. She anticipated it would take him half an hour or so to walk through the forest then time for the drive to the cabin. They probably had about two hours before they arrived.

"So why are we doing this again?" she asked.

"Because it's exciting." Mere smiled.

She wasn't totally wrong. Asha buzzed with energy and anticipation. She hated him, but she wanted him too. *You're pathetic.*

"And answers too, of course," Mere added.

"If Miles really is with them, then we can question him, find out what's going on. Like Avia said, I'll know in advance if there are others coming, and if there are, we can escape."

"And Asha can take her revenge," Avia said.

If only it were that easy. Asha turned to Ivy. "Did you know we were coming the other day at Avia's first cabin?" She worried that Clay had their location. As she'd noticed before, these girls were much too trusting.

"We were sleeping," Ivy answered. "We had a late night. It was your presence that woke me and the rocket was already coming."

"I was a bit hung over," Mere said. Her small grin lit her mischievous eyes.

Asha smiled, and Ivy turned back to Avia, who reclined against the kitchen counter again.

"I don't think it will come to revenge," Ivy continued. "Maybe because Clay is earth, but I believe him. I have no idea why, but I do."

Jealousy flared through Asha, and her stomach dropped. Two earth elements together made sense. Don't be such a girl. She shook her head and smiled. "Yeah, he got me with that too, and even after he'd already fooled me. I can only explain it as an insane urge to trust."

"Heavy," Mere said.

Even with a bullet hole in her shoulder, an army with unknown motives trying to kill them, and now five of their 'alleged' deserters on their way, Mere kept on smiling.

"I agree," Avia said. "I don't think it will come to that. I wouldn't have told them where to find us if I did."

The air thickened and tightened, peaking an hour later as tires crunched on the gravel drive announcing the men's arrival.

Ivy opened the door while the others stayed seated, watching her movements. Cole, the other firepower, carried Master Miles inside. Ivy gasped and snatched her bag from the table. He looked dead; the parts that weren't bruised and covered in dried blood were gray.

"This way," Ivy said clutching a first-aid kit and leading Cole to the guest room.

Clay followed Cole and Ivy. Asha's body clenched, and she let out her breath, but the tension still crackled, thrumming in the air. Rio and Aron waited awkwardly by the door for a moment before Aron closed it and Rio trailed him inside the room.

Cold reality hit Asha like a two-by-four straight to the face. This insanity was actually happening. She wasn't in her jungle anymore, and this wasn't some sex trafficker and his militia. She'd been at the Order, and she'd witnessed the dark and ancient forces against them.

Ages ago, she'd taught herself to pace things, because the moment she looked too far ahead, she risked panicking. She avoided her worst attacks by distraction, but she couldn't ignore the four men and the beaten Master who'd just entered their refuge. A man she'd never met, but who had separated her from her sisters and helped her escape the Order. Terror knocked the wind out of her.

Slow down, get the information, and focus on the next step. The fire in the hearth drew her, and she leaned into its warmth, taking deep breaths of warm air. Cole came back out and joined them in the living room.

Unlike her sisters' similarities, the brothers barely resembled each other. It was difficult to tell they were even brothers. Only Cole and Rio looked alike. In the jet, when Clay had identified the men as his brothers, she'd initially assumed he meant military brothers, but that was before they'd displayed their power.

Cole's black hair had red and gold highlights shimmering through it. His eyes were dark, black like hers. Rio's eyes were dark blue, similar to Mere's color when she fought, and his hair was such a deep black, the same blue of his eyes reflected through the strands. Cole and Rio had similar body types too. They were both about six feet and built strong. Aron's eyes were gray like Avia's, and his hair was the color of evening storm clouds. Aron was the tallest with a leaner musculature.

Based on body size and having wrestled with him, Clay was probably the strongest, with his height somewhere between Cole's and Aron's. They were all dressed alike in jeans, leather boots, black sweaters, and black coats. Their clothes were dapper but generic. They weren't exactly uniforms, but they were close enough.

Cole sat beside Aron on the couch, while Rio stayed by the door between the kitchen and living room, frowning. Mere took a seat in the chair beside the window, smiling at the men on the couch. Avia leaned back against the kitchen counter.

The silence was thick and embarrassing. No one spoke, but the energy swirled around them, causing the silent tension and pulsing vibe to grow even more.

Mere rose bravely, breaking the tension and the spell. "Well, we can all admit this is a bit awkward. There is the obvious question of trust on both sides, but more importantly, why is there electricity flying all over the place?"

Aron laughed, and Mere faced him then extended her hand. "I'm Mere and that's Avia. I suppose you've already met Asha. Ivy is still in the back."

Aron rose took her hand, their eyes locked and held before his smile grew. "My name is Aron, and that's Rio. I suppose you've already met Clay—he's also in the back. Oh, and he's Cole." He pointed to his brothers scattered around the room with his left hand, while still holding Mere's hand with his right.

Ivy and Clay came out, shutting the door. Cole got up, offering his seat to Ivy. Clay walked over to stand beside her near the fire. His eyes were solemn, but there was more in his look than just that.

She left his side and stood behind the couch, putting space between them, but the air tightened, drawing her back. She fought the impulse and remained where she was.

"Okay," he said, getting everyone's attention. "Master Miles is unconscious, and you can't speak to him yet, but there's one thing I promised him. The four of you must separate."

Her head snapped up. "I beg your pardon?" Her tone was sharp enough to cut.

"Asha—"

"No. Again, do you think we're stupid? You went through all that to come here and tell us we need to separate? No way."

"Why?" Mere asked.

"Master Miles says you're in danger when you're together. You can be traced. It's why he separated you in the first place."

Ivy frowned. "I can't believe we'd be safer apart. Are you sure?"

What was his game? To separate them was to weaken them.

"Why should we believe you or Miles?" Avia asked the group. "What's his role in all this? What's yours?"

"He is a Master of the Order—one of two. His brother, Master Heath, is the other. There is also the Grand Master, who is their father. Master Miles arranged Asha's escape from the Order, but you can't stay together. I promised him I'd find you and bring you this message. You've already been together for too long. He was very emphatic, desperate. There's so little time. You must separate."

"But we're stronger together!" Asha snapped. "It makes no sense. How could you think we would go for this? Trust *you*, after everything you've done? You're our enemies. We may have the same powers, but you tried to kill us. Why?"

"You have to trust me. We want to help, but you need to part."

"I'll never trust you. Whatever you claim now, you followed their *orders*," she snarled.

Her training and battle instincts required she pull back and take a breath, but she was angry, fired up, and looking to take everything out on this man. She should be looking for holes in the story, strategizing her own plan, yet she was unable to. She was too busy boiling with multiple but unfocused emotions.

Her hands clenched and unclenched into fists, and she ground her teeth. "You served them loyally. The massacre at my home? You're a monster. How many innocent lives have you and your brothers taken following *orders*?"

Clay recoiled as if she'd struck him. Tension crackled through the air.

"What's your problem?" Rio asked moving forward just a step into the room. "He said you invited us here—" His words were cut off as he slammed into an invisible shield and stumbled back.

"Rio," Clay snapped.

Ivy jumped up, her arms out. Rio swung around, glaring at Avia, who faced him from the kitchen.

"I'm sure you know nothing of being a monster, right Asha? Or taking innocent lives?" Cole whispered so only she could hear him.

The other fire power stared at her with his expression dark. His eyes as black as her own. They evoked such intensity, it sobered her like a slap in the face.

"Stop," Ivy shouted.

Asha finally tore her gaze away from him. Avia had her hands out, Mere looked worried, and Clay and Rio were fuming at each other.

Asha whistled a sharp, piercing sound. "I'm sorry. I shouldn't have said that. It was unkind."

Rio spun back to Asha. "Who are you to us?"

"Rio," Clay's voice was a whisper, but full of warning.

"What are we doing here Clay? We're putting ourselves at risk for this?"

Mere stood and marched to Rio staring at him narrow-eyed and glaring. "But now that you do know about us, you can see we mean you no harm. *We're* the ones who have the right to be suspicious. Hell, I was shot. Cut us some slack."

His frown cracked into a smile, and he winked at her. He shrugged at Clay before retreating to stand by the door.

"Why did you attack us?" she asked.

Clay scowled. "The Order wants you dead. Nothing else matters."

Asha snorted. "That's not good enough for me. I don't know who Miles is or why I should care." She glanced at Ivy. "Okay, yes. You think he's important, but we are not separating. It's madness."

Clay looked over at his brothers, and Rio shook his head ever so slightly. "We were adopted by the Order as infants. Technically, by Master Heath, but we were collectively raised by the Order. We were taught many skills, hence the surgical training. We learned to use our power, and when we grew up, we handled special assignments. We never questioned their system because we grew up in it."

Mere coughed, interrupting. "Okay, that explains very little. Thanks for that. But what is the Order really?" she asked.

"The Masters and Grand Master are like the high priests of the Order, and the Order serves the Four."

"The Four?" Mere asked.

Asha froze. She couldn't share Mere's doubtful expression. Cold shivered through Asha, chilling her heat.

"Yes, according to the doctrine, they're four gods who maintain balance and harmony and are responsible for the existence of the universe. The Order and all who belong to it are the Four's guardians. They are the ones who can find you, and they are the ones who will be coming."

No. Ice crawled up her arms into her chest, squeezing and taking her breath.

"Great, a cult?" Mere's laugh was full of sarcasm. It was more of a grunt or a snort.

"Closer to a religion," Aron said. "It's based on a mixture of magic and alchemical theories. The Four are believed to be ancient brothers. The four original men who achieved the power of gods. Immortal alchemists."

"So these *gods* are searching for us? But what do *gods* want with little old us?" Mere pressed, still smiling, still in denial.

Asha staggered, reaching for the couch to steady herself. Memories of dark ghouls and torture, electrocuting her, drowning her, cutting her up. "To kill us…" She gasped. "I've seen them. They're real—"

The ground lurched, and the cabin shifted like a tipping ship. The floor rattled, and the stone walls cracked as tremors shook the house.

"Clay? Ivy?" Mere and Rio shouted at the same time.

"It's not me," both Clay and Ivy shouted back.

It was a trap. *Damn him.*

Glass shattered, and the windowpanes fell like tinkling bells on the floor. Asha called flames to her hands automatically and turned to kill Clay right then and there for the last betrayal he'd ever commit against her. She rolled the flames, but he dove, knocking Ivy, who stood stunned and rigid, out of the path of a chunk of falling roof.

The rest of them had crouched, taking cover. Asha dropped her flames and darted to the front window, peering out through the shattered glass. Four cloaked shapes hovered outside.

Oh my God.

"They're outside. I can see them," she shouted over the violent shaking. Hitting the floor, she crawled over the broken glass back to the couch and unzipped the largest of Clay's bags.

Jackpot.

Giant fissures ran along the crumbling roof. More opened on the floor. The house bent like a cracked egg. She slid the guns across the wooden floor to all seven allies and rose from behind the couch, armed with a machine gun in each arm.

Like Rambo.

Her panic forgotten, she grinned at the mental image. Funny how it was only the anticipation of danger that terrified her, but once she faced it, she was in control, calm and focused.

Staying low, she ran to the door. She would deal with these monsters. Her power was back now, and it was her turn to repay them for the pain. She slipped outside into the darkening sky.

"Wait," Clay snarled from behind her.

Asha stalked toward the enemy but hesitated as she got closer to them. Were they men or ghosts…or gods?

Their black hoods hid their faces, and they hovered above the rolling earth. Ivy, Mere, and Avia stood with Asha. Her sisters were brave and strong, and she had them to back her up.

"Asha, no," Clay yelled again.

His voice sounded far away, a quiet echo in her consciousness. Her vision shimmered, and the sun was bright.

The same four cloaked men stood before her, but they were burning. A sword pierced her flesh, and she slumped at the sight of a purple-jeweled hilt protruding from her bloody chest. Her sisters were beside her, tied to posts, and dying. They were her sisters, but they were so much younger—hardly more than twelve.

More horrifying scenes of sacrifice flashed over and over—the victims were all too young. Their only crime being born with power others didn't have. She couldn't catch them all as clearly as the first. There had been sisters like them before, and they'd been brutally murdered too many times to count.

From babies to young women, these four creatures and the Order who served them had sacrificed them again and again. The visions ended abruptly, and she was back inside herself at Avia's cabin, her view normal again, only Asha's breathing had changed.

There was no shooting, no backup. She and her sisters faced evil personified. The ghouls rushed forward, blurring with speed, iron fingers squeezing her throat. They looked like vapor, but their hands were solid and ice-cold.

Asha caught the flash to her left. Avia ducked to the right once then dodged again, but the pale, wispy arm caught her too. The Four held them all trapped, hanging powerless in their grips.

Asha called her fire, but she could only struggle uselessly, her power blocked again. She fought to bring it on, but her spark was gone. Sharp pain sliced through her head spreading through her entire body.

No, no, please no. She screamed as her skin erupted in flames. Her sisters were beside her, their minds fused as if they were one. Their confusion and terror were hers. It was one thing for her to be scared, but her sisters' fear touched a new level of pain and torture.

A sob escaped Mere, and she rolled like water within the wraith's grip. Still holding her shape and features, but her body was fluid.

Ivy gasped, that sound followed by the most horrible cracking sound, and her body calcified into stone.

The three turned their dark hooded faces to the one still holding Avia. She wasn't struggling but hanging frozen in the hooded thing's grip. He shook her like a rag doll, and she started to fade in stuttering flashes.

It was over. They were defeated. The futility crushed her, and Asha screamed out in rage and despair. She couldn't fight, but she was still conscious and could grieve for the sisters she'd just met.

Each dark creature drew a sword and lifted it to deliver their fatal blow.

Buzzing filled her head, and strong arms wrapped around her. Clay tugged her burning body back. The moment he touched her, her power flowed back in, and the flames rolled over him enveloping and covering them both.

Yes... The flicker ran through her, and she grinned, clenching her teeth. She was back in control.

With all her strength and fury, she urged the flames on. They flared off her body up to the hand that gripped her throat, spreading up its robes, and bursting into a crackling inferno. Asha pushed her power harder, and the flames jumped and spread to the other three. Surging hotter, only their hooded heads were free from her fire. The iron grip on her throat loosened and she fell.

Clay caught her. "Are you all right, Asha?"

The Four stepped back, and the flames fizzled out. Her sisters were on the ground and had regained their natural forms. Rio, Cole, and Aron stood in front of them, shooting useless bullets that sailed right through the burning Four.

Electricity prickled the air. It was the same sensation she experienced right before she blew her hottest. She prepared for the shockwave, covering her ears.

"Take cover!" she screamed.

Clay covered her, shielding her. The ground shook violently, and white light flashed against her closed lids. A fraction of a second later, a snap echoed so loudly her eardrums should've split.

Disoriented as her senses returned, blurry and buzzing. The earth was charred, but the cabin behind her remained miraculously intact. Cole had shielded Ivy, and Aron had protected Mere. They should have disintegrated, except maybe her and Cole, *but even we...*should have felt it.

The Four were gone. Clay took off his coat and draped it over Asha's naked, blackened body. She wasn't hurt, but she was stunned and with her clothes burned away, exposed.

She looked for the others. Rio was on the ground, not moving with Avia beside him, her expression deadpan.

"Rio?" Clay rushed over, taking Rio's wrist, opening his eyelids. "What happened?"

"He pushed me, and I…it was an accident," Avia responded.

"What do you mean—wait, I got a pulse. Weak, but yes there it is. Rio."

He groaned. "Ow, mother fu—ow."

He opened his eyes and stared at Clay, his expression serious. "Wow, that'll give you the tingles."

Clay laughed and slapped him across the face.

"Dude, I said ow." Rio touched his cheek and smiled at Avia. "Is everyone all right?"

"All but you it would appear," Aron said.

Asha cocked her head and gaped at the brothers' light banter. Wholly inappropriate, but she'd seen it before. Boys handled their fear by making jokes.

Mere wasn't laughing anymore; she was shaking. "I saw them in my mind. They killed us again and again. I was powerless. I couldn't do anything. None of us could fight, we just died." She started to cry, her voice rising to hysteria. "What are they? Why do they kill us? This is crazy. It's not possible. None of this is possible." She gestured wildly around at the wasteland surrounding the cabin. "Look at this place."

Aron wrapped his arm around her shoulders, drawing her close. Asha was genuinely surprised to see Mere lean into him and close her eyes.

Umm?

"I saw it," Ivy shifted away from Cole. "It was terrible. We were killed over and over. It was so awful to feel death in a memory." Her fingers twitched by her sides.

Asha couldn't explain what happened, but she was certain Clay saved her life again—and with hers, her sisters' lives too. "What took you so long?" She gave him a small smile.

Even though she'd meant it as a bit of a joke, Aron answered, "Me too. I was at the window, and I took a few shots, but then you formed a line blocking my aim. I was about to dive out the window, but I couldn't move. I was in some kind of trance, but the murders, the massacre." He paused then said, "I saw it happen over and over in a hundred different ways—sometimes as girls, sometimes as babies. It was the Four, but Order members as well." He glanced at his brothers. "You did, didn't you?"

Clay and the others nodded.

"It was the most horrible thing I've ever seen." Aron's formerly affable expression evoked fierce violence now.

He had transformed from a cuddly puppy into a vicious wolf. It reminded Asha of how Clay had changed from helpful, charming doctor into Order guard.

"How could you have seen it?" Ivy asked. "Were you there? How could you have been there?"

"We weren't there," Cole said, his deep voice quiet. It was the first thing he'd said since he'd asked if she were a monster.

Ivy's head snapped up. "Miles." She ran into the cabin.

The rest of the group stayed a moment, staring around at the burned wasteland. Cole glanced back at the cabin door before he walked inside the house.

Moments later, she returned, calling them inside. "He's up."

They all filed inside the small house. Asha tugged on a pair of jeans, and green shirt Ivy handed her from her bag. Cole helped the Master walk from the bedroom into the living room and settled him on the couch.

"He shouldn't be moved—" One stern glare from Miles silenced Ivy.

"The Four were here." He panted from the exertion. "They found you—you must separate right now. They'll be back."

"Wait, wait, wait," Mere said. "We need to know what's happening first. I had a life a week ago, you know. Sure, maybe not a completely normal life, but I was safe and then one day I came home from the beach and it's all running, fighting, bullets, and fear. Don't get me wrong. I'm grateful I found my sisters, but now you're asking us to separate. You need to tell us what's happening first."

"You were supposed to stay apart. It is the only way." The Master croaked and paused to catch his breath. "Together you are a shining beacon. You draw them right to you. They have a trace on your essence. You must split up, and you must do it now. Apart, you are invisible to them."

Clay and Asha locked gazes. Her stomach dropped.

"But we just found each other. This is crazy," Mere cried.

"I was trained to take over as Grand Master. I have studied the Four and all that has been written about them. They will *never* stop. They have done it for generations, and they will continue to do so until the end of time. You are the sisters with power. You are their greatest fear and their greatest desire.

"How do we fight back?" Avia asked.

"You can't. You hide. But at least you have me, and them," Miles said, tilting his head to the brothers.

"And you are?"

"Your mother was a dear friend."

Mother?

"Who is she?" Ivy asked.

"Emma." He said her name quietly. "Her mother worked at the Order when Heath and I were children, and we all played together."

"What happened to her?" Ivy asked.

Master Miles studied her for a moment before he answered. "I'm so sorry, but she's dead."

"Did you kill her?" Avia asked.

"Avia," Ivy gasped.

"I loved your mother very much."

Asha glanced at Avia who shook her head slightly. She had picked-up on Miles's deflective non-answer as well.

Avia leaned back against the counter, her pale eyes studying the Master. She had a view of the entire room and all the occupants, with no space for surprises behind her.

How had she missed it? Avia evoked the behavior of a natural fighter, and though she may not have all the training, she had the instincts. She wasn't openly acting like it, but Avia was as wary as Asha was. She was grateful one of her sisters appeared more cautious.

"The sisters of the past never had any inside knowledge or warning as to what was coming for them," he continued. "None of them survived as long as you have, well past your age of power, and there have never been men with similar gifts. That is our edge and their new fear. It is different this time, and since they were here, and you still live, they know it."

"Wait, wait… I was there. How does the Order even exist? What makes you any authority?" Asha frowned.

"They are *the* authority. They control everything."

She snorted. The arrogance, even in this deserter was repugnant. "No, that's impossible. You could never keep that kind of power hidden." Her experience with military conspiracies and government cover-ups taught her something was missing from this story. "How do you keep the Order a secret?"

"I want you girls to understand, but it's difficult, I am so full of shame. They are brutality at its worst. Using torture, murder, and fear to force members' loyalty and submission."

"And the building?"

"Yes." He frowned. "The grounds, as you know, are vast and privately owned. On paper, it's a conservancy, but you've seen the building, and that's really the question, isn't it?"

She nodded. The grounds and building had reminded her of some fairytale kingdom, a really dark and evil kingdom. Avia shifted in the kitchen, but Asha refused to break eye contact with Miles. Behind the battered face, his eyes were sharp and his voice was steady.

"The Order is cloaked. A spell cast in the early days, I'm told, and it hides the building behind an invisible curtain. Members, Masters, and the soldiers can see it, but unless you cross the threshold with a key holder, it is invisible."

"I beg your pardon," Ivy asked from across the room. "Invisible? Spell? Magic? How does that work?" Her face was pale.

Mere snorted, but Asha pictured the Order and the grounds. How else could they hide it?

He winced and turned to Mere. "After what you've seen and what you are, can you still doubt magic?"

She dropped her head. "I doubt all of this."

"How does it work?" Asha asked.

"The spell? I don't know the details, except people can't see it or through it until they cross over."

The air was thick and heavy, and no one spoke. The cold chill returned. Asha worked to keep her breathing calm and even.

"They know you were successfully hidden and that the brothers have joined you."

"We saw it. We saw what they did," Clay's voice cracked. "They sacrificed children and infants."

Miles frowned at Clay. "The Order kills the sisters at birth for fear of their power. It is only when the Four need the sisters' full power that they risk halting the Order's hand to wait and sacrifice them. Those sacrifices increase their power and re-establish their immortality."

"How is this possible?" he asked.

Clay appeared sincere, but could he actually be as ignorant as he claimed? She wanted to believe him. She had to.

"Master, how could you be a part of that?" Clay asked. "And how could you bring us into it?"

"When we first discovered you boys, we were suspicious but curious. We adopted you to observe you and to see what your part would be. I convinced Heath and the Grand Master that you would be instrumental to the sisters' downfall and that you would be the ideal hunters to track and kill them.

"However, I hoped you would be part of their success. The Four are immortal, yet their hatred is so obviously fear born, you must pose some risk to them. Which means there must be a way to destroy them. We need to find out how."

"I don't understand," Mere said.

Master Miles shook his head, grunting in pain. "I have been searching since your birth, and I'm on the cusp of finding the answers we need, the answers we *really* need, but for you to survive now, you must separate.”

“Why didn’t the Four kill them?” Avia gestured to the brothers. “Why weren’t they threatened by *them?*”

Miles frowned. “I don’t know for the Four do not seek our counsel. If they had predicted you might all join together, I doubt they would have let them live.”

Asha met Avia’s eyes again. Interesting, another deflection.

But Asha was a bit calmer now, stronger. They’d gained some information, horrifying information, but knowledge was power and all that.

Boo, Asha, quit your clichés.

Her resolve slipped back into place, and she was ready for battle.

“So we must part,” Mere made the words a statement.

“Yes, one of you should go to the Pyramid of Giza where there’s been a recent discovery. It came just in time. Another must go to Rome and meet with an archivist from the Vatican Library, and the third to the ruins of Pompeii. I don’t care who goes where. Just get going, all of you.”

Avia cleared her throat. “Wait just a minute. You separated us once and now you’re doing it again.” Her voice was cold and accusatory.

“It is the only way to keep you hidden.” He glanced around the room. “How exactly did you get away?”

“Asha,” Clay said while collecting the weapons and bags.

Miles turned his dark gaze to her. “Fire alone? You won’t be so lucky next time. Now, let’s move. Come on.”

“You can’t go anywhere,” Ivy said. She scanned the destroyed cabin. “You are still too weak from the drive. We’ll have to make it work here.” To accentuate the issue, Miles coughed and groaned.

“I’ll stay to help you with Master Miles,” Cole said.

“You can’t stay here. The place is destroyed,” Mere said.

Ivy shrugged. “I can deal with it for a short stay. As soon as he is able, we’ll leave.”

“I’ll go to Rome,” Avia said.

Asha swung around. “You’re okay with this? You’re all just fine with this?”

“I am,” Avia said.

“What choice do we have?” Ivy asked. “I think he’s telling the truth.”

“I’d love to see the Pyramids,” Mere said.

“I’ll go with you.” Aron smiled, and she shrugged and smirked.

“That leaves Pompeii for us,” Clay said, but Miles had passed out.

"Excuse me?" Asha asked at Clay's brazen assumption.

"Oops, sorry. I meant to ask, should we go to Pompeii together?" he asked, suitably chagrined.

She returned her attention to her sisters and studied Mere and Ivy. "No, I'm not comfortable with this. We don't even know these men."

Clay frowned at Cole while Ivy repositioned Miles on the couch, laying him down and putting a pillow under his head.

"What else can we do?" Mere asked. "I feel like I can trust them."

"Are you sure you're okay with this?" Asha asked Avia again.

"Yes, it is our best option. We need to find out more if we can."

Her certainty was enough. Asha's instincts had played tug-of-war since this all began and allowing her sisters to make the right decision was a much better idea than trusting herself.

"So that leaves you and me," Rio said to Avia. His expression was tight, and his brow creased.

Her tone was firm when she said, "Fine, let's get moving. We can drive you to the airport." She nodded to Aron and Mere. "Ivy, there's another truck in the back shed. The shed is exactly like the last one. The keys are in the drawer by the back door. Please, make yourselves comfortable." She slipped into the bedroom and returned seconds later with a rolling bag. "Please take as many eggs as you can carry."

Asha smiled. So they were actually separating. She peeked at Clay, and he flashed a smile. *Okay, Mr. Bad Guy-Charming Pants. Let's do this.* "I want to check out the Order first."

"That's a good idea." His grin grew. "It would be good to see how the hive is buzzing."

Rio and Cole agreed.

"We can head to Italy after we do recon," Asha said, closing her eyes briefly. She was so tired, but her stomach fluttered.

Ivy rose. "Cole, would you mind helping Miles back to bed?"

"I'll send the information for my contacts in Egypt and Rome." Miles's eyes fluttered. "I'll send you all I have but be very careful."

Cole steered the Master to the bedroom.

"Take it easy," Rio said.

Cole nodded to his brothers before shutting the door.

Asha hugged Ivy and picked up a bag of weapons, following Clay and the others outside to the driveway. Rio and Aron got in the back of Avia's SUV, and Mere slipped into the front passenger seat, beside Avia.

Asha climbed into the passenger side of the shiny black car Clay and his brothers arrived in. She didn't know cars, and she didn't care what kind it was as long as it moved quickly. They headed down the mountain following the fading lights as Avia sped ahead.

Chapter Fourteen

Asha studied the departures board with Clay and the others under bright fluorescent lights in the airport terminal. Her body hummed with strange zinging sensations. She clenched against the urge to run.

"Unbelievable luck," Aron said smiling down at Mere. "There's a flight to Cairo in two hours. Enough time for some dinner before our flight."

"There's a flight to London leaving in forty-five minutes," Clay said. "I'll get us tickets."

"Okay, you four are set," Avia said and whipped back to Rio. "Let's go. It will be quicker if we drive. There isn't a flight until tomorrow."

Asha smiled at Avia and nodded.

"Take care," Mere said and hugged Avia goodbye.

"You too." She turned and studied Aron. "Take care of her," she said.

"Bye," Asha said and saluted, sensing Avia wasn't much of a hugger.

"Goodbye."

Rio nodded to his brothers, and Avia spun and strode toward the exit. Asha frowned. Avia was more anxious than she'd seen her yet. Even after hearing their destiny and facing the Four, Avia had remained stoic. Something had her rattled, but if she wasn't up for sharing, Asha couldn't worry about that. Avia appeared extremely capable in every way.

Asha was on her way back to the Order with Clay, and her nerves were stretched tighter than bowstrings.

~ * ~

Avia walked quickly for the terminal exit. They were wasting time and with no available flights, driving was their only option. Her mind was already running ahead to Rome.

"What's the rush?" Rio asked, catching up to her just inside the quiet parking lot.

She ignored him and plowed on leaving him in her wake. She

reached the car door several feet ahead. "There's someone, a friend in Rome. Armand, I need to get him to a safe place. It should take about eight hours to get there."

She was in the driver's seat already, putting the key in the ignition, and Rio stopped, looking at her through the windshield.

"I'll go without you if I have to," she snapped, irritated and more nervous than she could admit.

"You'll have to unlock the door first," he responded in a silky voice.

She narrowed her eyes and switching the button, unlocked his door.

He got in, smiled, and buckled up. "Well, let's go then. Who is it we're looking for?"

"His name is Armand." Shifting the car into reverse, the backs of her fingers brushed Rio's thigh.

Electric heat surged through her and sparked through her body. His body stiffened beside her, and she yanked her hand away so swiftly the gear slipped and screeched. She fought the urge to meet his eyes as she shifted the gear back. Aware he was smiling beside her, she frowned.

"So who is he?" he asked after a substantial pause.

"My music teacher."

"Your music teacher? You're driving like this for your music teacher?"

"He was a bit more than that. We became close." Her confession surprised her, but even more surprising, she continued, "I lived with him for a few years as a teenager."

She remembered how she'd just shown up on his doorstep. He'd been a stern and prickly teacher until the day he took her in. Since then, she viewed him as more of a grandfather.

"Are you worried the Four will go after him?"

"I don't know," she said. "There's still the Order, the Four's foot soldiers. They killed my sisters' guardians, Rio. Ivy and Mere cared for them."

"What about your guardian?"

Avia didn't respond. Her concern for Armand distracted her, and thankfully, as if sensing her reluctance to continue, Rio remained silent. She drove from Switzerland to Italy, breaking every speed limit on the planet. The tension grew thicker with every hour of the drive.

~ * ~

Clay sped through the dark night with Asha sitting in the passenger seat, staring out the window. She hadn't spoken a word since they'd landed and left the airport in the rental car. Her posture was hunched and turned away from him.

He fought the urge to touch her, tightening his grip on the gearshift and releasing it in silent rhythm with his pounding heart.

The continuous, hypnotic road drew his mind away to the last girl he'd cared about, and what the Order did to her. His white knuckled grip crushed the steering wheel.

Asha looked up. "What's wrong?"

"Everything."

"Yeah, tell me about it."

"I am sorry for all of this, Asha."

"Clay, I want to trust you, but you need to give me something. Something honest I can hold onto and believe. Because of me, my sisters are scattered around the world with dangerous men who were the enemy just days ago."

"What do you mean?"

"Give me something real. More than just the party line, 'we were raised to kill you but we didn't know.'"

His grip relaxed. He was in awe that they were here together when he thought he'd lost her. She was beside him now, questioning him, longing to believe his story, and he would ensure she stayed there. Her protection was his number one priority. Her destiny was everything to him because theirs were joined.

"Clay?"

It was inevitable. Of course she'd be having trust issues. "Okay, you're right. But I don't want to add any weight to the fear you must be feeling."

Her outraged face was adorable. Her wide black eyes were fierce, and her lovely mouth opened a bit on her gasp. A flush of anger crept into her cheeks. His stomach dropped and he swallowed past a lump in his throat.

"You're beautiful, Asha."

"Shut up, Clay. You can't protect me from this. You heard Miles. It's my destiny. I need all the information you have so I can protect *myself.*"

"I don't know anything that will help protect you."

"How do you know that? You couldn't possibly understand how important it is that I know you aren't lying to me or manipulating me."

"How?"

"I don't know. Confession? Did you and your brother have tests?"

Is she reading my mind? His grip tightened, making a squeaking noise on the steering wheel.

"Tell me about your tests," she said.

She'd picked up his reaction.

"You and your sisters had tests?" Clay asked.

"You tell me first."

"It'll only illustrate how far the Order will go to get their way."

"Tell me."

Damn. "Okay, okay. When we were sixteen we were a little on the wild side."

"I can imagine."

Here goes. "Well yeah, four guys cooped up behind stone walls could only stay sane for so long. Rio was the restless one, and he pushed us to go to the pub that first night. We snuck out and made it to the Fox and Hound. The village is average size, and the pub was busy. We met a group of nice girls."

"I bet," she said.

"They were a few years older and we all became friends." He looked at her.

She wasn't smiling anymore. "Continue with the test part of the story. I don't need the details on your *friendships.*"

"Cole fell for Anna pretty hard. She was sweet. But the rest of us just sort of hung out with them." *Shit.* He was acting like a moron. Just tell the story without emotion.

"Cole kept sneaking out to meet her, and we did our best to cover for him. But Paul discovered him and caught us when we were all at the lake one night." Clay's voice was already getting hoarse as his throat constricted. His chest tightened.

"What happened?"

"The soldiers arrived. I was too distracted to know or warn the others. We were knocked out and taken back to the Order. All but Cole."

Clay glanced over, and Asha's face was pale. Could she guess what was coming? "The Grand Master was there when we woke up. He told us they had our friends, and they were the perfect catalysts for our stunted power. We lacked strength and needed stronger motivation to kick them in. I had learned to use my power to search for people, for elements, and I was about to be tested.

"He was frightening, enraged, and Master Miles and Heath weren't there to help appeal to his mercy. He told us that our friends were buried underground and their air was fading. We had less than twenty minutes to find them and save them before they suffocated, buried alive. It was up to me to find them. Rio and Aron pleaded with me to find their friends. But I couldn't. I was terrified. I tried but I couldn't connect to any of them. Not even..."

"No, of course you couldn't. Under those—"

"But I tried, I wasted half an hour of useless time getting nowhere—"

"You tried—"

"Before I noticed Cole was missing."

Asha fell silent.

"I connected to him by the lake just outside the main building. We found him chained to a large rock. Anna was dead but still burning on a stake in front of him." Clay squeezed the wheel. "They burned her alive in front of Cole, taunting him to use his power to stop it."

"Without his hands?"

"It was my fault, all my fault. If I had realized Cole was missing, I would have found him immediately. I would have had time to save Anna and the others."

"The others?"

"Emily, Jennifer, and Rachel were there too. All buried beneath the stake. I felt the boxes—coffins underground. But I was too late."

"That is monstrous, but it wasn't your fault."

"Yes, it was. We are a set. It was our most fundamental lesson, and in my panic I forgot, and four innocents died horrifying deaths."

"I'm so sorry." Asha touched his arm.

He jerked, heat boiled from his core and he met her concerned gaze.

She looked away, brushing her hair away from her face and hiding her eyes with her hand.

~ * ~

Asha was so tense she was ready to snap. Her emotions were bouncing around like an insane person's. The drive had been a new kind of exquisite torture. Her mind had raced through all the events since she'd first opened the door to Dr. Brent's cell. How had this all happened? If she'd initially removed him and gone underground, would everything be different now? Her friends safe and her sisters still lost to her?

She'd stared out the window throughout the journey, hypnotized by the moon, barely blinking, praying for distraction from the energy building in the car. He glanced at her more than once, and her muscles clenched every time. She had to fight the urge to meet his eyes.

Her tightly strung nerves made her jumpy, but at least most of her fear had dissipated. Maybe it was because the Four couldn't trace them, or maybe with three powerful sisters, she was stronger and safer than ever before. Her connection to them boosted her confidence and soothed her fear. They would get through this together…but apart. She frowned at Clay. How had they convinced them to separate? It was crazy.

But then he'd finally opened up to her, and his story broke her heart. *Stop it; you don't have a heart.*

When she'd asked if they'd been tested, she meant if the elements had tested them. Like she'd been. But he told his sad tale, and she was moved. More than moved, she wanted to ease his pain and relieve his guilt. She touched his arm in an effort to comfort him, yet heat flared and sparks fired between them once again. *What are you doing? You're playing with...ugh.*

Clay jerked the wheel, and they were off the road and driving over fields. He drove to a small hill and stopped the car.

Her stomach dropped right out of her body and her skin hummed with electricity. "We can't stay here. We're totally exposed."

"It's the perfect place, a mile from the walls and the ground is flat enough for a clear view. That mound over there has a small cave facing the walls, and we can spy unseen from inside."

"A cave?" Asha's mouth dried, and something pulsed deep inside. They would be together in confinement. *Yikes.*

"I discovered it as a kid. It was a pretty awesome fort." Clay winked and got out of the car and jogged up the slight slope over to the spattering of small boulders. Despite herself, Asha smiled and took the scope and their packs and followed him to the entrance.

"Can you grab the other bags from the trunk?" Clay asked over his shoulder. She dropped their bags.

Yes, it was true. Chivalry was dead.

Stop whining.

She ran back to the car. Inside the trunk were two large duffle bags; she unzipped one and whistled. "You're prepared. How did you get these on the plane?"

"We have our ways," he answered.

"That's good." She hoisted a bag over each shoulder and lugged them up the slope.

Still crouched at the entrance, he spun at her approach and she skittered back startled, naturally mistaking his movement for an attack.

He grinned, and she scowled. She was jumpy. "I opened the cave up a bit to give us some more room. I'll stash the car behind that barn we passed a few miles back and return right away."

She swallowed and rolled her eyes away from his. He chuckled and jogged back to the car.

Asha was left out in the open under the cover of night but still exposed. The car's headlights cut across the wide-open fields as Clay drove back onto the road. She peered into the cave, and the bags slipped from her hands.

Leaning in to get a closer look she gasped. A bit bigger was an understatement. The hill was small and the cave entrance smaller, but inside it dropped and opened downward, deep and wide. She crawled in past the rock entrance, stashing the bags just inside and jumped off the ledge. Spongy moss carpeted the entire cave, making it soft and cushiony. She held a sphere of fire to light the dark.

It was larger than the average-size bunker but carved from stone. Wildflowers grew in little groups, scattered around the cave's edge. Asha dropped her hand, but the sphere still hovered. Her chest tightened. The vines growing up the walls with huge pink and white blooms were her favorite.

Seeing them here sent her mind speeding back in time, like a flapping film reel, and she was in her jungle again. The blossoms' sweet scent triggered familiar, sun-bleached memories that pressed at her loneliness and smothered her heart.

The sun couldn't touch flowers in there. Clay had made them or called them. She smiled as she admired the dark, underground meadow. It was the most unexpectedly beautiful setting she'd ever seen.

Too soon, his footsteps were outside the cave, and her stomach dropped. Her smile wavered. She swallowed past the obstruction in her throat, heat flowing from her core out through her body.

Her fingers shook, and the branches parted. "This is beautiful, I can't believe—" Her voice sounded hoarse. *Jesus.*

She turned, and he was coming toward her, breathing heavily. Her heart thumped in rhythm with his breath, and her body clenched. His flashlight blinded her in the dim cave.

Before she could step away, he closed the gap and dropped the light. It landed in the moss half shaded, casting their looming shadows on the wall. His body was millimeters from hers. So close, his eyes almost glowed. They glowed.

He stared down at her but didn't touch her. She absorbed the heat flowing off his body. The fire in her responded, surging. She couldn't stop herself. Meeting his eyes, she leaned forward, and his hand came to her cheek, touching her skin lightly with his thumb.

She gulped, and he cupped her face gently with both hands. His power rolled beneath his skin, barely restrained and pulsing. He bent, and her blood raced, heat flushed, and bubbled like molten lava. He brushed his lips over hers, a touch of silk, and she shook. Again, his mouth touched hers, and his tongue slipped gently between her lips.

He slid his hand around the nape of her neck, and she melted. Her body was liquid fire. She smoldered and flowed, but the urgency built, the lava boiling, and she tilted her head, leaning into his kiss. She raised her shaking fingers and gripped his shoulder to help keep steady.

Clay bent forward, wrapping his arm around her waist, and drawing her against him. Orange light flashed from above, the moment their bodies crashed together. His body ignited hers; his lips scorched her mouth. He broke away, kissing her neck, tightening his arm around her waist. His hand slid down around her throat, stopping on her chest above her beating heart. His lips slid down her neck, nipping her shoulder and following the path of his hand.

Asha couldn't slow her rushing blood or her pulsing reaction to his touch and his body. Tracing her fingers over his jaw, she slid them around the back of his neck and combed them up through his soft, dark hair. She arched against him, and his lips crept up her neck and back to her mouth. His tongue curled inside, and their lips crashed together. She pulled his shoulders closer, wanting more, and dying of the pleasure as her body floated weightless in his arms. She wasn't even sure if she touched the ground anymore. He squeezed, exhaling into her neck as he slid his hand from her heart to cover her breast.

Sparks flashed behind him in the dark, and her rubber legs gave out. Clay held her up before turning her in a perfect, movie-moment dip. The moss cushioned her as he laid her down, releasing an intoxicating aroma of fresh earth that flooded her nostrils. The sparks illuminated his glorious eyes as he leaned close, kissing her again.

She was crossing into dangerous territory, but she didn't care. She could barely breathe; her desire for him overwhelmed caution of any kind. A reaction like this was not something to walk away from. Regardless of where his allegiance truly lay, her physical response was too much to deny. She didn't think she could if she tried.

All her fear and suspicion were forgotten in the mind-blowing bliss. Nothing mattered except this. Well one thing did, and she was grateful for the momentary reality check. She pulled away.

"Clay," she rasped. "Do you have protection?"

He smiled. "My clothes are flame retardant, but I wasn't planning on keeping them on much longer."

Laughing, she smacked him. "That's not what I mean."

He rolled over, reaching into one of their bags and pulled out a small plastic square. Jealousy flared a moment. Why did he carry those with him? But he rolled back to her and the unwelcome irritation vanished. *For moments like these, duh.*

Touching their lips together, their mouths met in perfect harmony, the tension building and overwhelming her again. She slid her hands over his chest, touching the muscle through his thick layers of clothing, before slipping her hands under and up over his bare skin.

He drew his breath in sharply, and she tore her lips away and sat up. He paled, but she smiled, going for her best 'relax' look.

"Take this off," she whispered, tugging at his coat.

It was off in a flash, and he laid it over the moss behind her. She pulsed with anticipation but broke their stare-off by yanking her sweater over her head. She shivered as air blew across her bare skin. One of many downsides to her fire was running out of bras and underwear…well all clothes for that matter.

Clay froze, his hands on his shirt midway up his torso. She shivered from the shaded heat of his gaze and he tore his shirt over his head and tossed it aside.

As he reached for her, his hands stopped an inch from her shoulder. "What is that?"

"What?" she asked.

Ice froze the desire in her blood. Stung by the edge in his cold, chilling voice, she crossed her arms in front of her chest.

He took her arm and studied it. "What is this? You didn't have these marks in Colombia."

Asha finally looked up at him. His eyes were the soldier's eyes, fierce, violent, and scary, but his hands were gentle on her arm.

The damage the Four had done to her while she was a prisoner had scarred into mostly healed, red, welts, and she hadn't realized how ugly they looked. "The Four came to my cell the morning you brought me to my sisters."

"They did that to you?"

"I'm fine. Please don't ruin this."

His face softened. "They'll pay for it."

Yes, they will.

Leaning forward, he kissed her, and she melted anew. His kiss was tender, gentle, and protective, but there was more. Something softer and deeper than desire flooded her, but it came from him. There was love in it, soul-crushing love. Tears filled her eyes, her throat closed, but heat and fire still pounded beneath. He pulled away, and she gasped.

Kneeling, she studied him, motionless, panting, her heart pounding. His body was like a statue, solid and strong but carved with muscle.

He studied her. "Do you—?"

"Oh my God, yes."

Still holding her wrist, he tugged her back to him, and they slammed together. He took her lips, his hands roving everywhere, the skin against skin contact, burning.

Clay touched her face and her waist, and she fell back against his coat. She gripped his shoulders, dragging him on top of her and slid her fingers down his back.

He stopped, pried them from his back, and raised them over her head. His smile was trouble, and she loved it. She squirmed under him and flared at his wink. He held her hands together in his left hand and slid his free hand down her body, leaving fire trailing in its wake. Bending over her, he laid his burning lips to her neck, her scars. Her body jerked when his hand covered her breast.

He continued kissing down her neck, over her collarbones and across her chest. He paused, stroking gently and rubbing his thumb across her nipple.

She cried out in surprise, jerking again as his mouth closed over her other breast. She bit her lip to silent her cry.

A low crash startled her, and she craned her head back. Rock sealed the cave entrance. "But the air?"

He released her wrists and smiled down at her. "Plenty, more than enough." As he kissed her again, whatever her concerns had been, they vanished.

His lips were on her shoulder again. Her small moan echoed in the now enclosed space. *Aha.*

Clay bent his head and licked across her nipple and heat flooded low in her body. She gasped and gripped his hair, burning hotter, fighting for control over her power. She couldn't burst into flames, even though she already had. Metaphorically. What if she did lose control? She would kill him.

Clay licked again, and her body jerked, he rubbed his lips across it once, twice, before he took her nipple in his mouth, sucking. Her body lurched up, and Clay gripped her hip, pinning her down. His mouth continued to ravish her breasts while his hand stroked over her body and moved lower.

She could only hold his shoulders, panting with need and desire. The button on her jeans popped open, and he slid his hand inside. She blushed. She didn't have any underwear on. She'd burned her only pair days ago. He cupped her and traced his finger lightly over her trembling body, and she melted into his hand.

He clenched his jaw, the muscle jumping, as he slid his finger inside her. She came undone, spiraling and peaking and vibrating around his finger. He moved his hand stroking her and she squeezed his shoulders, crying out again. Spinning fireworks illuminated the cave, lighting the flowers and vines, illuminating the bright colors in the dark.

Panting, her awareness came back as her orgasm subsided. Her jeans had vanished. Clay knelt between her legs, stroking her thighs. He shifted, sliding lower, kissing her stomach, his fingers moving inside her again. She gasped again and gripped his shoulders, but he slid away, moving lower. Spreading her legs, he bent his head, his hot breath tickling her sensitive, throbbing body and driving her wild. He lowered his mouth to her, and she dropped her head back against the moss, rolling it to the side.

His tongue flicked out, and she jumped. His arm came around her legs, and he tugged her body closer toward him. Hot breath again and so close against her, she bowed with delicious anticipation before his tongue licked over her firmly and then softly. He groaned and she clawed at his shoulders, but he continued sucking, stroking. Her body clenched, and she exploded again and spun downward and then surged up again as another flash of light and pulsating pleasure swept her away. She groaned and gasped, trying not to blow up as her orgasm rose and fell again and again.

~ * ~

Clay crawled forward, his blood boiling and his body shaking. He studied Asha below him. Her eyes were closed, her face flushed, and her mouth opened slightly as she panted with pleasure. She was so real, vital, and alive. No longer a dream or an enemy, she was here with him, and he planned to keep it that way.

She writhed below him and yanked at his waistband. Rising up, she kissed his chest, licking his nipple as she tugged his jeans down. Slipping them off his legs, he couldn't hold his raging body back another moment.

He lowered over her. She sighed and wrapped her arms around his neck, arching into him. He lowered his mouth back to her breast, shifting his body between her open legs.

Regardless of life-shaking destinies, in this moment she trusted him, and he wanted her. She allowed him this pleasure and he would reward her for it. He wanted to consume her in a way he'd never felt. It was primal, fierce, and unnerving.

She opened her eyes and the black color seemed to spark with miniscule lights. He paused a moment before pushing forward, sliding inside. Her body enveloped him. She was soft, firm, and so hot.

God.

Clay sighed as he drove forward, pressing her back into the moss. He sank deep, their bodies fused together as one before he withdrew. She gasped, meeting each slow, deep thrust. Her body clenched around him, and his breath staggered as he held himself over her. He fought for control. He wanted to savor her, prolong this moment forever, but he craved more.

The ground quivered and rolled. Sheathed deep inside her, he worked to hold himself still. His hands shook as he touched her face. Sweat beaded on his skin, and he clenched his jaw.

Her hand moved from his shoulder to his cheek. Her eyes were flames. He bent and their mouths met.

Swelling passion erupted as their open mouths and tongues devoured each other. His body responded, out of control, as he thrust into her. A halo of fire burned against the cave walls spreading up. The ground pulsed beneath them. Asha's moans grew louder as she met his body, gripping his shoulders.

Hot coals burned again inside him, but it was deeper, stronger, and growing. He couldn't hold on. But he climbed higher and higher. Asha cried out, and her body sizzled and vibrated around him. His pleasure erupted with volcanic force and heat as he jerked and twitched, and they clung together, panting.

The ground calmed, but pulsed below ever so slightly, like a heartbeat in steady rhythm. The earth had literally moved in response to their union. He almost laughed. Asha was more than anything he could have imagined. He was done for.

He flipped over onto his back, pulling her with him until she rested across his naked, sweat-slicked chest. He studied her, grinning, and then looked up at the fire above them. She snapped her finger, and it shrank to a small burning star casting a soft glow down on them.

"I'm sorry, I didn't want that to happen," she said

The blow was like a punch in the gut; her words winded him. His smile crumbled, "Are you kidding? I've wanted that since the first moment I saw you."

She laughed. "No, I wanted *that*. I meant the fireworks, the beautiful flowers. They're gone. I could have hurt you."

His breath escaped in a gasp, but he smiled again. "That was nothing, kid. I can take it."

"Oh, you can, can you?" She laughed. "Is that a challenge?"

"Hell no. You could destroy me if you tried, but it would take more than that fairy fire to distract me from…" His eyes swept her naked body and his hand slid down her back. "You."

"Fairy fire?" she snapped, leaning away.

But he pulled her back, kissing her again. "Uh oh." he said through the kiss.

"Oh, yes." Asha sighed as she moved on top of him, and he slid inside her again.

~ * ~

It was late when Avia parked in front of Armand's house. The cobblestone street was quiet, and the old building's whitewashed, concrete exterior had dark windows on two floors. Stairs led up from the sidewalk to the familiar wooden door.

Crushing pressure squeezed her chest and her stomach dropped and flipped. Icy dread poured over her, and she swept from the car, leaving the door open. With the house key ready in her hand, she practically flew up the stairs, unlocking the door and opening it.

"Wait Avia, go slowly," Rio whispered right behind her and gripped her arm.

A zap shot through her, and she shook his arm off with a jerk, still moving forward, and praying Armand was upstairs asleep. The air smelled musty and metallic, and she gulped down rising panic.

She was down the hall in a flash, her hand on the door to his music room. Opening it, she had to grip the knob to hold herself upright as her eyes took in the grizzly scene. Armand was dead, tied to a chair. He had no face left. It was nothing but a bloody mess. They'd beaten him to death.

A broken gasp escaped her. Cold, hollow emptiness spread across her chest and through her body. She hadn't even crossed the threshold yet. *Why does time only slow during moments of horror and never joy?*

"Avia, I said wait." Rio snapped and slid past her, going to the chair. "Shit," he breathed the word.

Armand's blood hadn't even fully congealed. It still dripped from his body, echoing in her ears. It had happened recently. If she had only come sooner, she could have saved him. If she'd only remembered him a few hours earlier. *If only, if only.*

Rio turned around and walked back toward her, trying to block her view. He failed. He gripped her shoulders firmly. "This is bad, Avia. We have to move, now."

She was so far away, the humming growing too loud. It blocked out his voice. She couldn't tear her gaze away from the body. *The body? Why couldn't she react? Was this shock?*

"We can't help him. We'll call someone, anyone, but we can't stay here."

The entire scene was a trap, of course. It was so obvious, but she still couldn't move. Armand's destroyed body triggered her first moment of pure grief. She'd never lost anything that mattered, and she hadn't even guessed how much she cared until now.

Grief, like joy was an unfamiliar emotion. Years ago, child psychiatrists had tried to teach her to recognize emotions and empathize by showing her flashcards with cartoon faces on them. The face with tears and the arc turned down for a mouth was sadness.

Loud popping signaled the wave of gunfire seconds before it erupted from the walls and shattered windows. Rio grabbed her, breaking her out of her fog. She stood, but he shoved her, and she soared out the door. He drew his gun from his jacket, spinning back into the room.

Avia managed to throw her hands out in time to catch the oncoming bullets before they tore him apart. Hundreds hit her invisible shield, and it took all her focus and concentration to hold it.

But a squealing hiss warned of something even worse and the wall crumbled in flames. She forced all the air from her lungs and stretched her shaking fingers toward the wall. Her head splitting in agony, she held her shield against the rocket. The explosion crept forward in slow motion from the breaking wall, unfurling and rolling toward them.

Somehow, she contained the flashing fire and billowing smoke to the far side of the room, but the effort drained her power. Blood trickled from her left nostril—she was going to pass out.

"Rio," she screamed.

He twisted around, his blue eyes swirled and frothed like giant whirlpools, and in a blur he was diving toward her. He tackled her farther into the hallway and tumbled her to the side, covering her again. Water soaked her and rushed into the room with incredible pressure. It lifted into a huge wave, cresting and touching the ceiling as her hold broke. The house shook and a second squeal pierced the air, another rocket was coming.

"Come on." He yanked her up and shoved her ahead, splashing through the hallway and straight to the backdoor. The house shattered around them as the second rocket hit.

Avia drained the last of her power to blow the door off its hinges, clearing their way into the night. They sprinted through the small yard, past Armand's vegetable garden. Rio shot five soldiers waiting in the dark. They blew past the falling bodies as he dragged her out the gate and into the back alley.

Pausing against a neighbor's wall, and hidden by shadows, she looked up. People peered cautiously from their lit windows. The commotion had drawn a crowd. Well duh, they hadn't been very stealthy. She laughed.

Rio turned, his mouth open and his eyes wide. He reached out to her, but she jerked away.

Why was she laughing? Cold dripped from her scalp covering her, she shivered.

"Let's go," he whispered. Frowning and whipping back around, he walked forward.

Behind them the Order soldiers, disguised in Italian military garb, swarmed the shattered house. Rio signaled for her to follow him.

Two breaths were all it took. Two deep breaths and she was back. She shook her head. Revenge first. Rio could join her or leave her. She didn't care. She would kill them all for Armand. She shook her head again firmly holding her finger to her lips.

"Avia," he whispered sharply.

She ignored him and turned, walking back to the broken, stone skeleton of her childhood home-away-from-home.

"Shit," Rio swore behind her.

But he followed her, as she knew he would. Going back through the yard, purple mist swirled above the grass in wisps. She stopped short. She scanned the dark ground and the soldiers. Crouching down she clutched an empty uniform.

"What is this?" she asked horrified.

"Order soldiers," Rio said, scanning the rubble his gun raised and steady.

"Order soldiers? Where are their bodies?"

"The purple…it's them."

She didn't understand.

"Yeah, I know it's weird."

"Weird, are you kidding me? They aren't real?"

"Of course they're real. You've seen them. Asha's met a few of them. But when they die, they do this."

"Will you do this?"

"No."

In the alley back in Hong Kong, the purple mist had spooked her, but she had no idea what they were. This was bad. She closed her eyes thinking it through, but she couldn't see how men could become mist.

"Later, you talk." She jogged to the back of the house.

She could hear the monsters searching through the debris, and she tracked their positions by the sound. With a picture clear in her head, she mapped her approach. Twelve men were inside the room.

Rio flashed ten and two fingers, and she nodded.

With a deep breath, Avia entered the room rearmed with her power. Though previously drained, it was now back in force. She'd never replenished so fast. It had to be her passion, her desire for revenge refueling her.

Throwing her hand up, she called air, and three Order soldiers flew up, like puppets yanked by their strings. She was a tornado of cold, controlled rage. Her white hair blew wildly around her face, and she held them high a moment before pointing to the ground. They fell, screaming, onto razor-sharp glass and rebar spikes.

More soldiers, drawn by the noise, ran into the room. Avia slammed them into the wall. She curled her lips in a snarl and stalked toward them not hesitating as Rio shot three times followed by three thuds behind her.

She studied the soldiers' frightened eyes, and anger burst inside her. Sizzling energy sparked off her fingers, but it wasn't raging—it was steady and controlled. She couldn't shake Armand's beaten image—his fear, his pain.

She raised her hand and they rose, sliding up the wall. "This is going to be unpleasant for you," she whispered.

In Ivy's cavern she'd suffocated Mere and Asha without even trying. Avia took a deep breath, connecting to the air in their lungs and drew it out bit by bit. Their eyes widened, bulged.

Yes, that's right. This is scary. She held them immobilized, but they twitched and jerked, pinned against the slivers of the second-floor wall ten feet from the ground.

Lightning flashed in the dark sky above, reaching toward the soldiers. It didn't take much of her power. In fact, it was easier than it had ever been.

The men's fear wasn't enough to satiate her rage. The purest pain she could imagine filled her head. She focused her power, blew it out, and the screaming started. She let their anguished sounds fill her ears for three wonderful seconds then blew the air back until their bodies swelled and exploded in a spray of blood and gore.

Covered in splatter, she spun and faced Rio.

His expression was pale but resolute. "Let's go, Avia. More will come. We'll have to leave the car."

They ran through the purple mist and climbed through the broken wall. People gathered across the street watching the action. Rockets in this quiet neighborhood would definitely be unusual. Sirens sounded in the distance. Rio led her down the block and one brave person shouted at them to stop, but thankfully he didn't pursue them.

She allowed him to lead her, barely aware of their movements as they slid in and out through the shadows at a steady pace. They headed toward a small overpass where the bushes of the bordering park hid a dirt trail leading underneath. Rio started to climb down, his feet slipping on the loose soil, and he held out his hand.

She took his hand, genuinely pleased by his chivalrous gesture and grinned at him.

"Keep it together, Avia."

She recoiled as if he had hit her. For a split second, she had forgotten the only person she ever cared for was gone forever. Choking, she yanked her hand away. She'd never experienced this detachment. What a strange sensation it was. All consuming, and yet she'd momentarily forgotten him again.

Once, a long time ago, someone had told her denial was the body's shock absorber. Right now that described her reaction and behavior perfectly.

"We need a car and a place to go." Rio's sea-blue eyes were full of concern. "But maybe we should take a few minutes to let you rest."

Avia took a deep breath, mentally pulled herself together, and blew away the grief. A weight rose off her chest, and her eyes focused once more. "I don't need to rest." If she had stuff to deal with, she'd deal with it later. "I'm fine. Let's go."

"Okay, good. I'm glad you're fine, but you're covered in blood. You stay here. I am going to scout the area and find us another car. I'll be right back. Listen to me, Avia, *stay here*." Rio glanced back once then climbed up the riverbank into the night.

Avia wasn't fine, and she was sure he could see it. She was angry, no furious. Armand, sweet, feisty, old Armand. How could anyone hurt a human being in such a way, especially someone already old and frail?

~ * ~

Rio returned to Avia, sliding down the incline. He'd been gone only half an hour, rushing to get back. He was worried about her.

She sat in the exact position as when he'd left her.

"Avia," he whispered. "Here." He handed her the water bottle and tissues, so she could wash her face.

"Thank you."

"There's a bag in the car. A woman's bag. There should be a change of clothes."

"What happened to the woman?" Avia asked sharply.

"She and her boyfriend are in a bar. Don't worry, I was stealthy."

Cleaned up, Rio reached out to help her up, but she ignored him, standing on her own. He dropped his floating hand, surprisingly stung by her refusal.

She approached the passenger side of the old brown Honda while he got to work reconnecting the wires still hanging loose from the steering column. The car started, and he drove them through the quiet streets, maintaining the speed limit.

His skin grew warm under the weight of her gaze. "What is it? Are you all right?"

She was silent.

"Sorry that was a stupid question. Of course, you're not."

She cleared her throat. "I am fine. I told you that. But did you just hotwire this car?"

"So?" he asked.

"Where did you pick up that particular talent?"

Talent? "Oh that?" He relaxed. Maybe she appreciated the skill. "The streets." He chuckled, going for lightness. "I also have a knack for picking pockets and general street-guy-thuggery."

She smiled; she actually smiled. Something had definitely changed. Could she be thawing?

He had prepared for trouble when he returned, but if anything she was warmer. It unnerved him to see her rebound so fast from such trauma and violence, but considering he wasn't great with females in distress, he accepted her resolve gratefully.

"Really?"

"No, not really. We were never on the streets. It was the Order. They insisted a well-rounded education was the greatest advantage. I have to admit that it does come in handy from time to time." He glanced at her, sitting rigid and staring straight ahead, out the windshield.

"We didn't know anything about you and your sisters. None of us did."

Rio was disgusted beyond comprehension, thinking back now over all their lessons and missions. All their work had been preparation. They'd been trained to hunt these women.

His rage burned and grew after seeing Avia's teacher tied to the chair. Rio couldn't deny their part in the Order's plan. Though clueless about the actual intention, they were obviously weapons, raised to take out their masters' greatest threat.

He hated being used. Nothing infuriated him more. Driving through the tourist district, the traffic was heavy, even this late at night. He stopped the car across the street from the grand and suitably flashy, five-star Hotel Cavalieri.

Rio turned and grabbed one of the backpacks. Avia studied the bag and wrinkled her nose. It was a snobby flinch, but it pleased him. The reaction was genuine.

He pulled out some twisted and rolled up printed fabric.

"What is that?" she asked.

"You're asking me? It looks like a dress."

"No."

"Your clothes are a mess."

She looked down. "Yes, you're right."

Maybe she wasn't okay.

Rio got out of the car so she could change and took the other pack from the back seat. He opened it and tried not to laugh. Bob Marley shirts and board shorts.

Avia stepped out wearing a yellow sundress with big blue swirls. He swallowed. Wow. She looked like something from a fairy-tale. Young, soft, and vulnerable. Different from the woman he'd known up until now.

"We should dump the car and walk in." Pathetic though it was, he'd chosen the hotel to impress her, but she neither oohed nor ahhed, and her nonchalant walk was graceful and completely at ease.

All appearance of her grief gone, she thanked the doorman graciously as he took her backpack, and she sauntered rather seductively into the hotel.

Rio trailed her into the palatial lobby. The front desk staff greeted Avia enthusiastically.

Touché. He grinned.

"Ciao, bella Avia. My little bird, welcome, welcome." The paunchy, balding hotel manager beamed at Avia, shuffled around the desk, and took her into a huge hug.

Rio's grin grew at the man's pleasure in seeing her. He obviously cared about her very much, and Rio couldn't blame him. She was magnetic and beautiful, even if she was the most distant person he'd ever met.

"Carlos, listen," she whispered, leaning close. "I would like to stay under a false identity tonight. I am with a friend, and we must not be discovered or disturbed. It is critical."

He glanced over and frowned at Rio, who waited against the back wall scanning the lobby. Carlos was clearly concerned for his 'little bird,' and Rio wasn't exactly exuding Mr. Clean Cut and Charming.

Carlos beamed. "Franco, please get Miss Amelia and her brother up to their rooms," he said loudly to the clerk behind the desk.

Rio smiled again—brother meant separate rooms. Carlos was a sharp one.

Rio stood behind Avia while riding the elevator and took the chance to study her. She ignored him, staring straight ahead. He couldn't figure her out, but something had stirred the first time he spotted her from across the field. Unwelcome and unnerving, he was tense and edgy.

She was ethereal and unbelievably beautiful, but with power so strong, he wasn't ashamed to admit she frightened him. At their first meeting, he'd pegged her as distant and detached, and that hadn't changed after they'd all faced the Four. But then after finding Armand, her detached air disappeared, and there was love and grief. Though her grief was soon replaced with cold and calculated, ruthless vengeance.

He remembered her smile when he offered her his hand, so beautiful, so pure, and so out of place. Stupidly, he told her to keep it together, and at that moment, she'd shown emotion so raw—her heart broke before his eyes. He'd shattered whatever denial she needed, and it hit her all over again.

When he'd returned with the car, she'd been closed off, and her unreadable air had returned. But then in the car while driving, he had picked up on a moment, an opening. One he would try to build on.

He didn't want to go into his own, separate room. Pausing at their side-by-side doors, she met his eyes before she walked in after the bellman. Rio's stomach dropped, and his mouth dried at her absence. He scowled and opened his door. It had everything, a bed, a bathroom, and an adjoining door. The décor was extremely fancy; old-fashioned luxury done in cream, beige, flowers, and gold. He counted to five before grabbing his laptop and opening the adjoining door. Avia stood in the doorway.

Startled, he jumped, and she cracked a tiny smile. *That's an improvement.* But she'd suffered shock and loss tonight, and he needed to proceed with understanding and caution. She was prickly, and he didn't want to bleed.

Something, instinct maybe, told him to stay close, to make sure she was okay. He was relieved she'd opened the door. Knocking would have been intrusive and slightly pathetic.

She stepped aside, and he walked into her room, holding his breath. Allowing him in was another good sign, and he counted it as a victory.

She left the door open, and he strolled into the room and sat on the couch.

"Wow," he said. "Now *this* is a suite." It seemed his room was an attachment to Avia's multi-room splendor with a stocked bar and dining area, separate bedroom and living area, a hot tub on the huge outdoor patio.

Is that a Warhol? He studied the city view from her window; it was stunning.

Avia sighed, rolled her shoulders, and pointed to his laptop. "What have you got there?"

"Cole emailed me the details from Master Miles. We have to set up a meeting with an archivist from the Vatican Secret Archives. He is the only one who has seen the documents we need. I'll contact him now and wait to hear from him. If he is able to meet us, all the danger is on his side. I wonder how the Master convinced this man to help us."

Avia said nothing, just listened with the same detached expression on her face.

"Are you okay?"

"We need to tell the others what happened."

Rio held out his cellphone to her. She tilted her head to him, indicating he should make the call. He dialed Clay and Avia wandered into the bedroom. Rio craned his neck to see what she was doing. Clay's phone was off so Rio called Aron. His phone was off too. Next, Cole.

Chapter Fifteen

Mere exited the Cairo International Airport into the dry heat and desert night air beside Aron. He took her hand and led her to a waiting cab. She followed with a lovely fluttering in her stomach. On the plane, they'd hatched a scheme to act like a couple on vacation, but secretly they would play spies searching for top-secret intelligence.

She liked the challenge of playing a role within a role. It helped to transform her fear into excitement. Spies wouldn't be frightened of their mission. They'd take it on without emotion and get the job done.

She'd been beyond terrified after witnessing the forces against them. The Four, immortal beings they couldn't fight, who brought frightening visions of their destiny, and its futility. They were the most horrifying foes she could imagine. But she wouldn't let her devastating fear destroy her.

Fear wasn't a positive emotion, and she worked her ass off to stay positive. After everything she'd been through she wouldn't let even the Four and the Order sway her from positivity and light.

Long ago she'd made a conscious choice to face forward with joy, but she had to reinforce it, like a daily exercise, to steer herself against the darkness constantly drawing her back. Only recently had it become more natural, automatic. This adventure would not interfere with all her work; it would support it.

As Miles said, they may survive where everyone who'd come before them had not. He said it was different this time. They would stay hidden if they stayed apart, but it was an unfair sacrifice.

Separated from her sisters and paired up with Aron, she felt safe enough, and he helped by going along and making it an adventure and a game. It worked and took the weight away. She would enjoy this. She'd never been to Egypt, and despite the fact four evil gods out there were obsessed with their deaths, Mere was at ease and focused on their mission.

"We can go to a hotel near the pyramids," Aron said loudly.

She grinned at him, aiming for a loving expression as he opened the door for her, and the driver loaded their packs. Their cab driver recommended a luxury boutique hotel, operated by a friendly Swiss couple with a reputation for exceptional hospitality—a true oasis in the desert. She wondered what his kickback was for such a well-worded recommendation.

They arrived at a lovely, mosaic-covered building with curiously lush gardens for the desert. Large fountains and exquisite flowering bushes adorned the entrance in front of sparkling white marble steps.

Aron held her hand as she exited the car, and they climbed the beautiful staircase to the large, open reception area. Drawing her close, they approached the counter. He slipped his arm over her shoulder, and it vibrated with enticing energy. It was warm and drew her in, her body humming in response.

A lovely young clerk dressed in crisp white clothing checked them in, but her words didn't penetrate. Mere was too busy studying Aron's face. He charmed the woman easily with his kind, gray eyes and his seductive smile. Never breaking eye contact with the clerk, he trailed his finger over Mere's bare shoulder sending shivers through her. Whoa, who was this guy?

The girl grinned at her with an obvious *you lucky bitch* look as a bellman materialized beside them. He delivered fruity cocktails from a silver tray, his uniform, like the desk clerk's, blending into the open lobby's whitewashed walls. He ushered them upstairs and deposited them in a large, airy suite full of fresh flowers.

The door clicked shut, and she faced Aron across the room, alone for the first time since meeting at the cabin. She gulped and cleared her throat. "So, what first?" She took a dainty sip of her drink.

He smiled.

She could tell he was a warm person. *Warmer than Avia…she was like a Vulcan. Oh, wow that was really bitchy.* Mere shouldn't be comparing them just because they were both air elements. It wasn't fair. Would the others compare her to Rio?

"Let's see what's going on." Aron winked and opened his laptop. "Find a place to start?"

Though the brothers were apart, they stayed very well connected. Sadly, she and her sisters were not. Even though she'd just met them, she already missed them. They'd separated so soon after meeting. Could that be why the other sisters never survived? Had their love and attachment kept them together and drawn the Four?

"We've got the plans and contact info. It looks like we're set for some tomb raiding," Aron said, closing his laptop and leaning back against the couch.

His phone rang, and he showed her the screen. "Rio. Hey, what's up?" He listened. "What? Awful…"

Mere's stomach dropped and rolled.

"I'll tell her. Of course, I'll help her. We can come back here afterward. I'll talk to her and call you back."

Mere tensed and stared at Aron's pale face as he hung up. She was already expecting the worst, her hands tight in fists. "Just tell me."

"Mere, your family. We have to warn them, get them somewhere safe. Avia's music teacher was killed by the Order."

No. Mere fought the tears already welling in her eyes. *Poor Avia.* "Is she okay?"

"Mere, your parents, siblings?"

"You don't have to worry," she said. "I don't have anyone, not really. My parents died when I was twelve. The only other family I had was Father Austen, and he died a few days ago. I doubt my work colleagues and acquaintances would be targets for the Order. I didn't have any true friends. I couldn't." She cleared her throat and straightened her shoulders while lifting her chin. *Be stronger.*

Frowning, Aron bowed his head. "We barely know anything about each other, do we? I'm so sorry, Mere. The Order will pay for all of this, I promise you. Avia's teacher was well respected, so he wouldn't have been hard to find. Someone from the battle could have recognized her."

"Recognized her? What do you mean?"

"Avia is a musician, and the name of her teacher would be noted in a bio somewhere. The Order must have discovered him and used him as bait."

"Avia said she played the flute, but she never said she was famous."

"She is to some people. I have some of her music on my playlist."

"Really?"

He took the device from his bag and connected it to the stereo. Haunting, beautiful sounds filled the room, and she swayed side to side with the sweet, hypnotic music. It was incredible.

"There's something else you need to know. It's about the Order soldiers. Avia witnessed it tonight."

Mere listened in fearful awe to Aron's unbelievable explanation. But it made a strange kind of sense. How else could they have so many men at their disposal? It was the most utterly creepy thing she'd ever heard and she was even more grateful for the brothers' help.

"Call Rio back and tell him we're still on for treasure hunting, and send Avia my love," she said, closing her eyes.

Her mind swept away with the music as she half listened to Aron explain to Rio they were going to continue.

Mere's stomach flipped. Everything hit her at once—excitement and joy for discovering her sisters, but also an undeniable, crushing fear churned inside her. Even with her façade, the terror was still there underneath it all.

But there was also this powerful attraction. She had never experienced anything like it before, not even with the best surfers and cutest lifeguards.

What the hell, she might die tomorrow. Going with her role as a secret spy girlfriend, she would indulge herself. She wouldn't be able to resist his lure, but what had her stomach flipping, was whether he would be able to resist her.

"Are you ready for an adventure?" he asked playfully his gray eyes narrowing and darting around, looking shifty.

"Ah, yes, tomb raiding," she said, beaming. "I'm so in, but what are we doing exactly?"

"Join me on the couch, and we can go over what Cole sent."

Her stomach churned again, but she sat beside him. They read the email listing the instructions, locations, and contact information. They searched and found a website and map of the pyramids' excavation plans.

"According to Master Miles, there are secret catacombs running under the Pyramid of Giza. We'll meet our contact at the site. He's the dig director, and he's made a discovery of great importance to the Master."

"Contact?" She laughed. "Perfect."

"We have to text this number and give him the time of our tour. He'll be waiting at the pyramid."

He was indulging her, making it fun, like the adventure she desired.

He leaned forward, speaking with a hushed tone. "We have to get in there." He pointed to the screen again. "These are the sketches of the tunnel we need to find. We follow the tour, get in, commit some theft, and get out."

She studied the map...*wait.* "It didn't even occur to me. We need Ivy or Clay. They're the earth elements. Avia couldn't be underground. She kind of lost it, and if those drawings are any indication, we'll be in much more cramped quarters than she was." What an idiot, how could she have forgotten?

"I'll be fine. I don't have a problem with small spaces, and we won't need our elements. The Master has done all the work for us. We just have to follow the map and his instructions. Our contact will get us in and out. It'll be easy."

Mostly reassured by his confidence, she smiled, "Okay, if you're sure. It sounds fun, even if there is limited risk." Her voice held a flirtatious lilt. She was testing the vibe and seeing if he would respond in kind.

His eyes twinkled, and he glanced with the shifty eyes again, making her smile. "The plan is this," he said in his hushed voice. "When the opportunity presents itself, we detach from the group, get in and find whatever we can, and get out. The chamber we need is still being excavated and the dig director has done work for the Master in the past."

"A secret source?"

"Yes, apparently the Master has quite a network of people out there, searching for information and following up on leads. The director's name is Marvin Trigger. He'll take us to the vault and get us out safely. He has all the proper credentials."

Mere frowned slightly. "So we barely have to do anything?"

Aron flashed her a leg-weakening grin before fixing a fake, but somber expression on his face. "We're still stealing ancient artifacts and robbing a pyramid. And hey, with luck our escort may not show, and then we'll really be on our own."

"Well, I guess we can hope for that." She laughed, but it trailed off into silence.

She snapped her attention to the most luxurious suite she'd ever beheld, and she was dressed in jeans, a tank top, and her usual bikini top instead of a bra. This wouldn't do.

She was inappropriately attired for her surroundings and the part she intended to play. "If you'll excuse me, I need to go to the lobby for a few things."

Aron was surprised but stood as she slipped on her plastic flip-flops. She blushed as she took her frayed, old Velcro Billabong wallet from her pack. Hiding her childish accessory, she darted out the door.

She was back in forty minutes with several bags. "There's a lovely boutique in the lobby, and I wanted to pick up some necessities," she said, smiling at the question in his eyes.

"You must be hungry. How about some room service and a bottle of wine?"

"Perfect. I need to get cleaned up after the flight. I'm going to take a bath."

"Great. Dinner will take time, and I can go over the plans."

"I'll be back soon," she said, slipping into the bathroom with her bags.

Now that was a tub. The large bathroom was spacious and airy, with a huge marble bathtub and a separate, standalone, double-headed shower encased in glass. She sat on the edge and turned on the tap, testing the water. She needed to calm herself and wash away the film of travel grime coating her body.

Aron knocked gently. She'd left the door open a crack, and it swung open. "Um, Mere? I ordered dinner. Some falafel, vegetables, and kebobs."

"What? I can't hear you." He repeated the details more loudly, but she still couldn't hear well over the pouring water. "I can't hear you. Come in."

He walked in, and she shook the water drops from her fingers. She stared up into his dark, stormy eyes and gulped. The distance between them shimmered and constricted, urging her closer to him. One step, and he was there, his hand reaching out to her face. She breathed a sigh as his hand cupped her cheek ever so gently. He was so big, but his hands were so gentle on her skin. His thumbs stroked her cheek, and his fingers brushed her hair back from her face.

Shivers tickled over her hot skin, and her body clenched. Pounding, rushing blood filled her ears, shifting the sound of pouring water into a low hum. He bent and his lips touched hers, a tender brush. She sizzled as a weight dropped inside her, pulsing out through her body. Aron opened his mouth, his tongue gently touching hers.

Mere loved kissing—she always had—but it had never been like this. Her body purred, and he wrapped his arm around her firmly, holding her against him, the other hand still cupping her face. Passion took over with tidal force, heat pouring through her, her blood rushing so loudly through her ears she couldn't think. Even breathing was difficult.

He deepened his kiss, his mouth against hers hot and firm and she moaned with pleasure.

Instantly, he dropped his hands and backed away paling visibly. "I'm sorry. I shouldn't have intruded."

"I invited you in."

"I wanted to ask if white wine was all right."

He seemed nervous.

"Are you sure you weren't trying to get a peek at me naked?" She smiled, but her stomach was doing back flips. His kiss made one thing abundantly clear. He wanted her as much as she did him.

He frowned.

"White wine sounds lovely. I'll be out in a moment. Thank you, Aron."

He slipped out, leaving the door open a crack. Mere stripped, kicking her casual clothes into the corner and slid into the tub and under the water immediately, letting the soothing heat wash over her and clear her lust-filled head.

Even with the extreme stress and danger, her mind kept wandering to Aron outside the door and her distracting level of attraction and desire. She was well aware of her emotional extremes. She felt attraction, lust, and love deeply and easily. Hell, she'd been in lust with a lifeguard she'd only spoken to once before.

She'd been cursed with a fickle heart and a short attention span. Her desires tended to get her into trouble. Despite all her training, she had done her fair share of damage, usually due to her frequent emotional swings. Could she handle something with a man this hot?

When her breath ran out, she came up for air. Eager to be in the next room with Aron, she swiftly shampooed, washed, buffed, and dried herself and her hair with the fluffiest white towels she'd ever touched. The rich red and orange patterned silk robes hanging on the door matched the room's décor, but she ignored them. Maybe later.

She took the lace one-piece bra and panty thing from the bag and bit off the tags. Much fancier than what she was used to, she slipped on the silky, sexy garment and did a spin in the mirror, quite pleased with the effect. It was doing the trick. Her confidence and brashness grew.

She dug through the bag with her brand new make-up. Though she never wore it, without doubt a super spy would, so she opened the selection of tubes and bottles she'd bought downstairs.

Made up, she unwrapped the simply elegant, but still sexy dress the woman in the shop had recommended.

"Perfect for a hot date on a yacht, sexy, but still sophisticated," she'd said.

It was a low-cut, sapphire-blue, fitted sheath, and she admitted after putting it on, it looked fabulous on her, hugging her slight curves perfectly. She might not be able to fill out a dress like Ivy or even Asha, but Mere was confident she rocked it anyway. She spun toward the full-length mirror, but something was missing.

Oh shoot, the shoes. She had forgotten to complete her ensemble. This outfit needed shoes, and she didn't have anything suitable. Oh, well. She'd just have to fake it. It wasn't as if she could pull off looking sexy in heels once she took a step anyway.

She grinned and took the towel off her head and let her black hair fall in damp waves across and below her shoulders. Pouring out a pouf of mousse, she ran her fingers through the silky strands and checked one last time in the mirror. Quite surprised by the make-up's effects, she smiled. *As good as this can get.*

~ * ~

Aron paced. His heart beat too fast. He hadn't intended to interrupt her or kiss her. Raking his fingers through his hair, he closed his eyes and shook his head violently. *You're behaving like an animal.*

He'd only wanted to ask it she preferred white or red wine, but the moment he saw her sitting like some seductive mermaid on the side of the filling tub, he'd lost control.

And that kiss, my God, never had he reacted to a kiss like that before. He needed to get control. The room service arrival gave him a much-needed distraction. The waiter set the table on the balcony, and Aron tipped him generously for his speedy efforts. He shut the door and turned as Mere made her entrance.

Oh shit.

His mouth went dry, and he dropped his hand from the door. He couldn't say a word. The dress, her hair, her eyes—he was in trouble.

The desert air blew through the billowing curtains. Heat and heaviness built in the air, as his blood raced faster through his body.

She walked forward, her steps hesitant.

"Wine?" he asked, backing up.

"Yes, please."

He took the wine from the ice bucket and poured the amber liquid into two glasses. She took the one he handed her and went outside onto the patio. He followed her out.

She leaned against the barricade, and the breeze lifted her hair into a swirling black cloud as she gazed out over the pyramids. He gulped and looked away.

"They're amazing, but we're going to go under them? Are you sure you'll be all right underground? Avia had such a difficult time."

Aron clenched his jaw. "I'm sorry Avia has trouble with it, but I got over my fear when I was younger. It was part of my early training. Clay helped me through the toughest trials, but the work paid off."

Mere angled her body toward him, and he mimicked the movement—he couldn't help it, her body pulled him in. "I just don't want you to suffer. It should be Clay or Ivy doing this, not us."

"You said you wanted to go to the pyramids," he said. "It's okay. Even if it's tough, I'll manage. I've been through worse." So much worse.

He turned away from the view and stared at her. His heart hammered in the building tension. He tucked her hair back, grazing her cheek.

Taking the glass from her shaking hand, he put it on the table.

Unable to stop himself, he needed to taste her again. But he made no move to touch her. He held himself back and closed his eyes. *Don't do it.*

The air moved slightly. He opened his eyes and looked at her lips. She touched them with the tip of her tongue.

He placed his hand on her shoulder. Her skin was silk. He slid his hand up and around the back of her neck and dragged her against him. Her mouth was perfect, soft and warm, and too inviting. She pressed her body against him and he groaned pulling her in tighter.

He gripped her hip and squeezed as shocks went off like fireworks through his body. She wrapped her arms around his neck, stretching up and rubbing against him. His urgent desire to tear off her clothes and stroke every inch of her body overwhelmed him.

Her kiss consumed him, and his body took control as he burned with barely contained fire. He pushed her back against the railing, and leaned in closer, his hand at her neck while the other slid from her waist, burning a trail up until it hovered an inch from her breast. She moaned and the sound penetrated past the ringing in his head. *What are you doing?*

He stopped, drew back, and placed his hand awkwardly on her shoulder staring at her mouth.

"Jesus," he said, shutting his eyes.

~ * ~

Aron backed away and Mere bit back a frustrated scream.

Please don't stop.

He took his wine from the railing and handed hers back, avoiding her questioning stare. He gulped his down, went through the billowing curtains, and returned with the bottle. Not a great sign.

She sipped her wine, and the cold liquid soothed her dry throat. Her heart still hammered, and her body still throbbed. Why had he stopped? She could never have paused in the heat of that. She wanted it, and she'd assumed he did as well. But she'd been wrong and she hated that.

He filled his glass again and held the bottle up. "More?"

She nodded, still disoriented. He topped her glass and placed the bottle back on the table, avoiding her eyes again and leaned against the railing to stare at the pyramids. She drank the sweet dry wine, perfectly crisp, but doing nothing to soothe her frustration. She faced the view as well but shifted a glance his way. His eyes were closed and his head bowed.

"We just met," he said.

Duh. She remembered; it was just yesterday. They'd faced each other across a battlefield, and one of his brethren had shot her. Frankly, she thought she was handling it all rather well. Apparently he was not.

"I'm not behaving in a very gentlemanly manner."

A gentleman was the last thing she wanted. Screw embarrassment. She touched his cheek. He jumped, opening his eyes and faced her. His eyes were cloudy, the dark charcoal swirled with light gray fog. She backed away and withdrew her hand. Her own eyes swirled and she'd seen her sisters' eyes change and move, but the brothers? It was a sign of power.

The wind flowed, and she swung her gaze out to the dark dessert. "Aron? Are you okay?"

Cold air blasted her, knocking her back a step before dying away. He blinked, and his eyes stilled. His smile didn't light his eyes as he straightened and rolled his hunched shoulders back. "Sorry, yes I'm fine. But I think it would be best if we get some rest for tomorrow. Take the master suite. I'll see you in the morning."

Mere almost dropped her glass as Aron walked inside and straight into the smaller bathroom and shut the door.

She gulped down the rest of the wine. *Don't do it, don't, don't, don't. Put it down.*

She turned and placed the glass on the table. Hurling it against a stone wall might have been a splendid but temporary release of her frustration, but it could ruin the image she'd so carefully crafted if he busted her acting so immaturely.

As she walked past the door to the large master suite, the shower was running. She smiled past her scowl. The abrupt end was disappointing, but at least she was having an effect on him. In bed she laid awake tense and cranky before finally falling into nightmares about pyramids and ghost-like figures.

Chapter Sixteen

Asha woke up with a start. Clay was on the ledge above staring through the scope. "Anything interesting?" she asked.

"No, not really. It's strange."

"I'm starving," she mumbled. "Do you have any food in there?"

He reached into his bag and tossed her a large protein bar. She snatched it from the air and saluted him with it. "Ugh, I hate these things."

"Good catch." He dragged his bag closer and peeked inside with his eyebrows raised. "I have a present for you."

"Pardon? A present?" She choked on the mouthful of chocolate, peanut-butter sawdust and tossed the bar aside. "What?"

She frowned, but her smile sprang back on the moment he lifted out her sword, her beautiful, ridiculous, ruby sword.

She gasped. "How? Oh my God, how?"

He passed it over, and she slipped it in and out of her old back-holster. She hugged it.

"I kept it."

"Thank you," she said. It was her old friend, and she hadn't realized how much she missed it until it was back in her hand.

"Where did you get it? I've never seen a sword like that before."

She stiffened a bit, her grin wavered. "I picked it up in Columbia years ago."

"Your guardian, the one Master Miles placed you with? What happened to him?"

So now it was Clay's turn to question her. He gave her a gift, and she was feeling blissful. It was a logical tactic.

"I care about you, and I want to help. Whatever is happening out there, I need you to know, I..." He hesitated then said, "I am worried."

Warmth rolled through her, and she crawled forward and kissed him. The shrill ring cut through her building passion. Clay's phone. Rio. Asha listened, her body already clenched anticipating bad news.

"Christ," Clay said, shaking his head. "Was it Paul?" He paused.

"Yes, she's right here." He passed the phone to her. "It's Avia. She wants to talk to you. Her friend was murdered by the Order last night. He was beaten to death."

Asha grabbed the phone. "Are you okay? What happened?"

Avia's voice was the same, no anger, barely any emotion. "Yes, I'm fine. He was my music teacher."

"I am so sorry. Are you sure you're all right?"

"Yes, I assure you I'm well, but Rio tried to call last night. Clay's phone was off. Are you okay?"

Asha's cheeks warmed. "I didn't know it was off. I was tired so I was sleeping."

"I had to call you. The Order soldiers are not human, or they are, it's not totally clear. I saw their dead evaporate into purple mist. The soldiers are part of their power. They can recycle their armies."

"Are you serious?" Asha glared at Clay, and his eyes widened. "Have you told Ivy and Mere?"

"Yes, Aron already told Mere."

"What do you think?"

"We agreed to continue."

"What? Is that smart?"

"The explanation doesn't change our destiny, just how much we can trust them. For now we need them, but we stay in contact and watch them."

Asha swallowed. Her stomach swooped, and her head spun. *Betrayed.* "Thanks for the heads up." Her grip tightened, squeezing the phone.

"Are you going to be okay?"

"I'll let you know."

Asha still stared at Clay, her rage building like sparks in her belly. He looked down seeming to be cursing under his breath.

She dropped the phone to the moss. "Tell me about the soldiers."

Chapter Seventeen

Avia sat at the table in a fluffy, white hotel robe eating grapefruit slices for breakfast. Rio knocked then came through the adjoining door, fresh from the shower—shirtless in jeans. She had a restless night caught in a tornado of unfamiliar emotions.

Despite her need to get things back under control, there was no call for rudeness. He saved her life back at Armand's, and she could no longer doubt Rio's sincerity. She still had difficulty believing his story about the mist. But after gods, elemental power, and everything else, was Frankenstein's army really that much of a stretch? It only made their enemies more frightening and more powerful. A disposable army was an invincible army.

He appeared genuine, and until he did something to prove otherwise, there was no reason to be unkind. The tension between them was too tight, and she had to relieve it somehow. Perhaps being friendly was the answer.

"Good morning," she said, greeting him as he sat across from her. "Are you going to try Clay again?" They hadn't gotten through last night.

After she and Rio hung up from speaking with Clay and Asha, a soft tap came from the door. Avia stood, but Rio jumped up scowling and stalked past her to the side of the door and peered through the peephole.

He opened the door. "Carlos, good morning."

"Good morning, please come in," Avia said.

Carlos frowned at Rio but stepped inside with a tray. "Good morning, my dear. Here are the things you requested." He held out a shopping bag.

Clothes. "Thank you."

"This was dropped at the front desk for your guest."

Rio grabbed the envelope. "Who left it?"

"A *bella* child about eight or nine-years old."

Avia looked at Rio. He opened the envelope.

"Very suspicious," Carlos said. His laugh was as jovial as a mall Santa Clause.

She smiled at him. "Thank you. We were expecting this, I suspect you are going off duty soon?" She guided him to the door.

"Yes. I have arranged a car for you. Just ask for Amelia Ashburn's car at the valet."

"You are too good to me. Send my love to your family."

He kissed her on both cheeks and left the room with a curt bow to Rio.

She leaned against the door. Carlos had been so wonderful. He was quite possibly the only person left in the real world she had, or could have, a human connection with. She opened the door.

"Carlos?" she called.

Halfway down the hall, he spun and returned to her door with swift steps. "My dear?"

"I've had some trouble recently." She reached out at his rising pallor. "I assure I can handle it, but you are a true friend. Avia is dead. You may or may not hear about it but know that it is not true. I am safe."

He was concerned; she could read that. "That man?"

"No." She smiled. "He is an ally. You don't have to worry about me. Thank you."

Giving him a warm smile, she shut the door.

Rio cleared his throat.

"What is it?" Avia asked.

He extended the small slip of paper. Two numbers were scrawled on it: *41.96667* and *12.66667*. "Is that all?"

"Yes."

"Latitude and longitude?" she asked.

"My guess too." Rio went to his GPS and plugged it in. "Okay, here we go. Yes, you were right. The *Cimitero Accatolico,* but why send us this? It doesn't make sense."

"Fear," she said.

She took her bag into her room and changed into the garments. Much better.

He waited by the door.

"Let's go." She grabbed her shoulder bag and followed him out to exit the building.

A valet pulled the gleaming black Lincoln up and shuffled around to open the door for her. Rio got in and drove them along *via Cai Cestio* to the cemetery.

Inside the grounds she trailed Rio who referred to the GPS for guidance. "Just ahead." He pointed to a flat tombstone.

She leaned over. Percy Bysshe Shelley. *Ozymandias.* *"I met a traveler from an antique land..."*

He looked around. "Where is he?"

Fear. "He won't be coming. I suspect he'll have hidden it nearby." She studied the ground.

"How do you—"

"Here. The ground's been disturbed recently." Her mind spun with options and choices.

Rio went to his knees and drew back a loose flap of grass behind the grave. "There's something buried here."

"Yes, a poet," she said deadpan.

He paused and met her gaze, his grin spreading. "Was that a joke?"

She nodded, surprised, but impressed with herself as he pulled out a package wrapped in plastic with books and scrolls inside. "It can't be this easy." Avia scanned the area, her smile fading. *Where is everyone?*

"I was thinking the same thing. I was prepared for a trap."

"What? Why didn't you tell me?" she snapped. *Whoa easy, you anticipated one too.*

"Relax, it wasn't...well, at least it isn't one yet."

She frowned, but opened her bag and Rio stuffed the package inside. "Let's get back to the hotel."

He strode ahead and scanned the tombstones as they returned to the car.

~ * ~

Clay tensed as if Asha had slapped him. *Shit.*

Of course she would question the soldiers' origins. It was only a matter of time. But she hadn't picked up on it, and he was grateful. Now he was in trouble. *Coward. You should have told her; you should have told her everything.* Asha was a powder keg, and he suspected her reaction to the truth would be explosive.

How do you explain the unexplainable? "I don't really know how it works."

Asha stepped back. "Don't lie to me."

He raised his hands. "You must understand. They weren't unusual to us. We were surrounded by them since childhood."

"What happens after you kill them?"

"Their bodies turn to purple mist," he said, rushing his words. It sounded ludicrous, and it was why he'd kept it from her.

"What are you?"

"No, my brothers and I aren't like them. We're normal. They are like ghosts in flesh form." Her face remained expressionless. He couldn't tell what she was thinking.

"You're not normal!" she shouted.

"I have power, okay yes, that's not normal, but we are not like them."

"How do you know that? Do they know they'll turn into mist?"

"They must obey. We have free will."

"Where do they come from? What are they?"

"Only the Masters know. They are more difficult to kill than men. A headshot is the best way."

"Brains. Basically your army is comprised of obedient zombies."

"It's not my army. They are not zombies, but the mist seems to tie them to the Order. When they die they disappear, and there's a mist."

"How could that not tip you off to something being wrong?" She frowned. "That brutal test?"

"We grew up in it, and we never questioned it."

"Do you not have a brain in your head? What's wrong with you?"

Clay rose. "Look I am sorry for not telling you earlier, but we're with you now. And yes, standing outside and saying it out loud, I understand how unbelievable it sounds, but what more can I say? I am ready to find out how to stop them and help you. We, my brothers and I, see it clearly now. We are on your side."

"This mist…they are the men? But what is it? Their souls? What happens to the mist?"

"It is tied to the Order. It returns and new soldiers are…"

"What?" She paled.

He didn't know what word to use. "Created?"

"Avia said recycled. How could you lie about this?"

"Lie? I haven't lied."

"This is what is hunting me, and you didn't tell me. They're immortal ghosts, or whatever, and you didn't think to give me that information? What kind of game are you playing? This is my life. My sisters' lives."

"Asha."

"No. How do you keep doing this to me? I wanted to trust you. Even against all my instincts, I thought there was a chance I could. But I was wrong, as usual. I don't trust you. I don't trust your brothers or any of this. Read a book. Absence of necessary information is how tragedies occur."

"I'm sorry. I was worried if I told you—"

"How do you expect me to trust you after it took Avia's discovery for you to tell me about something this important?"

"I'm sorry. It was wrong."

"You've lied, manipulated, and controlled everything since the moment you arrived in Colombia. You're a henchman, a thug. You came from nowhere and threw my life into…whatever this is? A life and death battle with ghosts and gods and sacrifice. Jesus, do you hear how it sounds?"

Clay had blown it. He was in trouble. He could see in her face and her posture she was pulling away.

"I can't do this, Clay." She brushed her hair back from her face and rolled her eyes to the roof of the cave. "Jesus, I can't believe I slept with you."

He swallowed a lump forming in his throat. "Asha stop, please calm down."

She went rigid, and her face flushed. Her irises spun red flames. *Uh oh.* "Don't tell me to calm down," she growled through her gritted teeth.

He took an involuntary step back. "I'm sorry. But can you blame me for not telling you?"

"Of course, I can blame you. Honesty first, confession. That's how you build trust. Not by hoping I don't find out."

"Okay, you're right. I'll tell you everything. What do you want to know?"

Asha's eyes stopped spinning, and she uncurled her fists.

Chapter Eighteen

Mere's eyes fluttered open, and she jerked up, looking around the huge room. It all came crashing back: Father Austen, her sisters, the Four, and Aron. Jumping out of bed, Mere strode naked across the room to the shower.

Under the cascading water, her tension eased, and her stuttering heart slowed. The hot water and steam spun around her like a whirlpool, and she lingered for twenty minutes before leaving the bathroom in a fresh fluffy towel.

She dressed in her tan shorts and black tank top—the perfect Lara Croft outfit. She checked out her reflection. If only she had Lara's boobs. Mere smiled at the image and grabbed her running shoes from her pack on the way out.

Aron brought their waiting breakfast trolley onto the balcony where they drank coffee and nibbled on pastries and fruit before packing a bag with the mission's essentials. She was polite and kept the act up. She wasn't going to let him see her so affected by him. Desperation was not an attractive quality.

Miles's notes went in the bag first, followed by maps, water, flashlights, and ropes. Aron also packed a large sketchpad of paper and charcoal, two small hand shovels, two headlamps, two knives, two guns, and finally, two apples. They left the room hand-in-hand and headed to the elevator.

He had sent a text to Marvin Trigger from the lobby before they checked in with the tour group leader. They climbed aboard the fancy tour bus, with air-conditioning blasting, and sat beside huge windows among excited tourists chattering and checking their cameras.

She was relaxed sitting next to him and was more excited than nervous. He held her hand, and his touch passed peace and serenity into her. It was surprising. A different sensation than last night's passion. It evoked safety and security.

They exited the bus with the tourists at the site entrance, and a young man of average height and build approached them and identified himself as Marvin, the dig director. He appeared to have all the necessary laminated credentials clipped to his pocket, and they all shook hands.

Mere studied him. Credentials aside, one could never be too careful. The Order had proven themselves ruthless and resourceful. He appeared to be in his mid-thirties, handsome, but with shrewd eyes. He fit the dig director vibe well in his khaki uniform, covered in a light layer of dust. Even his glasses had a brown film covering them.

The tourists' excited energy stoked her blood, and it flowed faster through her body.

"All right then," Marvin whispered as the tour leader led them into the dark pyramid. "We will go with the group then split off once everyone is occupied."

In the King's Chamber, while the visitors were busy oohing and aahing, Marvin inclined his head and drew them away from the group, past a wooden barricade to a descending path. They took another tunnel, going deeper, leaving the tourists' din fading behind them until it was silent.

A gate and another barricade blocked the end of the tunnel. He fumbled with his keys before opening the lock with a click. They trailed him into the darkness, and Mere's concern for Aron rose, praying the dark confinement wasn't too difficult.

The tunnel narrowed even further, and they had to hunch over to navigate the tiny passage. Even she started to freak a bit, but they finally emerged into a large cavernous room with a crudely made bridge, sturdy enough to push a wheelbarrow of supplies across.

Marvin gestured. "Cross the bridge and follow the passage. You will find what you're looking for at the back, through the wall. Be quick. I'll wait here and make sure no one discovers you. The dig is on a break. You won't be able to remove the tablets; they are far too large. Gather as much as you can with shadings. The tour will be leaving the pyramid in forty minutes. It is all the time you have. Now go, and again, please hurry."

"Thank you," Mere said, taking his hand and squeezing it. It was cold and clammy, and she had to fight not to snatch hers away.

Aron seemed to be all right, staring into the dark. He was steady, and she took it as a sign he was handling the confined surroundings. She led the way to the bridge, and they moved across to the tunnel on the other side. They had to crouch again, but she shuffled forward, determined to locate their treasure.

As they crept through the tunnel, Aron paused behind her, and Mere did the same, halting her pace to close the gap.

"This passage is tiny so we must be close," she whispered, trying to relieve the tension

"Yes." His voice was tight, so maybe he was having trouble after all.

She walked a bit farther, and the passage curved and opened a bit. Wheelbarrows and tools lined the walls, and she paused again for Aron to catch up. She waited and strode beside him, impressed with how well he handled it. The place was suffocating even to her.

"There it is, right ahead." He pointed, and his finger shook just a bit.

Rock remains and debris leaned against a wall with large holes in it. The broken wall showed another cavern behind it, and they climbed through to cross to the opening in the back wall. Mere slipped into the smaller chamber; it was only about ten by ten feet.

Aron would have to bend, but he didn't hesitate and climbed in behind her, taking the paper and charcoal from the bag. Bricks and paving stones were spread across the ground and resting against the wall.

"How are you doing?" she asked.

"I'm fine. I'll get the stone shadings, and you take the pictures." He handed her the camera and bent to rub the stones with charcoal. He didn't have to tell her to hurry. His tense body said it all.

Taking the camera, she crouched closer and snapped a picture of the first stone. The flash blinded them both.

"Sorry. I'll warn you next time so you can close your eyes." She rushed to get the remaining photos. There wasn't much time, and she needed them to be clear.

He worked fast, shading the stones of interest and storing them carefully in plastic bags within the pack.

Something clinked outside the hole in the first chamber. "Did you hear that?"

He didn't even stir. He was hunched down and rigid. She stood and faced the opening. Movement outside, like a scuff and a strange popping noise. A dart hit her in the chest. "What the—?"

It stung a moment, and heat flushed through her. She twisted, searching behind her for Aron's help and caught a hazy glimpse of him standing and staring past her at the cave entrance. She didn't understand, but she couldn't connect to another thought before she fell and darkness washed over her.

~ * ~

Asha turned to face Clay. His green eyes almost glowed at her.

The sight had an unwelcome, but sobering effect. If he was providing an opportunity for interrogation, she had to take it. She managed to separate her feelings of betrayal and anger, her own stupidity and embarrassment, from her desire to know more, to learn everything she could.

She focused on her subject. "How did you find me?"

"I knew you before I found you. Colombia wasn't the first time I saw your face. Growing up…" He paused, running his fingers up to his temple combing them through his hair. "You were in my dreams."

She scoffed. *He can't think I'll fall for this now.*

"Seriously, hear me out. I had recurring nightmares of you burning. It was why I couldn't follow my orders and kill you at your base. I was half in love with you before you even walked through that cell door in your compound."

"Give me a break."

"Really, I am telling the truth. I loved you before I even met you. I love you now, Asha."

"That is bullshit. How did you find me?"

"Master Miles gave me your location as *la Reina Guerrera*. I didn't know you were anything else."

"Who is Miles?"

He was silent.

"Who is he? Who are you?"

"As Miles said, he and Heath are brothers. The Grand Master is their father. Miles was cold and cruel. Heath too, but Heath seemed more human. Miles was the strict one, and he used some harsh methods to help us control and strengthen our power, but it worked, and we are stronger because of it. The Grand Master frightened us. He had more brutal designs on our power." Clay's eyes shadowed, and he clenched his jaw again. "I don't know anything about their mother. There are no women in the Order."

"My mother?"

"They kept women as cleaning and cooking staff but there are no women inducted as Order members."

Her growl was internal.

"How did you justify your world to yourself? How could you not question the Order and everything about it?"

"We were not part of the faith, but the security side. We were on the outside. They were waiting for us… to be ready, but if I had known what they were after, I would never have…"

Asha was going to scream. He wasn't giving her anything. "This is crap. I want to know what you were up to behind those walls. I'm not stupid. I want to know the Order's plan and how you and your brothers are being used to carry it out.”

Chapter Nineteen

Avia glanced up as she drew the plastic-wrapped contents from her bag. Rio walked in through the connecting door that now seemed to remain open.

She unwrapped the plastic and scrolls tumbled off a pile of three books. The one on top looked like a faded, leather journal, engraved with a symbol. Ice chilled and prickled her skin. Her mind clicked and churned through memories, trying to track it. She studied it; the design of four triangles pointing inward, their tips touching was familiar somehow.

"How do you know that symbol?" he asked.

"I don't," she whispered. Her cold, physical reaction to a symbol she recognized, but had never seen, was unusual. "But it means something."

"It's the ancient symbol of the Order."

Avia took the book to the couch and flipped through it. It was a diary from the 1800s. "It was written by a previous Grand Master. He wrote about the Four." It was exactly the book they needed. She read the first entry.

"I'm going to order some lunch."

Avia nodded, distracted and already deep in the mind of a former Grand Master. The author wrote with a fearful tone. He was forbidden to keep any written record, but when the Four had shown themselves on the eve of his inauguration as Grand Master, he had been terrified of the true force he'd worshiped. The Four were kept vague and metaphorical in all the teachings, and with their presence, he questioned his faith for the first time.

The author wrote of four immortal gods with evil magic—single-minded in their hunger for power and revenge—and they existed only to be worshipped and hunt the goddess sisters to gain their gifts. He acknowledged the blood on his hands, the blood of the guilty and the witches he had helped to slay, but there were others—many others who had showed no sign of guilt. His fear alone kept him loyal, and he did the job that was required, but kept the diary as a passive testimony of his guilt.

She dropped it in disgust, wiping her fingers on her skirt. She went back to the table and looked over the scrolls and the other books.

Rio hung up the phone and stood beside her, and she fought the urge to shift away. His presence was difficult for her. After being on her own, it was unnerving.

"Well?" he asked.

"I've just started. I need to keep reading." She passed him a book, carefully avoiding his touch. "You can help."

He took the book as if it was a dirty sock. "Really? Homework?"

"Yes, read."

She pushed aside her suspicions about how easy it had been to discover their haul and focused on the first scroll. "It's all here," Avia said, frowning. "Everything."

"Oh yeah?"

She read the scroll, translating for Rio in case he didn't speak Latin. He'd said they were educated by the Order, so he probably did. Their ilk reeked of Latin speakers.

He stared with one dark eyebrow arched.

"Four brothers, there's no indication when they lived, were obsessed with the natural elements and according to this were the very first alchemists. They hungered to harness the power of earth, air, fire, and water, and managed with faith and magic to master them. They used the elements to cause destruction and chaos. Motivated by greed, they yearned to live forever, manipulating the elements to control the universe.

"They succeeded and created an elixir of life in order to achieve immortality, laughing at Mother Nature and her laws—they gained more and more power—never dying. With control over the four elements, they desired but one thing—control over the fifth—the Quintessence. Obsessed with controlling the natural world with their supernatural power, the magical fifth element eluded them."

Rio scowled. "Magical fifth element?"

"I don't know." She scanned further down. "Okay, Mother Nature, the true ruler of the elements, sought her own balance against the Four's imbalance. The first women with power were born. The sisters faced the Four as young girls and came close to defeating them. The Four experienced something new for them—a threat. They feared the sisters' power might surpass their own and that their natural gifts could defeat their learned ones.

"So, they hunted the girls, sacrificing the first set of sisters with their dark magic. With that sacrifice, they gained enough power in the aftermath to cast one very important spell. If the sisters had reached their age of power and were united, the Four could locate them. Since then, every time the Four succeeded and killed the sisters, their power increased." She put down the scroll.

"Whatever this quintessence was, it was the Four's goal?" Rio asked.

She picked up another scroll. "It was mentioned in here; I just scanned it. It's described as the life force. It can only be achieved by the balance and unity of the four elements. It sounds more like a metaphor than something real."

"We thought the Four were a metaphor. If it is something Miles had us searching for, then we should just go with it."

"Okay, so if we can find, or achieve this quintessence, it might help us? Is it possible to use a life force as a weapon?"

Rio stood. "We need to tell the others what we've found."

~ * ~

Asha was ready to pop, and Clay knew he had to be very careful. If he didn't give her enough she was gone. But if he gave her too much she'd kill him before she took off.

She looked away, but she still listened. He had to confess. She may hate him more for it, but she wouldn't accept anything but the truth. Plus it erased the risk of more unhappy discoveries in the future.

"Since we were children," he started, "the Masters continually pushed us to achieve higher levels of power. Sometimes they were harsh, but we were always together. We always had each other for help. I'm sorry you didn't have that. Cole had a hard time with his power. I imagine it was even more difficult for you considering your strength."

"Get to the point."

"We were warned there would be others with power. They would be stronger, and they would kill us. We also believed they would be brothers, not sisters. We've been preparing for the fight since we were old enough to train."

"You knew about us?"

"No, we knew there would be others like *us*, who would threaten our power and defeat us if we faced them. It was foretold. Master Miles and Master Heath pushed us to prepare us, but they also had me searching for the others. I started years ago. I used my power to try and find elemental energy."

She dropped her head. "You just said Miles gave you my location."

"No, you were an accident. But once I met you, I found your

sisters." He cringed.

Her head snapped up. "The hits, the battle, Avia's cabin." She narrowed her eyes. "You weren't reuniting me. You were going to kill my sisters."

He paused, swallowing his fear. *You're going to lose her.* "Yes."

~ * ~

"You *were* going to kill us?" Asha had to repeat it because there was no way he'd said yes. "You weren't reuniting me with them?"

"No, Alex had me take you out of the Order, but my ultimate objective was to kill the targets. I assumed they were your sisters, though I wasn't specifically told. I couldn't have guessed you'd never met them before."

"And you were going to do it?"

"I thought I was. My brothers knew nothing. To them it was just another mission."

"Oh, just another mission?" A slow burn flickered low in her body.

He'd admitted it. He had ulterior motives. Her vision tinted red.

She turned away, closing her eyes. *Don't look at him, breathe deep.* "You were going to take innocent lives because you were told they were a threat?"

"I couldn't do it. You saw. I didn't strike one blow against you or your sisters."

"I'm leaving, I'm calling my sisters and telling them to abort this ridiculous alliance. I've been so stupid." She spun around, and her rage poured over her. All of it, everything she'd held in since the beginning was going to come bursting out and he would pay the price.

He raised his hands. "It's too dangerous. You can't unite with your sisters or you'll draw the Four."

"Why? Because that's what Miles says? Bullshit. You killed my friends, kidnapped me, drugged me, tracked my sisters, hunted us, and used a web of lies to separate us." Her hair fluttered as the flames rippled over her arms. "I'm done."

"You can't—"

She narrowed her eyes at him. "Stop telling me what I can't do," she screamed. "Give me your phone. Right now!"

Clay's puppy dog look wasn't working, but just to keep her rage heightened she looked at the ceiling again. The last thing she wanted in the throes of her temper was his emerald-eyed spell calming her anger.

He pulled the phone out just as it rang in his hand. Asha's stomach dropped.

"It's Aron." He answered. "Whoa…what?" Clay's body was

stiff, his face pale.

Cold icy dread covered her anger, and the flames puffed out. Something was wrong.

"Get the others first. We're at the cave." He hung up the phone.

"What happened?"

"It's Mere. She's gone. They were ambushed at the pyramids. They got her."

Terror froze Asha where she stood. Memories of her imprisonment returned. *No.* "We have to get her now. We can intercept them before they get her inside." She spun to the exit as rocks shifted and crashed over the entrance, drowning them in pitch blackness.

She called her flames to flicker from her fingertips lighting the cave. "What are you doing? Open it."

"You can't charge out rashly and take on the Order alone. We need reinforcements."

Would she ever trust anyone again?

"Open it" Flames rolled over her hands rippling up her arms.

"No."

"I will blast it open, and you'll go with it." Asha turned and fired at the entrance. Fire rushed over the stones heating the cave and casting it in a red scarlet glow.

"You might not want to burn out our weapons. We're going to need them." His voice was calm, detached.

She turned back. He looked like the soldier he was, cold, hard, and evil. Vines shot from the dirt and wrapped around each wrist and pulled them together. Asha laughed. Flames burned the vines away.

"Is that the best you can do?" She lunged forward. *He's the enemy. He's the enemy.* She chanted it over and over as she pushed aside sentimental feelings and slipped into soldier mode, her rage and fear for Mere in full control of her actions.

Asha attacked, drawing her sword and hit dirt, soft dirt. She spun and kicked, but she struck more loose soil rising in a pillar. Stabbing her sword forward—more rock. Her sword spun out of her hand, but she turned and kicked out again. Sand exploded into clouds. The columns rose too fast to get through, knocking her back but not hurting her.

Her inability to connect with her target drove her mad, and she flailed, trying in vain to hit him and strike one blow. It was no use; he was tiring her out by using her own temper against her.

"Asha, calm down." He grabbed her shoulder.

She wrenched away. "They have her. You have to help me get her now, you don't understand. They hurt me and they'll hurt her too." Tears filled her eyes.

She pulled back, sent the fire out in a wave and flooded the entire cave with burning heat. Turning, she rushed through the fire to the entrance, clawing at the stone. Pulling the flames to her hand to focus the heat. She held her palm against the stone. White-hot fire cut through like a blowtorch.

"I don't want to hurt you Asha, but I can't let you go out there alone."

"As if you could stop me. I'm stronger than you."

"The others are coming to us. We will re-group and go in with a plan."

"You have me trapped outside the Order. You have Mere on her way. Separate us and weaken us. I knew it was wrong to believe you. This has been the plan all along. I should have killed you when I had the chance."

"When you're rational, you'll understand this is the smarter plan. I said I don't want to hurt you, but if you force me, I will do what I have to, to save your life."

"Hurt me? How? You disgusting, arrogant zombie—" She threw her hands out, but a rocky wall rose defending him just in time.

Her blasts were weak. They hit the stone leaving only a scorched black mark. She blasted fireball after fireball until the wall was nothing but smoking rubble.

Enraged and fearful for Mere, Asha wanted to kill him, but as she prepared for the final blow, she froze. An icy chill returned and crept over her, and she lowered her hands fell. She couldn't do it.

She choked. If she couldn't hurt him… The dream in the cave came back to her. She was compromised.

Could she be so stupid as to be in love with her enemy? She shook her head. *No.* It was lust, just lust.

Or was it love? It had to be. Otherwise she would be able to finish him. Writers described love like this… but it was worse… and better. *Damn it, no.*

She raised her hands. *Do it. End him.*

Clay shifted then threw something small at her. It stuck to her chest, and the flames on her hands went out, leaving the cave dark. What the hell?

She touched it as a numbing agent sped through her limbs. She pulled a tiny ball from her skin. Prickly on one side, smooth on the other, tiny hooks grabbed at the tip of her finger. Her head spun. *No.*

She swayed and went down.

Chapter Twenty

Ivy was in the kitchen grinding herbs for tea to help boost Miles's immune system. He was asleep upstairs in the large master bedroom of the safe house. He was out of danger and healing exceptionally well. Her healing ability was good, but not that good. She suspected her connection with her sisters had something to do with it.

They'd left Avia's cabin as soon as Master Miles regained consciousness. He'd insisted it was better to risk moving than to stay. To prove his point he'd stood and walked to Avia's truck himself. They drove to Nice, where Miles had a secret townhouse, and he settled upstairs. He had slept there on and off, since.

Ivy studied her herbs. They were close to dust. *Oops.* She was too aware of Cole, sitting behind her in a wingback chair in the large living room.

The chair creaked, and his gaze burned through her back.

She turned around and met his eyes, staring at him with unflinching focus. For the last three days, she had tended to Miles and kept the subject of any conversation with Cole on Miles and his needs.

She'd postponed her interrogation because she had to be smart and strategic. She only had one chance. Their lives depended on the vital information these two might have, but as secret societies went, their members weren't really known for spilling details upon request. Her sisters needed her to be alert and seek signs of lies, betrayals, or hidden agendas. She'd observed Cole since her sisters left, but to her frustration, he'd revealed nothing.

His hair was striking, black with thin veins of red and gold streaking through it like lava moving under the cracked crust of charred earth. His eyes were similar to Asha's, so dark they were black. He was beautiful, but she'd seen plenty of beautiful things.

The floorboard creaked behind her, the only sign Cole had left his chair and made it across the living room and into the kitchen.

Here we go. It's time to get some answers.

"How is he?" he asked.

"Why don't you ask him yourself?"

He was as silent as his earlier movements.

"You haven't gone in there once. Your only interaction with him was while we drove here."

Cole shrugged. "You seem to have it under control."

"I'm surprised you don't have more questions for him." Ivy studied him out of the corner of her eye, and he shifted, standing stiff and rigid.

"I don't think I can face him."

His response surprised her. She hadn't expected such honesty.

"It's all so unbelievable. I don't know how he…how they managed to hide the Order's true motivations, everything. We were idiots. We never questioned it or the cult mentality." He rubbed his face, running his hand around the back of his neck and shaking his head.

She forced herself to be unmoved by his quite possibly feigned ignorance. "They managed it somehow. Miles said it—they—were invested in you. They must've assumed you were no threat and could help their cause. Otherwise, they would've killed you too, right?" She paused. "But for some reason only the women were hunted and killed."

Cole frowned. "What are you saying?"

"What I'm saying *is*, they had you under their roof, but they raised you and educated you, while they continued to hunt us and all the others who came before. The girls *you* saw."

A muscle jumped in his jaw. "They hid that from us. They were our family. I could never imagine anything so dark as killing babies or young girls. It's biblical in its ferocity. I'm sick—I can't tell you what it does to me knowing I served them, but I have a new purpose. I'm on your side and your sisters' side."

Ivy snapped, "If Asha hadn't made it on that jet and been on the battlefield you would have killed us."

He shook his head.

She continued, "Mere was shot. Any one of those bullets could have killed us."

"I told you we are on your side. How could you doubt it after what happened yesterday, what I saw them do to you? I was there too. How could you doubt we would want to join you and help you fight?"

Ivy listened to his deep voice, trying to pick up something, just a hint of nervousness or dishonesty. He walked over, standing behind her. She waited.

"Let's be straight, shall we?"

"I am being straight," she said, whipping around to face him.

Cole held her gaze a moment then backed away. He seemed

cautious, concerned.

"There is something else we need to discuss," he said changing the subject. "Asha and Clay."

True. She'd seen the connection between them on the battlefield. It was Asha's warning that stopped Ivy from killing Clay and his brothers. Asha's tone had been frightened then she'd said she loved him.

Ivy had been shocked by her slip of the tongue at the time, but after Mere and Aron and the heat Ivy felt around Cole she was concerned.

"Do you feel it?" he asked.

Yes. She frowned. "Yes, and we need to know why."

"You saw the others. There's something going on here. I'm uncomfortable with these pair-ups. When Clay mentioned leaving the Order, I had serious doubts. Going against the Order is an automatic death sentence, but the urge to find you overwhelmed them. I don't trust it."

"*You* don't trust it? How do you think I feel?"

"There's something deeper, far beyond attraction," he said.

The phone rang, interrupting them, and Ivy answered it, grateful for a break to catch her breath. It was Rio.

He told Ivy they had a lead but assured her it wasn't necessary to wake Master Miles. She hung up and returned to the kitchen, smiling. "They've found something promising."

Cole and Ivy switched on Miles's computer and opened the e-mail with Avia's translated excerpts from the scrolls.

Chapter Twenty-One

Mere reached out until her fingertips touched a smooth, cold stone wall. She recoiled in shock. *Where am I?*

She wasn't where she should be. She was alone. Her eyes adjusted, and she could see the small cell's layout. She was on a metal slab on the left side of a small room. The sink and toilet were on the wall to the right of the door. Something was very wrong; she was in trouble.

She touched her fingers to the wall again. It was cold and moist—clammy. Dampness spread over her skin and seeped inside her. Turning away, she wiped her hand on her shorts.

There was no water—yes there *was*, she'd just touched it. But she couldn't connect to it.

She'd been in a cave, under the pyramid, and someone shot her with a dart, a drugged dart. Aron. The door unlocked. She prayed she could take this one out, clear her way, and maybe she could escape.

The door swung open, and a man switched on the overhead light. The harsh fluorescent glare flickered before momentarily blinding her. He was in his late forties, wore black robes, and scowled.

She was at the Order.

She tried her power anyway.

Nothing happened. No matter how much she tried, she couldn't sense the water in his body, and she couldn't freeze him. She sat up, drew her knees to her chest then searched again—nothing. Asha had warned them that something in this place blocked their power.

"There is no use. You are powerless here," he said.

"I am never powerless."

"Which one are you?"

"Water."

"What's your name?"

"Mere."

"Well, Mere, my name is Heath. *Master* Heath."

"I've heard of you, you're Miles's brother. What happened to Aron?"

He didn't answer her.

"Why are you after us? What have we ever done to you?" Her fury poured out of her. Anger overtook the fear, and she was thankful for it. "We don't want any part of this. We didn't ask for this. Let me go and leave us alone."

"No, no, that won't be happening. But I am curious. How much do you know?"

Mere glared, praying, though she knew it was useless, for his death.

He studied her. "Yes, I am Miles's brother. I'm your Uncle Heath, and I truly regret our family connection. But it *is* your destiny to die. And yes, the fact that you're my brother's daughter does make it a bit awkward. Your mother was a lovely woman. We were friends, and I cared about her very much."

"Miles? Yeah, right."

"He didn't tell you? That surprises me. How else did he get you to trust him?"

She glared. *It's a lie.*

"It's true. Why else would a Master of the Order defect from his duty? He separated you and continues to protect you—because he is your father. But it changes nothing. You and your sisters, and now Miles too, will have to die."

He smiled. "Of course, I understand your confusion. How could you, or anyone for that matter, really accept the importance of their death? Well, not these days anyway. As long as you live, you and your sisters shift the balance we must provide."

Was he serious? "I'm so sorry to tell you this, Uncle, but you're insane. You're a cult leader, nothing more, and you've had way too much Kool-Aid. I don't know how you and those monsters you serve could believe this, but they are ancient, primitive, and wrong. We are no threat to you or to anyone."

"Oh, my dear niece, *you* are wrong. Hundreds of thousands have fallen at the sisters' hands over the centuries. We've been cleaning up their messes since the beginning. You are the raw elements personified. You are powerful and very destructive, ticking time bombs, each and every one of you. The scars on this earth are the proof of what I say."

"What do you mean, *scars*?"

"I'm afraid you won't get a chance to find out." He shook his head. After exiting, he locked the cell door.

Mere exhaled. She rushed to the sink and turned the tap, dipping her fingers into the stream, touching the water as it ran over her skin. Searching for the smoothness, usually comforting, but it was different, it was heavier, without energy. Her stomach dropped, and she crumpled to the floor sobbing for her peace—her element.

She wiped away her tears. Okay, she was alone and imprisoned without her power, but she wasn't powerless. She would *not* be a victim in this dark and cold place. She was strong, and there wasn't much that was darker or colder than the deepest water that ruled her element.

She'd always had to fight against her dark side, because like the ocean, it could be deep, black, and fathomless. Since the day her worst nightmare came true and her family had died all around her, she had been forced to battle against her inner demons. She'd witnessed Asha's guilt while she shared her story. She had opened up, but none of them had shared their stories. Mere's own guilt surrounded the day her power reached full strength.

She closed her eyes, letting the anger fill her and took strength from her rage. Jarred from her thoughts, she opened her eyes as the wall cracked in the silent cell and she bolted up. The floor around her erupted into huge flames reaching the rocky ceiling. The heat burned her skin, and she coughed and choked, gripping her throat. The flames crackled, and her vision blurred, the heat cooking her until her skin turned red and blistered.

The shock of a hundred thousand volts blasted her, and her body jerked hard enough to break her back. Cuts from invisible daggers sliced her skin, and the fire kept burning. Too much. Unbearable pain pulsed with the closing darkness. But there was no peace in the dark. She suffered the visions of sacrifice, the past sisters, and their brutal murders playing over and over.

Mere didn't want to see it and closed her eyes, but it played in her mind and ripped her heart apart. Again, it was throbbing pain and crushing fear with each vision, and she begged for the finality of her own death just to stop it. One ending finally fading to peace.

The visions stopped, she was back in the cell, the fire still circling the slab, burning her. "Just kill me!" Her shriek tore her scorched throat.

A low chuckle echoed behind the flames, and she forced her eyes open, panting and stifling another scream.

"You remember us, don't you?" His voice was cold, deep, and familiar.

She stiffened as the flames parted, and the Four walked through. Her vision blurred, but they approached, and she cringed and fought backing away. One translucent, smoky hand reached out toward her. *No, no, no.*

She leaned back, but he grasped her throat squeezing until tears filled her eyes, and she gasped and gagged. She shook in his grip, repulsed and disgusted at its touch, fighting and clawing at the twisted white hand.

He lifted her up to his hooded face, and she stared into the hood through tear-filled eyes. It was Cole then Aron. Aron's beautiful face twisted in hate and rage choking her. "You will die, but not yet. When we are through with you, you will greet death gratefully."

Mere's heart broke. The chance he had escaped and found her sisters was how she'd kept it together. But he was there with his brothers hurting her. Her sisters wouldn't be coming for her. Asha was right. They'd been fooled.

The brothers were the Four. "Leave us alone, please," she pleaded.

Aron tossed her back, and she landed on the slab, her burned skin tearing and she rolled stifling her screams.

He laughed. It was colder, dismissive, evil, but definitely his. She couldn't breathe. Were her sisters there too and trapped?

Mere had trouble thinking it through, past the anguish, but one thing was obvious, she was dead anyway. Her sisters, her brand-new sisters—she prayed they were safe and free before she lunged toward the fire.

Before the fire closed around her Aron's hand gripped her around the calf and dragged her until she was back on the slab. Shackles floated up and clamped around her neck, her wrists, and her feet securing her to the metal shelf.

"You will not die yet." He bent, his eyes swirling again but they were frightening and hate filled. His lip curled in a snarl, and he pressed his pointy, white withered finger into her chest.

It pierced her, sharp as any needle and she screamed, the agony too much. He stared into her eyes and pushed deeper, touching her heart with ice.

She stopped screaming, stared into eyes of a man she'd hopelessly fallen for, and pleaded, "Please, just let me die." She whispered the words, as darkness dragged at her until she finally passed out.

~ * ~

"Jesus Clay, did you have to knock her out?"

Ivy?

There were fingers on Asha's throat checking her pulse.

"You didn't see her. She went nuts. She didn't believe you were coming, and she wouldn't wait. I had to stop her from charging the wall." Clay's voice.

"Maybe you should have been more honest. I suspect Asha has more difficulty with trust than any of us."

Avia?

"Asha, Asha wake up. Are you okay?"

Ivy? She was there. Asha could hear her voice through the buzzing. She opened her eyes. She was still in the cave, but Ivy was there. He told her the truth. "I'll be fine once I can kill Clay."

Ivy turned. "She's pissed. I don't blame her."

"Mere."

"We're going to get her now. We just need a plan." Ivy squeezed her hand.

Asha stared at Clay across the cave. He handed the bags of weapons to his brothers. He drugged her. Like Father Sean, he couldn't control her, and he couldn't beat her, so he'd put her down like an animal.

Not now.

Her anger was there, but it wasn't nearly as paramount as her fear for Mere. "How long have I been out?"

Clay nodded to Rio and Cole, who took the bags to the mouth of the cave.

"Clay?" she snapped.

He glanced up but didn't meet her eyes. "Twelve hours."

An inner scream built and erupted, splitting her skull. Her brain was going to explode with the screeching, buzzing, and swirling cries inside her head. Twelve hours? She had been locked in that place for twelve hours. An image of her face floated before her, her mouth opened wide in a scream of pain and terror.

They were all so calm. How could they be so calm? They didn't know. They didn't know what they'd do to her. Rage and fear for Mere consumed Asha, and her mind ran far away.

No. Keep it together. She needs you. She needs all of you.

Clay was beside her, holding her shoulders as tears filled her eyes. "I'm so scared. They're going to hurt her."

"We're going now."

She needed him and his brothers for what was coming. "Will you help me save her from these assholes?"

"Nothing would make me happier."

Rio came inside with Cole. Miles followed…and he was on his feet.

"Excuse me, but how are you better?" Asha asked. His recovery was impressive, almost miraculous.

"Ivy's power—"

"Fine. Aron?" she asked cutting him off. That wasn't important right now.

He stood, rigid against the wall by the opening.

"What happened?"

"We were darted," he said, running his hands through his hair. "When our guide and I woke, Mere was gone."

"What do you think?" Asha asked Avia and Ivy.

"We believe him," Ivy said.

"We must go in without power," Avia said.

"Our power works," Rio said.

"You're not as strong as us. We need *ours*." Asha's temper flashed.

"Their power will have to be enough," Avia said. "If they go in and draw the Order soldiers into a fight, we can get Mere. We'll have to see how the rest of it goes." Avia was her strongest ally and a decent strategist.

Miles and Clay answered Asha's rapid-fire questions about the Order's security and boundaries and within minutes they had the beginning of a plan.

"What the hell. It's a suicide mission, but it will be exciting," Rio said. He cocked his gun and winked at Avia.

"Clay can you get us in?" Asha asked.

"Yes."

She spun. "We're going. Now."

Chapter Twenty-Two

In position outside the Order, Asha spied the two guards at the gate. She shifted her rifle and took aim, listening for the others' voices through the earpiece.

"I have it," Cole said.

"Got it," Rio said.

"Got him," Aron said, almost growling.

"Okay," Asha said to Clay. "Three, two, one."

Zombie brains.

She fired with four other muffled shots in the distance. "Again, three, two, one." She raised her gun and found the guard in the gate tower. "Again, three, two, one." And twelve men died.

She ran after Clay and Miles toward the wall. The others joined them while Clay pushed the barrier until it cracked and opened.

They entered a small, walled garden. Something so beautiful and serene was starkly out of place on the dark eerie grounds. It was like finding a bright, multicolored orchid in a muddy swamp.

Ivy gasped. The wall and the entire Order only appeared to them as they walked through it. Magic cloaked it until they crossed over the boundary.

"She's on the lowest level," Clay whispered.

Asha trailed him, and her sisters followed her. Cole and Rio were in the back guarding the rear. They walked through the grass, beside a small pond until they reached the far wall.

"Okay everyone, here we go. Be prepared and remember the Four will know once you have Mere."

Clay parted the wall, and they slipped through. They had to pause behind the door before he opened it and brushed the tapestry aside. "It's clear. Go."

Cole, Aron, Rio, and Miles dashed down the left hallway. Cole hesitated, the last to go before he went, covering his brothers.

Asha was right behind Clay, and he led them in the opposite direction to find Mere. They slid along the wall to the door. Clay opened it, and they all spiraled into the Order's depth.

Traveling the stone steps lower and lower Asha's steps got less graceful. Deep underground, the bottom dungeon corridor was the same level where she'd stayed.

Clay stiffened. "Shit," he whispered before bolting down the hallway.

She sprinted after him. He was already opening the wall of the last cell.

"No," she gasped, shoving past him and going through the hole.

The entire room was on fire, but she couldn't control it, and she couldn't get past it. It was too hot, and it burned her.

"Clay," she screamed. She had to back out of the cell.

Mere was laying on the slab, limp, eyes closed, and Asha's breath caught. Her sister's skin was burned and bloody. Clay ran through the flames, ripped the chains from the wall and lifted her. He shielded her with his body the best he could, bending over as he carried her out.

He laid her down outside the cell, and the flames flashed out. Asha covered her mouth to stop her screams. Mere's skin was blistered red with deep cuts everywhere. She had a black stab wound on her chest. Iron shackles still gripped her neck, wrists, and ankles.

Ivy seemed to hesitate to touch her, but she repeated her name, trying to wake her. "She's breathing, but she's unconscious."

Avia passed Ivy her trench coat, but with the chains, they couldn't get it on. Anything on Mere's skin would cause her pain.

She was really hurt.

Asha remembered the torture, and seeing Mere like this snapped something inside her. Her heart? Her control? She didn't care. The monster inside raged, clawing at her barriers.

She opened the gates. "Carry her. We're going," she snapped, already moving.

Gunfire erupted in the distance. Clay draped the coat over Mere and picked her up. Asha strode ahead, and he guided her toward the Order's center.

She growled as the first soldiers finally appeared, coming around the corner. While she didn't have her power, she still had her skills and her weapons. She sprinted forward drawing her sword, and attacked first slicing one through as another fired, and Clay spun, shielding Mere.

Avia raised her gun, shot and hit one. Asha's momentum kept her spinning, and she threw out her left arm chopping the last one across the throat. Withdrawing her sword from her first victim, she stabbed it down in an arc and twisted it in the second falling man as his head hit the ground. Ivy ran up.

"The gunfire will bring more," Asha said handing Ivy one of the soldiers' guns. "Clay needs to carry Mere. You need to help us shoot our way out of here." Asha severed the throats of the guards to be safe. "Aim for their heads."

Ivy took the gun, meeting Asha's eyes. They were fierce, glowing green. She nodded.

Asha picked up the rest of the guns. Clay was already armed and occupied. She handed one to Avia and slipped one over her head and one in her waistband. He told her where to go, and she took the lead again. Around the corner, three more guards ambushed them.

Avia came close to losing her head as a bullet hit the wall beside her ear. Asha responded instantly, blowing the shooter away with a bullet through his visor and between his eyes. Ivy hit one of them in the chest, but before Asha got the last one, he managed to take a shot at Clay. He grunted as blood splattered the shining black wall and the whole building shook, almost knocking them to the ground.

"I'm hit," Clay yelled. His leg buckled, and he fell to one knee still holding Mere and didn't drop her.

"What was that?" Avia shouted her eyes wide.

"It just grazed me. I'm fine." He stood, shaking and limping on. "Let's go."

Ivy ran to him, tearing off her coat. Another two soldiers darted at them, and Asha burst forward drawing her guns as she ducked under their assault, sliding forward on her knees and shooting each one in the forehead. The bodies dropped as more rounded the corner. She was in soldier mode again and acting on autopilot.

Ivy knelt before Clay and pulled her belt around his thigh. "Can you walk?"

He nodded and stalked forward protecting her sister as she charged ahead, free to expel her rage on those who would destroy them.

He pointed down the hallway toward two huge, guarded doors. Asha shot twice and the guards fell before they could draw their guns. She yanked the heavy door open then entered an enormous room, trailed by Avia, Ivy, and Clay. The timing was perfect. The door across the room opened at the same time, and Aron, Rio, and Cole walked in, followed by Miles.

"Traitor," the Grand Master yelled from the dais, jumping to his feet. "Kill them!"

The guards, standing on either side of the dais, raised their guns, but Aron and Rio fired, killing the Order men before they could aim.

Asha charged into the room, kicking another guard and knocking away the gun he was raising. She swept his legs out from under him and when he hit the floor, she finished him off by stomping on his windpipe and shooting him in the head.

Cole shot the last guard in the forehead before he could touch the trigger. It was all over in seconds.

"Clay?" Aron called across the room.

"She's alive." He answered the unasked question.

"Jesus," Rio said.

The Grand Master staggered back, falling into his chair. Clay placed Mere beside Ivy. The sound of her chains clanged and echoed in the huge room. Blood still dripped down his leg, but he stood in front of Mere, protecting her from the men on the dais.

Asha'd been shot in the leg before, and it hurt like hell, but with Ivy's belt he would be all right…as long as he stopped bleeding.

"Stop this at once," the younger of the two men on the dais screamed.

"Don't kill him, any of you," Miles boomed from across the room. "None of you touches Heath."

Asha flinched. "Are you serious? They are both responsible for this."

"No," Miles said, his voice echoing through the room.

Master Heath smiled. "Oh Miles, you have become so much more sentimental than I ever thought possible. Your daughters have caused such a profound change in you. We are enemies now, yet you spare my life?"

Daughters?

The Grand Master set his evil, glaring expression on her. "My granddaughters—disgusting."

What?

"Oh? You didn't know?" he asked. "Yes, this weak, pathetic traitor, once a Master of the Order and heir apparent to its powers, is your father. He is quite evil and is capable of darker things than your vapid minds could possibly comprehend. Do you think he has risen to his position without doing as all Masters must? It was your father who found and captured the last set of sisters."

He turned to Miles. "You and Heath were so young then, remember? We all witnessed and celebrated their sacrifice. It was the greatest day of our lives. And today we will relive our celebration, this time with your daughters as the sacrifice."

Asha spun, and Miles's gaze bored into both Heath and the Grand Master with so much venom, she flinched. Ivy backed away, her eyes wide.

Miles didn't deny it. He was rigid a moment, but then he bolted forward running for the dais. He leaped onto the stage, and the Grand Master leaned back…a flash…a knife.

Heath shouted a warning too late, and the knife landed, stabbing Miles in the chest. He fell back, hitting the floor with a sickening thud.

Asha raised her gun, aiming it at the Grand Master, but a crackling hiss came from behind her. She turned. Avia's hair blew and danced in white wisps around her face. Dust swarmed in the center of the room, and the Four materialized before them.

"Finally, I will see it. I will see the four witches sacrificed by the Four." The Grand Master's gleeful squeal was coated with madness.

A cold shiver rolled through Asha, and her stomach fell away, but before the Four could take her mind, she spun back, aimed, and pulled the trigger. The Grand Master's glinting eyes widened in shock as he collapsed back into his chair, and blood poured from the bullet hole in his chest.

Clay grasped her hand, and she squeezed his for reassurance. Her rage calmed, and power flowed through her. She was aware of the earth, the gardens outside, and roots swirling like snakes below. Rio, Cole, and Aron were shooting, but their guns were useless. Fireballs flew from the four dark figures coming at her.

Clay yanked her into his arms and turned shielding her. The blasts struck him in the back, but she was protected in his embrace. The fire burned on Clay's body. Her power didn't work here, but she felt something, her spark was back. She could feel it. Joined with Clay, she had her power. "Hold on," she whispered.

Asha sucked in a deep calming breath, tempering her fear and blew out. Flames ran along the black floor and small flames licked at the Four's robes. She wasn't very strong, but she could feel her power through Clay, connected to him.

Cole flicked his lighter and sent fireballs, but they failed to connect and passed right through the Four, not even singeing them.

"Pair up," Asha yelled. "I have power."

Ivy ran over and before Cole could try again, she linked her arm through his connecting them, but leaving their hands free. His next round of fireballs connected and the Four's robes burst into crackling fire.

"I feel it," she yelled. "It's working." The ground shifted and cracked. Rough stone pillars rose up and surrounded the Four, trapping them.

Asha couldn't charge forward and cut them up; she had to stay with Clay. She followed Ivy's lead and linked her arm through his. His power flowed, and Asha felt it like a pulse in his body. She reached out pushed at the flames burning on their robes. They surged from red to white. Avia hadn't moved since the Four appeared. Asha turned to her. "Help us," she said, trying to snap her out of it.

Avia stood beside Aron and grabbed his shoulder. He fell to his knees, his arms limp at his sides. His eyes widened then squeezed shut as a lightning bolt shot from his back through the Four without connecting. She squeezed again, and another bolt flew through the Four. The air in the windowless room rustled, and she moved her hands around Aron's throat and choked him. Her hair flew around her face, but her expression was cold and still.

"Take it easy," Rio yelled over the crackling of electricity and fire.

Aron's mouth had opened in the pained grimace of a silent scream.

"Avia, stop," Ivy shouted.

Mere stirred on the ground. She rolled over and rose. The chains hung, swinging from her body. Her eyes were solid black. What did they do to her?

"Avia," Rio shouted, yanking her hand off Aron's throat. He fell forward with two charred smoking holes in his back. Had Avia killed him?

Mere's black eyes were empty and expressionless as Aron dropped and laid still. *That isn't Mere.*

He wasn't dead. Getting up, he crawled over to Mere. He gripped her ankle from his position on the floor. She twisted, pulling back, her eyes squeezed shut as she kicked out. But he held on and wind blasted from his fingers, forming a small, flickering shield.

She stood still with her head tilted back and her mouth slack. Water erupted from the floor and rose into a wall stretching across the room. She dropped her head forward.

Shit. Now her eyes were white, hollow holes. Ice shivered through Asha's blood.

The Four's attack of fire, stone, ice, and wind pummeled through Aron's shield and past Ivy's pillars. Mere's wall turned to ice and while it was their final protection from the assault, coming in short, stuttering bursts, flames rolled over it, and it cracked and shattered.

Mere closed her eyes and blue-tinted lightning sparked and covered Aron and spread to her body. He reached out and bolts shot through his shield hitting the Four. Her chains dropped clanging to the ground.

"We're stronger together," Ivy shouted.

She grasped Clay's hand connecting the two earth and two fire elements. Vines burst through the floor, growing, reaching, and entwining around the Four, holding them. Rocks and boulders exploded from Ivy.

Power surged stronger as giant fireballs fired from Cole and out of Asha's chest, a beam of white flames shot forward. The fire caught, and she pushed it as hot as her remaining energy allowed.

They hadn't gotten anywhere. The fire didn't seem the burn them, and the stone and rock Ivy fired at them bounced off. But they were holding the Four back.

"We need more juice," she shouted.

Rio pulled Avia over, and Asha took his hand. Aron stood and grabbed Avia's, which connected all eight of them in a chain.

Fresh energy rushed over Asha. Her fire blew stronger, hotter, and it turned blue. Cannonball-sized rocks and razor-sharp twigs burst from Ivy, impaling and pounding the Four. Lightning bolts shot from Avia's chest to cover them in a flashing, electric net. Water flowed from Mere's chest and froze into ice, stabbing their enemies.

Anchored by the brothers, her and her sisters' elements pounded the Four. Strange shivers tickled through Asha. Her fire flashed from blue to white and pulsed from her body as new energy vibrated through her. It wasn't her power; it was her sisters combined. She felt each one as the energy spread through the chain. This was what the Four feared.

It was wonderful. All her fear and anxiety vanished as the white light enveloped the Four, holding them still and halting their attack.

Clay glowed beside her, with Ivy and Cole. Six white beams blasted the Four, shining as bright as the stars. They'd gained an advantage.

Avia gasped, and the light stuttered and dimmed, and that beautiful, heavenly peace disappeared.

No, no, no they were getting somewhere.

She screamed, and Asha winced, the sound penetrating like knives into her head. Their light flickered then went out.

Silence thrummed for a second, and Avia was blasted off her feet and into the air. She crashed far behind them against the raised dais. Horrible laughter echoed through the chamber. The Four were free.

Rio turned, jerked his hand away. Asha gripped it harder.

"No," Aron said, and he clamped the hand Avia had released from around Rio's wrist. The stuttering light flared then returned.

Even stronger than before, it caught the Four again—holding them still and motionless.

They thrashed and spun. Melding together, they became one in blurring speed, and with a squealing hiss, vanished into dust.

Silence.

Asha dropped Clay's hand then ran to Avia. Rio and Ivy were already kneeling beside her.

"What happened?" he asked.

"She's breathing," Ivy said.

He took Avia's wrist, and her eyes snapped opened. "I'm fine," she said, sitting up. When Rio offered his hand, she refused it and got to her feet. "I said I am fine."

Miles struggled to breathe with the knife still stuck in his chest. Asha looked for Heath. He must have vanished during the fight.

Ivy knelt beside Miles. After removing the knife, she pressed her hands over his chest. Blood pooled between her fingers. "Cole, help me."

He was beside her in a flash, bending over.

"Touch here." She guided his finger into the bleeding wound. "Can you feel it? Touch there and seal it."

"How? I can't call the fire."

"You just did. Try Cole. He won't survive more than a few minutes. You must."

He bent his head as he let Ivy hold his hand inside Master Miles's chest. Cole closed his eyes and clenched his jaw.

A second later, he snapped his head up and yanked his hand back. "I did it. It's closed."

Mere.

Asha turned back to where she stood like a statue, her eyes white and eerie.

"What's wrong with her eyes?" Avia and Ivy stood beside her as they stared at Mere's white eyes.

"I've seen that before," Clay said.

"What is it?" Asha asked.

"I don't know what it is or what it means, but the first day you were a prisoner here, you looked the same."

Mere snapped her gaze to Aron, who still held her hand. Her body swayed, but he caught her before she hit the floor. Ivy touched Mere's neck for a pulse as he cradled her in his arms.

"What happened to her?" he whispered.

"I don't know. We need to get her out of here."

His back was red and burned. It was ugly, but he didn't seem to care. Avia's attack use of Aron had been vicious. She was far too powerful to lose control.

Like you're one to talk. But what happened to Asha in the chain? Avia's scream had evoked pain, while Asha experienced… how could she describe it…divinity? Exultation? Avia's reaction was puzzling.

Though the Four were gone, Asha wasn't confident they'd been defeated. If they were gods, then by definition, they were immortal. She'd killed the Grand Master, but Heath had escaped. Their fight wasn't over. They'd rescued Mere, and that was all that mattered. Everything else could wait.

They left the grounds. Cole carried Miles, and Aron carried Mere. They approached the cars by the cave outside the wall, and he placed Mere across the backseat of one of the SUVs. She whimpered and rolled into a fetal position.

Asha rushed forward, but he leaned in. Mere's scream was so sudden, so full of fierce, raw pain, Asha jumped. The sound was anguished and terror-filled, and it tore at her heart.

He backed away, his eyes wide and hands out. He dropped to the ground seizing. Clay fell beside him. Cole set Miles down, and he and Rio followed, all four jerking on the ground.

"What's happening?" Asha yelled, her voice shrill.

Avia ran to the car grasping Mere's shoulders and shaking her. Asha'd never seen Avia move that fast or look that worried.

"Mere. Stop," Avia screamed into her face.

Mere's eyes were black and fierce, and her lips curled back revealing bared teeth in a horrifying snarl.

What happened to her?

Clay stopped twitching, and his eyes bulged.

"Mere!" Avia's voice was so loud Asha had to cover her ears. "Take them and go. There is something wrong with her. She's going to kill them."

Fire and ice battled under her skin, and Asha's legs gave out. She fell to her knees beside Clay. He laid rigid on the ground gritting his teeth. "Mere, no!"

"She's scared, confused," Ivy pleaded. "We have to help her."

"No, she's lost it. If you don't go now, she'll kill them." Avia's fierce tone urged Asha into action.

She gripped Clay's hand, but he clamped it closed and squeezed so hard she flinched. His eyes, the green color and black pupils, were gone. They were pale, foggy white, and terrified. Her heart stopped. *No.* She whipped around, heat rushing through her body. Her heart slammed against her ribs.

He jerked again, and liquid flowed from his open mouth.

"Please, no." Asha reached for Mere inside the car, but Avia shifted between them blocking her view with her back.

"Stop," Avia shouted, shaking Mere hard.

Clay's grip loosened. Asha lowered her face close to him. His eyes were still milky pale, but the green color was back.

"Go now. Hurry." Avia still faced Mere, who was fighting to get past the shield. She blasted it with a swirling flood. Avia held her hands out, containing it. "Go. I can help her, but she is too dangerous right now. I will contact you as soon as I can."

Asha helped him off the ground, and Ivy pulled Rio and Aron up. Cole's face was clenched, but he assisted Miles.

"Let's go, Aron," Clay said.

Aron's face was anguished, but he got in Clay's car with Rio and Cole. Asha took the black car Avia and Rio arrived in with Clay and Miles. They drove away, leaving her two sisters alone and outside the Order.

~ * ~

Master Heath returned to the Order to salvage what was left. He found the earlier battle damage repaired and the Grand Chamber restored to its usual opulence. The Grand Master's body—his father—was missing, and he shuddered to think what the building had done with it.

Inside the Grand Master's bedchamber, he glanced around the huge, ornate room. The massive, luxurious curtained bed made him think of kings and dukes and men with power. He studied the desk. His father's small laptop sat beside his wax seal amid papers, pens, and books. The entire place was both old and new.

A rustle disturbed the air behind him, and the hair on the back of his neck prickled. The same unsettling and familiar sensation came over him. No, it couldn't be. He'd seen them disintegrate under the force of the white light.

Another chill crept up his neck, this one colder than the last. Suddenly unsure, he spun and beheld the frightening, familiar forms. As always, unless in battle, they stood shoulder to shoulder, black beside black.

Heath dropped to his knees, bowing. "My lords, I believed they'd defeated you."

"They have not. It is as it should be, and as Grand Master, you must continue. They are the ones we have been waiting for, and we will have them."

About the Author

Courtney Shepard lives on Salt Spring Island on the beautiful coast of British Columbia. As a mother to a young child, her days are filled with wonder as well as writing. The *Unbalanced* series is a passion project that began years ago.

Courtney loves to hear from her readers. You can find and connect with her at the links below.

Website/Blog: http://www.unbalancedseries.com/
Facebook: https://www.facebook.com/unbalancedseries
Instagram: https://www.instagram.com/unbalancedseries/?hl=en
Twitter: https://twitter.com/CAShepard76

Thank you for taking the time to read *Unbalanced*, book 1 of the Unbalanced series. If you enjoyed the story, please tell your friends, and leave a review. Reviews support authors and ensure they continue to bring readers books to love and enjoy.